KFIR
LUZZATTO

ONCE AWAKENED

PINE TEN

Pine Ten, LLC
205 N Michigan Avenue
Chicago, ILL 60601

Fist publication, July 2019

ISBN: 978-1-938212-83-3

Books by Kfir Luzzatto:

CROSSING THE MEADOW

THE ODYSSEY GENE

THE EVELYN PROJECT

HAVE BOOK, WILL TRAVEL (With Yonatan Luzzatto)

AN ITALIAN OBSESSION

EXODUS '95

CHIPLESS

ONCE AWAKENED

The Tessa Extra-Sensory Agent series:

TESSA (Tessa Extra-Sensory Agent Book 1)

THE OTHERS (Tessa Extra-Sensory Agent Book 2)

HUNTER (Tessa Extra-Sensory Agent Book 3)

The DEAD & BUSY series

#1: ACCIDENTAL LAZARUS

#2: PHANTOM LOVER

#3: MICE

#4: THE ACCOUNTANT

Table of Contents

PART ONE
Beginning

"My name is Richard Luster, and this is my testimony ... Oh, this is stupid!"

"It's protocol. Start reading it again."

"All right, but it's stupid. My name is Richard Luster, and this is my testimony. I swear to relate the whole truth, knowing that willful false statements will be punished by imprisonment or fine, or both."

"Good. Start your relation from the beginning."

"I will. I want to tell you this more than you want to hear it. But what's the sense when I know that you won't believe me?"

"Try me."

"Very well. This will take some time ..."

CHAPTER 1

I gazed at the disheveled man sitting in the chair usually occupied by my upper-class clients. I shouldn't have let him in. His expression was one of mild despair, but he didn't have crazy eyes. I wish he'd had them. I could have sent him away if only he had had crazy eyes.

"Why are you here?" I asked for the third time. Not that he hadn't answered my question, but I guess that I was hoping for a different answer.

"I told you. You're the only one who can understand. I had to speak with you before they got to me. It's a miracle that I have managed to stay alive for so long. The moment I walk out of here, my hours are numbered. But I don't care anymore. Not now that I know what I know about the Vargos."

"You know that they betrayed my trust and pushed me away. I'm done with them. I forgot that they existed. I don't want to hear about them," I said, but I knew that he would force me to listen.

His demeanor made it plain that he wasn't going to leave before he had said his say.

"Listen to me!" he almost yelled. "You're the only one who can save us."

"Who's 'us'?"

"Everybody. The world. Humans. You decide. I don't know why, but you're special to them. Since they made me their slave, they made it plain that you can't be touched, that no harm can come to you, and that you must be left alone. I never managed to get my head around it and could never get an explanation from them, but, obviously, they're not going after you like they have to others. That's why you are the only one who can unmask them and tell the world what they are."

(He told me plenty more, and I'll relate everything to you, but that will have to wait until you have the entire background, or you won't understand.)

"How do I know that you're not delusional?" I said after he concluded his tale. I gazed at him intently, trying to gauge his reaction. "Forgive me for asking, but the immediate conclusion should be that you are out of your mind. Your story is crazy; you realize that."

"You will know. I think you know it already, and you have known all along. You're just in denial. But I must leave now—I've placed you in grave danger already by coming to you, and the more I stay, the greater the danger. When you hear that I am dead—probably hit by lightning," he added, with a weary smile, "you will know that everything I said to you is true. It may take a day or a few minutes, I can't say, but they will get at me, that's for sure."

The man got up, nodded, and turned to leave.

"Wait! What's your name?" I cried. A part of me didn't want to know his name, but if his story was true, I needed to know it.

"Right, I didn't tell you. I'm Benjamin Richmond, Certified Public Accountant. That's how the papers will refer to me. Good luck," he added.

He lasted two more days. Electrocuted in his hotel room; careless with the coffee maker, the newspaper said. But we'll go back to that.

I can't believe how improbably this nightmare began. How usual, boring, and commonplace was her first approach to me. She sounded like any other prospective client who calls, fishing for free information, mentioning that someone with an unfamiliar name had recommended me to her.

"We have asked around for the best patent attorney in Israel and have been told that you are the one," she said.

I ignored the flattery—a common tactic of many prospective clients—one that, nine times out of ten, is followed by more or less pressing pleas for a discount—you know, like "Mr. Whatshisname said that if we mentioned his name, you would give us a reduced rate."

"Thank you," I answered somewhat brusquely, brushing the annoying, insincere flattery aside, "but let's see if I can be of any help to you at all."

"Let me tell you this: What we have is big, it's huge, and we will not settle for anything less than the best. I am a lawyer myself, and I know what it means to hire good advice. It makes all the difference."

"Yes, yes. I won't argue with you on that," I said curtly, "but I would like to know what I can do for you."

Her voice was loud and coarse, with what sounded like a Polish or Romanian accent, though I couldn't be sure. By now, she had me annoyed. I hate people who talk loudly over the telephone and particularly in the morning. And I hate people that waste my time over the phone, beating about the bush. I have too much of that crap in my profession. But her voice now went down to a whisper; all of a sudden, it changed from its initial dislikeable joviality into a worried, almost frightened murmur.

"Mr. Luster," she said, "I must trust you, I know. But please understand that I am worried, very worried."

"Yes ...," I prompted her, after the pause that followed became too long.

"Would you think me mad if I told you that my husband has discovered the cure for cancer?"

I was indeed starting to get the uncomfortable feeling that this lady might not have all her marbles. But I realized that she might be overstating it like many clients who exaggerate their technology's value but still have something not to be discounted. I decided to let the conversation continue for a little longer.

"I am afraid that I'm not in a position to judge," I answered, "given that I don't know who your husband is and what his qualifications are. Perhaps you should tell me a little about him."

"My husband is a scientist, a great scientist. He is a specialist, a gynecologist, at the Holy Mount Hospital in Jerusalem. He also runs a research laboratory with a grant that he has obtained from a foreign institution—and very few young doctors receive those grants. That's how talented my husband is. So, during his research, he has stumbled upon this huge find, and the important thing is that it has always been out there for everybody to see, and nobody has ever paid any attention to it. It is so simple that even I, who am not a scientist, understood it. Now you see why we need the best patent attorney available to protect this invention?"

I felt relieved. Professors always drop in with cures for all kinds of illnesses, most of which eventually turn out to be far less important than initially thought. But they are not usually nuts. Stuffed shirts, yes. Empty shells full only of themselves, absolutely. But mostly not insane. I had no reason to believe that this particular doctor was crazy, and I was willing to suspend judgment. I would not hold it against him that his wife sounded annoying, particularly if the invention was really good. After all, this was the year 2000, the new millennium with all its fantastic scientific advances, and it was about time that we found a way to beat that damn illness. In fact, it seemed like everybody was working on it.

"Okay, I get the picture. I will be ready to meet with him and review the data, and we can pick it up from there. Please bring him to my office, let's see ..." I started looking through my calendar.

"But you don't understand. We need you to come to our house, and I mean immediately. He can't go anywhere before this invention has been protected. It's too big a thing."

"Yes, but I meet clients only in my office. I don't meet with anybody anywhere else unless there are compelling reasons for it."

"But there are—very compelling reasons. You see, I haven't told you the whole story. My husband is frightened by what is going on at the hospital. People have heard of his breakthrough research, and strange things are happening. He's very close to a nervous breakdown, and I can't bring him all the way to your office in Tel Aviv. It may kill him. He is in such a state ..."

Her voice broke as if she were about to cry. I don't cope well with crying women, as a general rule, but this was business, not social, so I decided to hold my ground, at least for a while longer. I wanted time to think. This sounded quite unusual and potentially interesting, but I didn't want to rush into anything.

"Look ... I don't think you've told me your name."

"I am Paula Vargo, Advocate Paula Vargo."

"Okay, Mrs. Vargo. This is what we do. Give me your phone

number, and I'll think this over. Then, I'll give you a call and tell you what I have decided to do."

"When?"

"Tonight. Sometime after nine. Give me a number where you can be reached then."

"I'll give you my home phone. I work from my home."

I took down the number and hung up. Something was disturbing in the conversation I'd just had, but much as I tried to capture it, it escaped me. I decided to forget about it for the time being and to get some work done.

That had been a busy day if I ever had one, and Paula Vargo and her husband got pushed into a corner of my mind, from which they popped up once more while I was driving home. I ran the conversation through my mind again. My instinct told me that I should find a good reason to say to the Vargo woman that I was too busy and couldn't afford the time, but I was too curious to simply ignore her. No, she had left me with no choice but to find out what it was all about. Curiosity—the drug that had made me go into the profession to begin with—was pushing me too hard to resist.

That night at home was one of our regular exhausting evenings. Our son, Elan, who is eight years old, smart, and opinionated, and his sister Dana, who is five and very persistent, were at each other's throat. At last, Elan was sent to his room, and Dana fell asleep on the couch, and I managed to get my wife to myself for ten minutes and tell her as much as I knew of the story. Becky is a chemist, of the matter-of-fact, feet-on-earth type, and can be counted on to bluntly give her opinion.

"This woman sounds like a crackpot," was her swift and merciless verdict. "There is no such thing as 'a cure for cancer.' Cancer is a generic name for many diseases that behave differently and react to different cures. That's why what she said to you doesn't make sense."

"I know, I know. I'm sure that he hasn't found a universal cure for *all* types of cancer. But assume that he has found a cure for one. That's big enough."

"Then why didn't *he* call you? Why did he send his wife, who is no scientist? It doesn't sound right."

"I gather she's protecting him. He is frightened by his discovery and doesn't know what to do next. He needs a guiding hand, and perhaps I can help."

"And I also don't like that bit about you going to their house," she continued as if I hadn't spoken. "Why on earth can't they come to you? Then you can judge if they are real or not."

"I know that this is unusual, but it sounds intriguing ... and we are talking about a practicing doctor ..."

"Or so she says," Becky pointed out, dropping the towel she was using to wipe the dinner table, only to pick it up again to start wiping it once more. She worked it so hard that her knuckles went white, and I wondered why she was so uptight. She had been unreasonably jealous before, and I hoped that this was not going to be one of her bouts of jealousy.

"So she says, and I have no reason to doubt it. What good would it do to her to lie?"

"I don't know ... call it feminine intuition. I have a bad feeling about this. It lends seriousness when a doctor is involved, and that could be her way to talk you into going there."

"Yes? And for what purpose? Murder me?"

"Worse. To waste your time. I really think you shouldn't go."

"Look here. I know that this is a million-to-one shot, and probably nothing will come out of it. I'm not kidding myself into believing that there is a big chance that this guy has found a real cure for cancer. I'll be the first to admit that I have been tricked into wasting a lot of time if and when I reach that conclusion. But how do you think I'd feel if I let this go and in a year's time it turned out that it was real? If there is even a minuscule chance that this is as big as it sounds, it would be foolish not to be part of the team. This could be an opportunity to do something really meaningful, such as comes your way once in a lifetime. Are you telling me that I should let it pass without even checking it?"

"If you put it that way, then there is nothing more to be said. Go, make a fool of yourself, and have fun. But keep your eyes open." Becky knew when arguing with me was useless, and she realized that my mind was made up. She wasn't going to fight me over this, but she damn well wanted to go on record telling me what she thought of it. She switched off the main kitchen light, signifying that, as far as she was concerned, the discussion was concluded.

"For the time being, I will only go and meet these people. If I smell a rat, I will come straight back without wasting any more time," I promised.

"All right. As long as you remember that."

I have great respect for Becky's feminine intuition. I always take it very seriously, but intuition cannot be entirely disconnected from the facts. She hadn't spoken with Paula Vargo, so she only had what I told her to go by. I resolved to talk to her again about it, but I had to make the call first.

"Mrs. Vargo?"

"I was waiting for your call," was the quick answer.

"I have thought things over and have decided to give it a shot. I'll come to see you and your husband tomorrow morning at ten o'clock. Give me the address."

"I knew you would," she said simply, and gave it to me.

When I finally got up to our room, Becky was just coming out of the shower. She was as beautiful as the first time that I had seen her. In fact, aging, she had grown more beautiful. And sexier. I had thought that passion would fade after years of marriage, but she managed to turn it on every time without effort. Her slim body, which had returned to its unblemished self after each birth, worked like a magnet on me. Her dark honey-colored eyes always seemed to promise delights, and I could get drunk on the smell of her long, brown hair alone. That's how lucky I was.

"I bring peace offerings—tea and cookies," I said. That was something I had learned even before Becky and I were married: Room service was the best opening for a peace conference with her, and it worked every time. She smiled and took the tray from my hands, put it on the bedside table, and then came and kissed me. She likes to take unbelievably hot showers, and as a result, her body still radiated heat.

"I'm not mad at you," she said.

"I thought you might be," I said, pulling her to me.

"Not mad, just worried because the story didn't sound right to me. But since you made amends ..." She left that dangling. I knew what she meant, so I gently pulled the towel she wrapped in, but she slapped my hand.

"Go and take a shower, first," she ordered. "The tea will be waiting when you get back."

I practically ran to the shower. Becky always knows how to push my buttons.

CHAPTER 2

The address I was looking for was in a beautiful neighborhood, on the outskirts of Jerusalem, in a sleepy part of the city. At ten in the morning, few people were around. The house was located at a bend of the road, slightly below street level, on a hill's slope. It was partly hidden by trees and shrubbery, and I almost missed it. I didn't find the entrance to the car park and had driven on and parked far away. I was walking quickly, not because I was late, but to get out of the windy street and the cold, which, in late October, the bright sun was doing little to mitigate.

Down a few stone steps, I stood before a door and studied the nameplates. A huge ceramic plate, in really bad taste, occupied the best part of the upper portion of the door. The names on it were Adele and Mordechai Fleishman, and by the look of it, the Fleishmans were the landlords. So the Vargos are renting the house, I concluded. That didn't come as a surprise. The neighborhood was an expensive one, and practicing MDs are not rich people, as a rule.

Below the Fleishmans' plaque, and slightly to the right, as if trying to keep to themselves, I spotted my perspective clients' nameplates. The first one, of weathered metal, said: Daniel Vargo, M.D., Specialist (Obstet. & Gynecol.).

The second one, smaller and made of bluish plastic material, simply stated: Paula Vargo, L.L.B, L.L.M., Attorney at Law.

I tried to picture the Vargos and concluded that he must be stocky, with a small mustache and hair oil. She, I was sure, must be tall, elegant, and blonde. A classy lawyer married to a high-profile physician, right out of any Jewish mother's dream.

I rang the bell.

Well, I was certainly right, at least in part, regarding Paula. She was tall all right, almost a head taller than I, and blondish, sort of. And she affected a fashionable skirt with a matching cardigan. But she was by no means classy. She was coarse in appearance, matching her voice well. Her high cheekbones and rosy cheeks were more reminiscent of a barefooted farm girl than a Slavic princess. She looked thirty-five years old or so, but something in her appearance seemed to change every time I saw her, and she could have been forty-something or much younger. I don't really know, I never asked. Also, as I soon discovered, she had a tendency to be too damn familiar.

"Reechee! How good of you to come. Do come in, please. If you need to refresh yourself, the bathroom is over here," she said, jabbering and pointing at a door. "I have put in fresh towels for you. Coffee? Tea? Make yourself at home," she said, steering me through the hall, into a well-lit sitting room.

Standing in front of the broad window that faced a white sofa, one could not help being held spellbound by the breathtaking view of the hills outside the city. I moved my gaze back to her to remain focused.

"My name is Richard. Plain Richard," I said. I dislike nicknames, intensely so. And at my age—I am almost forty years old—I resented having the bathroom thrust at me. I had taken an immediate dislike to this woman.

I sat on the white sofa, facing the French window with the gorgeous view of the hills, and she sat beside me.

"Nice view you have here," I said, trying to ease the tension.

"Yes. Beautiful, isn't it? I told Daniel when we came here—we used to live in Paris before, when I studied law—that this is the only house I can live in. I wouldn't move under any circumstances. Well, please sign here."

She handed me a piece of paper, which I took and read. It was headed "Contract" and contained five clauses. All of them were written in exceedingly bad English. They described the attorney-client relationship between us, my secrecy obligations, and Paula and Daniel Vargo's undertaking to exclusively use my services as a patent attorney.

"Look here, Mrs. Vargo ..."

"Paula," she corrected me.

"Look here, Paula," I said with difficulty, relinquishing some of the distance that I had hoped to achieve. "This is a bit premature, you know. I haven't yet consented to take your husband on as a client, and I don't think that we can sign a retainer agreement before I do. Where is he, by the way?"

"He is here, in his room. I have asked him to stay away until we conclude the legal parts of our arrangement. Then you can talk to him."

"Yes, but we don't have an arrangement—at least, not yet. I will have to talk to him to get an impression of the status of his research and to see whether I can be of assistance to him at all. I will not undertake to assist him unless I am convinced that I can help."

"But of course you can help. I know you can. You are the best."

"Well, thank you for your confidence, but I wish I were as sure as you are. I simply don't know. So let me talk to him first."

"Okay. I'll trust you ... up to a point. Daniel will explain to you in general terms, but then if you want to get any more details, you sign the agreement."

"Fair enough. Let's get going."

She rose swiftly and disappeared along a dark corridor, from which she emerged two minutes later with her husband. Daniel Vargo was anything but stocky. He was as tall as Paula and lissome, almost fragile in appearance. His delicate features, topped by butter-colored hair, were effeminate, and his gaze was vague. While I had guessed that Paula's accent had a Polish or Romanian ring to it, Daniel's was unmistakably Romanian, as if he had given up trying to mask it. My parents' neighbors had come from Romania, and I had grown up hearing them speak.

"Mr. Luster," he said, in civilized contrast to his wife, "I am so glad that you agreed to come. I have heard so much about you from Paula that I feel like I know you already."

I had to make an effort to remind myself that Paula had also met me for the first time a few minutes before. He made us sound like old acquaintances.

"My pleasure. But, please, call me Richard. It's easier if we get rid of formalities."

"Then you call me Daniel, okay?"

"Okay. Now, Daniel, I would like to get down to work if you don't mind." He nodded silently, throwing a quick glance at Paula, who had curled up on a matching couch right in front of him as if to keep watch over her husband.

"How would you like to proceed?" he asked. "Do you wish to

ask me questions?"

"I would like you to tell me the whole story, in your own words. Please assume that I know nothing and speak to me as to a layman."

"Where would you like him to start?" interjected Paula.

I turned toward her, annoyed. "The beginning would be a good place," I said, ungraciously. "May I suggest that you let Daniel collect his thoughts and tell the story in whatever sequence he pleases. If I need him to explain any particular point to me, I will ask him. At this time, I need him to speak freely and without interruptions, in the way that is the most convenient for him. Only so we can get somewhere. Please go ahead, Daniel."

As Daniel gave it to me, the whole story is quite technical, and I don't think that the specifics would add much to my relation. I can go into more details later if needed. The essence of the story is that while doing research using fetal tissue extracts, Daniel noted that a particular protein is present in an abnormally high concentration in the fetus when a natural miscarriage occurs. Daniel then started thinking that, perhaps, that protein could have a regulatory function in the differentiation of the cells in the fetus, which has other implications. His lab, which he had rented from the hospital using the money from a research grant, was running another experiment simultaneously with ovarian cancer. He took the extract from the aborted fetal tissue and put a few drops in three Petri dishes with cancer cell cultures, and when he came back three days later, the tissue had gotten back to normal. No cancerous cells could be found anywhere in any of the dishes.

"I couldn't believe my eyes," Daniel said, sounding moved as if he were experiencing it all over again. "I tried again, and again the tissue was regenerated to a normal state, and no cancer cells could be detected.

"I didn't know what I should do next. I came home and sat in the dark here on this couch, for I don't know how long, and thought the whole thing over and over again. I couldn't get away from the conclusion that I had found the molecule that regulates life and death. I took two Valium pills but couldn't calm down. I woke Paula up and told her all about it. I asked her if she thought I was mad because I couldn't grasp the enormity of what I had found. My life has been hell ever since."

"The hospital has got wind of Daniel's work," Paula said, "we don't know how. The only one who knows something is Daniel's assistant, Tarun, but Daniel trusts him, and therefore so do I."

"Maybe you both are being naive," I ventured.

"No," said Daniel, brushing the possibility aside with his hand. "I don't say that I'm not naive as a rule, because I am—that's why Paula is always watching out for me—but Tarun owes nothing to the hospital. He is a post-doctoral biology student, and his salary is paid by my research funds. Besides, Tarun is very trustworthy and will never do anything to harm our research or me. You'll see for yourself when you meet him."

"But he may have said something inadvertently, without intending to cause any harm," I suggested.

"That may be," said Paula, "but whatever the cause, the fact is that the hospital knows that Daniel has accomplished a major scientific breakthrough. They don't know what it is, but perhaps they imagine it has to do with cancer since ovarian cancer is one of the projects on which Daniel's lab works. The hospital management is absolutely furious with Daniel for not telling them and because he will not share the fame with them.

"Daniel probably made a mistake because he told them that he was going to get a patent on his invention and refused to tell them what it is or to add their names to it. They can't make him, can they?"

"Of course they can't," I said. "As long as Daniel made his invention outside his work hours and using funds unrelated to the hospital, they can stake no claim on his invention. Daniel gets paid to treat women with gynecologic problems, not to find a cure for cancer."

At this point, I was already hooked on the Vargos' side. The hospital's management was behaving like bullies, not an uncommon occurrence in large organizations.

"Perhaps I should give them something. Maybe I should add their names ..." Daniel started to say.

"No," Paula said emphatically. "We've been through this before. You can't give in and lose your well-earned fame. You know them. The moment you put their names on your paper or patent, they become the heroes, and you are pushed back into the background. I won't let that happen."

"Paula is opposed to any compromise," Daniel said, turning to me with a disoriented look, "but I don't know. They've canceled all my outside clinic hours for the next two months, using some procedural excuse that I don't even understand. And if I have no clinic hours, I don't get any new private patients. Pregnant women like to go for extracurricular medical advice to the same physician who sees them at the hospital on their regular visits. If they take that away from me, I won't get any new clients. Maybe you don't know it, but nobody can live on a hospital salary. We all rely on private practice for our living."

"I understand it, but Paula is right. Once you give in, there's no way back. They will take possession of your invention, and you'll lose your well-earned fame and profits. And if they are as vicious as you picture them, they will eventually also get rid of you because seeing you around will always remind them that they stole it from you. No, you can't give in, but you do need some good legal advice regarding your employment agreement with the hospital and how to deal with them."

"I told him that we should sue the hospital," said Paula. "I even started to draft a complaint."

"I don't think that this is the right way to go," I said, leaving no room for discussion. A lawsuit would bring it all out into the open and could unleash God knows what forces.

"Then what do you suggest?" asked Daniel.

"I know nothing at all about labor law, but I have a good friend who does. I suggest that you talk to him and let him try to sort things out with the hospital."

"But we have no money, Richard," said Paula. "As you just heard, the hospital is making sure that our bank account gets hit."

"I understand. I'll talk to him and see what we can do. You may have to agree to retain him on a contingency basis if you can't pay now, the same as you suggested to me. Are you prepared to do that?"

"Do we have a choice?" asked Paula.

"Quite frankly," I said, "I don't think so."

"Okay. Let's do it, then," she said. "And how do you plan to proceed?"

"I will have to start getting all the experimental details to see if we have enough data to file a strong patent application. But first things first. I'll give you a call once I have spoken with my friend, and we'll take it from there."

I got up and walked to the door. Daniel and Paula both followed me.

"I can't tell you how much we appreciate what you are doing for us, Richard, but now is the time for you to sign that contract before Daniel gives you specific details," said Paula.

"It needs rewording a little. For clarity. I'll do it and will bring a signed copy when we next meet."

"Great! I knew when I called you that you were the right choice. Thank you."

"I haven't done anything yet," I reminded her. "I'll do my best, but I don't have a magic wand to put things right with. You'll have to be patient."

"Oh, we are patient, Richard. You can't even imagine how patient we are," she added with a smug smile.

It was the first time I had seen her smile in that way. So far, she had always kept a worried countenance, which became the gravity of their situation. But now she was smiling as if she didn't have a care in the world. A shiver ran down my spine, and for a moment, I felt a tension in my arms and neck and a buzzing sound in my head, possibly a nervous reaction after the stress of the day. Paula kept smiling at me.

"What's the matter, Richard? Are you feeling well?"

"I'm fine," I hastened to say, and turned to leave.

There was something unnerving about her smug appearance. I didn't like it.

I had to explain things to Becky, and I didn't relish the idea of having that conversation. Still, it had to be done. Luckily, she had friends over for coffee and gossip, and then we had to put the kids to sleep, so I managed to put it off until bedtime. I sneaked up and into the shower and then waited for her in bed.

"We didn't have a moment for ourselves all evening," I said when she joined me in bed.

"Did you see that Walter woman?" she asked directly.

"Vargo," I corrected her.

"Walter or Vargo doesn't matter. Did you see her?"

"I did, and I met her husband."

"And?"

"And he's very impressive. I think he may have made a real discovery. His wife is more annoying than I imagined, but he seems a nice guy."

"So?"

"So, I think I'll check his invention out to see if there is any substance to it."

"It doesn't feel right," she said.

"Why?"

"It just doesn't," Becky said stubbornly.

I propped myself up on my right elbow and gently massaged her shoulder with my left hand, in my best soothing manner.

"You're being unreasonable," I pointed out. "You haven't seen Daniel Vargo and have not heard anything about his discovery, so how can you express an opinion at all?"

"Have it your own way," she said. She turned on her side, giving me her back, and clammed up.

CHAPTER 3

I got up the next morning feeling nervous. Things had been tense with Becky lately because of her mood swings. That was mostly due to money problems that were not my fault. Since Dana's birth, Becky had been a stay-at-home mom and lately had complained about how she felt caged. On the other hand, she didn't seem able to find a job that she might like or trying very hard to find one. To contribute to our family's finances—or at least to feel like she was doing something useful—she had started bossing me and "taking an interest" in my work and schedule, which had brought about some friction. But that didn't mean that she or I had fallen out of love. I really wanted her to feel better about herself but didn't seem to find a way to help with that, and I was constantly worried that we were growing apart.

Becky has always been a perfect mate for me, just as I had pictured that my wife would be. We had met through a common friend and had clicked immediately. She had the uncanny knack of making me feel like a high-school boy in love, hormones included, even now that I had become the father of two. But lately, there were times when Becky felt to me like a ticking bomb around which I needed to tiptoe to avoid setting it off. That morning I had to be doubly careful because my first meeting was on behalf of the Vargos, with the labor lawyer I was hoping would help them.

"Going to the office?" Becky asked.

"Yeah, I'm stopping at Yoel's on my way there—a couple of loose ends I have to tie up."

I hate it when I need to lie to Becky, but I wasn't actually lying, just not giving her the whole truth. Yoel was a labor lawyer, one of the best, who knew everything about employment contracts, a topic on which I was by choice completely ignorant. That's why I came to him with what by then was promising to become my little personal mess.

Yoel was waiting for me behind his maddeningly clean desk. After greeting me, he lifted an eyebrow and waited for me to speak. I exposed the situation as clearly as I knew how without getting bogged down with technical details, but I noticed that his eyebrow had remained lifted.

"This is a great opportunity for you, Yoel," I said, speaking as temptingly as I could manage. "You may not only take part in this exciting project, but you stand to gain a lot from it. If the drug that will be developed is as good as the preliminary results would seem to indicate, it will make billions, and you will have a nice two-point-five percent. It's a steal."

"So you say, and I hear you, but I wonder what's inside the nice package that you are handing to me."

"Well, I'm sure that a lot of work is involved and no end of trouble too. This is a hot potato. But I thought that it's the kind of thing you like."

"Yeah, how considerate of you. And you say you're in it too?"

"Of course," I said. "I wouldn't dream of getting you into any trouble I wasn't already sinking in myself."

"Okay, then I'll look into it. But if this turns out to be some stupid academic brawl, I walk out."

"It's a deal," I said, relieved that he had agreed.

"All righty. Now give me all the details."

I told Yoel all I knew, but that was not nearly enough to get started on.

"Let's get them over here for a working session," I suggested. "It's time for them to leave the house."

Despite much protest on Paula's part, the Vargos showed up at Yoel's office at the appointed time on the morrow. I counted that as a small achievement because Paula had become almost religious about their need to meet their lawyers exclusively in the privacy of their sitting room.

"Listen to me, Paula," I had said without hiding my impatience. "You have no money, but on the other hand, you do have a messy case that most lawyers won't touch. I'm handing the best labor lawyer there is to you on a silver plate, and you get difficult? I'll expect to see you in Yoel's office at eleven a.m. sharp, or else I'm out too."

"But you forget that Daniel has made this great scientific breakthrough, probably more important than antibiotics," she had said. "That should amount to something, shouldn't it? He should be treated with the respect he deserves."

Paula was really starting to get on my nerves by then.

"Daniel is a great guy, I agree, and maybe he's going to be hailed as the greatest scientist of our era—if we don't mess this up, that is. Now make up your mind. I can't do that for you. But if I don't see you here tomorrow, it's goodbye."

I had hung up, knowing that they would come. They had no choice, really. And come they did. Daniel chose to sink in a comfortable armchair in front of Yoel's vast and clean desk, and Paula sat upright in another one beside him. I had taken a chair at the side of the desk to be able to see the three of them.

"After I met with Richard yesterday," Yoel started, "I made a few phone calls. One of them was to a friend of mine at the Ministry of Health. He is a very dear and old buddy who's always ready to help me out. But this time, the moment I mentioned your name, he told me to back off and clammed up. The only words I could get from him were, 'You don't know what you're dealing with. Let's not talk about him anymore.' So, what have you been doing to stir the ministry that much?"

"This is real persecution," Daniel said, looking really worried this time. "The director of the hospital is a very influential person with strong political ties. That's all I know. I'm not too familiar with hospital intrigues, you know," he added. "I usually keep pretty much to myself; I do my job and mind my own business."

"You're right that he has a strong influence with the ministry, and apparently, he is using it. After I spoke with my friend, I made a few more phone calls and more guarded inquiries. I'm sorry to say that rumors have it that they are contemplating putting you before an ethics committee to ask for a suspension of your license to practice medicine."

"What!" This was Paula, who jumped out of her chair. "But they can't do it. They have no cause."

"Don't they?" asked Yoel, looking at her askance. "Look, Daniel ... and Paula. If you are not a hundred percent candid with me, I can't help you. You understand that?"

"I understand," said Daniel, "but I really have no idea of what they have against me ... except, of course, that I wouldn't tell them what my discovery was."

"They are using that argument too. The hospital claims that, since you refuse to disclose the nature of your discovery, they can't be sure that it isn't something that belongs by right to the institute. Therefore, they work under the assumption that you are stealing from the hospital."

"I told you so," Daniel said, turning to me accusingly as if it were my doing. "I knew that it would get to this."

"Who exactly are 'they'?" Yoel asked.

"My direct boss, the Head of Obstetrics, and the General Manager of the hospital."

"Names?" Yoel demanded. Daniel gave him the names of two well-known professors, Cooperman and Abramov—so well known that even I had heard their names mentioned before.

"You see, Yoel," said Daniel, "we must get a patent application filed as soon as possible. This is why we went to Richard first. Once we file the application, they will understand that it's all over and will stop crucifying me."

"Yes, but we've been wasting a lot of time," Paula said to me reproachfully. "We should have filed the patent application by now."

"Paula," I said with ill-concealed annoyance, "you really don't know what you're talking about. Filing a patent application is not merely filling in forms, as you lawyers like to do—pardon my generalization," I said, turning to Yoel, who nodded, smiling graciously. "Doing a reasonable job—I'm not talking about the best possible text, mind you, merely an adequate one—will take days and probably weeks. We must keep you going in the meantime, and this is where Yoel comes in."

"Yes," said Yoel, "but, unfortunately, the problem with the invention is not the worst one. I think that we can keep that at bay for a while. We have other problems. Tell me," he said, turning to Daniel, "have you completed all your examinations to become a specialist in obstetrics?"

"Well, practically ..."

"A 'yes or no' answer would be helpful," said Yoel, eyeing him narrowly.

"You see," started Daniel, "in order to become a specialist, you must pass two sets of exams—Part A and Part B. I did my Part A exams a long time ago, and I went to the Part B exams only six months ago."

I could tell that Daniel was beating about the bush and was starting to get a strong feeling that something was really wrong here.

"And ..." Yoel prompted him.

"And I was very successful in all the parts of the exam, only in the oral questions I was tricked into giving one wrong answer, and therefore I didn't officially pass that exam."

"Meaning you flunked it?"

"Officially, yes."

"Officially is what counts," said Yoel. "The reason why they are summoning you to the ethics committee is that it appears that you have been impersonating a specialist, while 'officially,' as you say, you are an intern."

Yoel was right. I remembered seeing the nameplate on his door that identified him as a "specialist."

"Look, Yoel," Daniel said, looking desperate. "I have much more experience than anybody else at the hospital. I am allowed to carry out procedures that only specialists perform. Everybody knows that it's only a formality ..."

"Formalities can be deadly," said Yoel. "In this case, they give them the excuse they need to go after you. And there is no point in discussing whether this is right or wrong. It's the way it is. So let's face it and start planning our defense."

"You mean that you will help us?" Daniel asked, looking relieved.

"I will help you, as long as you promise never to lie to me again. If I catch you lying, you're history. Agreed?"

"Agreed."

"Now, in what ways have you been impersonating a specialist? For instance, did you make any statements in a form you filled? Is it stated on your stationery or visiting card?"

"No. It isn't written anywhere, except on my door. And, of course, I have told patients that I specialize in obstetrics, although not that I am 'a specialist.'"

"Think well. I don't want some paper that you don't remember having signed to come back to haunt us. Did you use the title on a scientific paper? In a personal letter? Anywhere else you can think of? No?" he added when Daniel kept shaking his head. "Then, this is simple. You go straight back to your house and remove the stupid sign from your door. There is a good chance that they may have taken pictures by now, but let's hope that they haven't thought of it."

They got up and left quickly. Yoel was working wonders on Paula, I noted. She had kept unusually quiet and had protested only weakly and sporadically.

When the door closed, Yoel looked at me with an amused expression on his face.

"It's a nice mess that you have landed on my plate, Richard."

"Well," I said, defensively, "don't say that I didn't warn you beforehand. But what do you want? No risk, no gain."

"Yeah. I'm not complaining, but this is no regular brawl

between egocentric doctors. They are after Daniel big time. My friend at the ministry almost begged me not to call him again for as long as I live. We may be putting ourselves on the lepers' list. But this makes it all the more interesting," he added brightly. "Now tell me, when do you think that you can get a patent application filed?"

"I really don't know. I haven't seen the data yet. If what Daniel has already gathered is good enough to file at least an initial application, I can do it in a few days. But if he needs to run more experiments ..."

"Well, be quick about it."

"I will, but how are you going to get him off the hook on the impersonation charge?"

"I'm not worried. If he gets rid of the door sign and if they have no photographs—which I'm sure they don't have, the self-confident paternalistic bastards—then all they have are rumors. You can't take someone's license based on a rumor, not even for one day. Daniel's story is good: he says that he never said that he 'is' a specialist, only that he 'specializes.' If he sticks to his story, he's off the hook."

"Good," I said, relieved. "I'll get busy right away." I got up and walked out. Then, I remembered that I hadn't thanked Yoel at all. I poked my head in again. Yoel was already engulfed in a voluminous file.

"By the way," I said from the door, "welcome aboard."

Yoel waved his hand as if to say, "don't mention it," without shifting his gaze from the file. I saw myself out.

CHAPTER 4

It was getting late, and the shadows in Daniel's living room were becoming longer. I was tired and unhappy, but, mercifully, Paula was not around to worsen the situation. She had a headache and had gone to lie down.

We had been going through Daniel's data for two hours, and I found them inconclusive. Daniel was undoubtedly a bright person, but he was the most confused and the least organized researcher I had ever seen. His data were written in three different notebooks but not in any chronological order. He had the habit of keeping his notebook at home, safely away from the university buzzards. Every time he carried out a new experiment at the lab and had forgotten to take it with him, he started a new notebook. That had happened three times already. Then, when he remembered to bring a notebook with him to the lab, he kept picking up any one of them at random, causing all his data to be mixed in a messy sequence that Daniel alone was able to follow, and even he only partially. If you added to that the fact that he often forgot to date his experiments, you had something out of a first-class nightmare.

"I believe that this is the experiment from which I took that point, you see," he said, pointing at a curve he had sketched on the back of a page. "Yes, this is definitely it."

"Forget it," I said. "Even if everything you remember is a hundred percent correct, we only have qualitative results. We don't have a full characterization of the protein, and we don't have any concentration-dependent results. That is the information that we must have if we want to prepare a decent patent application. We must generate those immediately, and that will take quite some time."

"What are you saying, Richard? Do you mean that we can't file a patent application?"

"Not a good one, no. I must have an idea of what additional data will become available and when. We must start planning the experiments. For instance, we will have to do some work to isolate and characterize the protein."

"I don't know if we can do it," said Daniel doubtfully. "I don't have that kind of equipment in my laboratory, and, as matters stand now, I can't very well ask the hospital to lend it to me. They used to be cooperative before all this started because my sponsor is paying good money to let me rent the lab from them, but now ... I don't know what can be done. And besides, I don't have the manual skills to do it. Tarun does most of the lab work."

"Let's go and talk to Tarun, then. How much does he know about this mess?"

"Very little. He knows of my discovery, of course, and his name will go on all published papers since he deserves it. But I haven't told him about my problems with the university; I didn't want to scare him off."

"Well, you have no choice now. You must tell him everything

if you want him on your side. Things may become nasty soon, and if he doesn't know what's going on, he may run. Can you arrange for us to meet now?"

"Why, yes. He should be at the lab right now, running some new experiments. Let me check."

He got up and spoke briefly into the telephone at the corner of the room.

"We are lucky. He's at work. I told him to wait for us and that we are on our way to him. Let's go."

As we walked through the parking lot next to his lab, I watched Daniel and tried to gauge his mood. This was the first time he had gone back to the lab since his argument with his boss, and I thought that he was behaving well, despite his apparent anxiety.

"Are you okay?" I asked.

"Yes, thank you ... I think. We go down this way," he said, and led me to a side entrance that opened to bare concrete steps. We descended two flights of stairs and then walked a short distance along a corridor. At the entrance to his lab, Daniel took a key and unlocked the door.

"We keep it locked at all times, even when we are here. This is what it has come to; we must guard against our superiors to make sure that they don't steal the fruits of our work. Tarun ..." he called, opening the door.

"I'm here," a voice came from under the bench that ran along a narrow room, cluttered with equipment of all kinds. A large refrigerator stood beside a centrifuge, and a small incubator occupied most of the wall opposite the entrance.

Tarun was small and dark-skinned. From his accent, I guessed that he was Indian, but then he gave me a complicated story that made him Pakistani, after all. He was lively and smiled incessantly; his eyes betrayed intelligence. I liked him immediately.

"Tarun," said Daniel, "this is Richard Luster, my patent attorney. You can tell him everything as if you were talking to me."

"Pleased to meet you, Mr. Luster."

"Call me Richard, please. Nice to meet you. Daniel speaks very highly of you."

"Daniel is always flattering me. I really don't deserve it."

"Tarun," I said, getting down to business, "we need your help in organizing the data. Here is what Daniel has so far."

We started going through the data, and it was soon apparent that Tarun wasn't getting from it anything more than we were.

"I'm sorry," said Tarun at last, "but I can't help you with the characterization of the protein. That is way beyond my expertise."

I looked at Daniel. He was no candidate for it either.

"Do you know anybody who can do it for you, Daniel?"

"Not really."

"Then I'll have to think of something." I already had an idea about who was going to do this for me, but I didn't want to tell Daniel before I knew that he was ready to help.

"And you, Tarun, had better start working on organizing those experiments right away. We don't have much time. And one more thing: the hospital is doing its best to make life difficult for Daniel, and they may try to get at you too, to scare you into leaving his employ. If anything happens to disturb your work, call me at any time. Is this clear?" I handed him a notebook page with my office and home phone numbers on it.

"Yes, Mr. Luster ... Richard," said Tarun, looking worried.

We thanked him and left to make our way back to Daniel's house.

"He seems a nice guy," I said.

"He's the best. Absolutely the best. I'm sure that he'll be a great help."

We reached the house, and I asked Daniel to let me make a phone call in private. The call was to a friend of mine at a university in Tel Aviv. He owed me big time for something I did for him in the past, and he was going to pay for it now by working on my protein. He agreed immediately to help me, but he shall remain nameless since he broke virtually every rule in the book. Let's call him "Yair."

"Good news, Daniel," I said, getting off the phone. "I have a friend who is capable of characterizing that protein of yours. What he needs is some raw material to work on and your gel data. Can you give me those?"

"Well ... I'll have to prepare some fresh extracts—I have used up all I had, but I can get those ready in a couple of days, even if it means going to the lab again. But is it safe to let someone else know about it? Won't he steal it from me or tell others about it?"

"I can vouch for him, and I have explained the need for secrecy to him. You needn't worry about that. He's a hundred percent trustworthy."

Daniel was looking out of the window, toward the hills that were lit with a myriad of small lights. When he spoke, it was in a sad, bitter tone.

"So, you may devote yourself to healing mankind, but that doesn't count. You can be the greatest scientist of the century, but you still have to go and do menial work because recognition won't come to you easily. Nobody cares if you have found the cure for cancer. You still have to go to the lab and do your own dirty work. This is very disheartening."

"Yeah," I said, with an ill-concealed lack of sympathy, "life is hard, and then you die. Talk to you tomorrow."

He was starting to get on my nerves almost as much as his wife, with his self-pity and his megalomaniac view of himself. But then, I reflected, he lives day after day with Paula, so what else could I expect? I left, banging the door behind me.

I drove pensively to Tel Aviv, keeping low speed on the turns of the road. The drive from Daniel's house to mine took a little less than one hour, and I needed the time to reflect and plan ahead.

That night I had a row with Becky. She decided that it was a good time to remind me that she had warned me.

"I told you so," she said, the moment I stepped into the kitchen, where she was washing the dishes.

"You told me what?"

"I told you that this woman, Paula, was bad news and that you would be wasting your time."

"How do you figure that? We don't know yet that I am wasting my time. We are still in the initial stages of the work, and the project looks exciting and promising." I knew that I sounded too much like a salesman, but I was on the defensive.

"It's promising to send your practice down the drain, that's what it's promising. Do you remember that you also have other clients and that you have other things to do, apart from holding Mr. Vargo's hand?"

"Of course I do," I retorted, "and I am dealing with all of them. Oz is taking care of things back at the office." Oz was my trainee and was actually doing his best to hold the fort while I was away. Some day he will make a fine patent attorney.

Becky turned her back to the sink and threw the towel toward its hook, missing it by an inch. "I bet he does," she said sarcastically. "Do you know that your clients started calling here, complaining that you don't call them back and that they haven't been able to find you at the office for days?"

"You always have a few cheeky clients who call you at home.

They should know better."

"And, of course, they should talk to Oz—only he has been calling me three times a day, almost in tears, trying to get in touch with you. What do you have a cellular phone for?"

I looked at my cell-phone, surprised to see it switched off. I had no recollection of having done it, but perhaps I didn't want to be disturbed when I discussed the data with Daniel, and then I forgot to turn it on again. I put it on the kitchen table without turning it on.

"Yes, I'm sorry. I didn't notice that it wasn't working."

"It seems to me that you haven't noticed that you have not been working either. I suggest that you go to the office tomorrow morning and start picking up the pieces."

In Becky's lingo, "suggest" was a euphemism for ordering, so I didn't argue, also because that was precisely what I had planned to do on the morrow anyway.

"Of course," I said, "I'll report to the office first thing in the morning, ma'am," I tried to joke. Becky gave me a quick side glance and then got back to her washing-up. I could tell that she was not amused, so I went straight to bed.

CHAPTER 5

The next morning I got up early, eager to get to my office and deal with the backlog. Becky had woken up before me to prepare the kids for school. She had made coffee out of habit, I guessed, but she wasn't talking to me. I really thought that she was overreacting. I sat in the kitchen, looking at her making sandwiches in a marked manner.

"Becky," I started out, tentatively, "I don't see the need to make such an issue out of all this. After all, it's only work."

"Only work? It doesn't look at all like it."

"What do you mean?"

"I mean that if you have a thing going on with that woman, Paula, I'd like to know."

That jealousy again. She had her back to me, but from her voice, I guessed she was almost crying—something she didn't often do. I got up and grabbed her by the shoulders, turning her toward me quickly. This thing had to be dealt with right now before it got entirely out of hand.

"You must be kidding!" I said, with a feeble attempt at a smile.

"I'm not kidding at all," she answered seriously, without looking me in the eyes and feigning to go on with her wrapping of the sandwiches. "There is no other explanation for your behavior. You neglect your work, your kids, and me and spend all your time with these Vargo people. What do you want me to think?"

"Look here," I said, trying hard to make my voice carry my feelings, "I loathe this Paula. I hate her guts. I find her the most disgusting woman I have ever met. She is coarse, lacks grace, and gets on my nerves. But her husband seems to have discovered something really great, and I try to forget that she exists because the project is so important."

She was softening, but I could tell that she wasn't yet convinced and needed more reassuring, so I went on, telling her all the obvious things she knew already, but wanted to hear from me again and again, every time she felt insecure.

"Besides, what makes you think that I would ever look at another woman? You know I'm not like that."

"Says you."

"Says me, and I'm the one who knows. I haven't ever looked at another woman up to now, not because I'm blind, but because I already have all I want to look at here at home. Let me show you tonight," I whispered, not wanting the kids to hear. "I'll bring cookies," I added, which made her smile for a moment, relieving some of the tension.

"That doesn't mean that you won't be tempted when you're thrown together with a beautiful woman day after day," she objected, but I could tell that she was no longer really mad.

"You're off the mark. I wouldn't look at her even if she were a beauty, which she isn't ... but I forget that you haven't seen her.

That's the problem. Once you see her, you'll understand how silly this is."

"Mm ..." she said, sounding unconvinced. "I'll suspend judgment for now. But if she turns out to be gorgeous ..."

"Don't worry. I am safe here. She is a gargoyle."

Becky went back to the sandwiches and the kids, looking much more cheerful than she had for a while. I collected my strength, something that lately was really needed to make me go to work, and hit the road.

The theoretical fifteen-minute drive to my office took close to one hour. It was eight-thirty when I left home, peak hour, and I wasn't used to driving to my office so early in the day. I usually took it easy in the morning and never left home before nine-thirty, reassuring myself that it didn't matter whether I left home earlier or not since leaving early would only mean spending extra time in the traffic. That morning I was proven entirely right, but by nine-thirty, I was at my desk, going through a pile of messages. So many had accumulated over the last few days that I didn't know where to start. Eventually, I threw all the notes aside for future consideration and got down to finishing some urgent work. I felt much better after my talk with Becky that morning, and I was soon able to get up to speed with the file I was working on. As soon as I started to concentrate, of course, there was a buzz on the intercom.

"Yes, what is it? I asked not to be disturbed," I said reproachfully. Lia, my secretary, knew me well enough not to disturb me on the rare occasions when I issued formal orders to be left in peace.

"I'm sorry, Richard, but I have Advocate Dayan on the line, and he says it can't wait. Want me to tell him you're not available?"

"No," I sighed. "I'll talk to him."

"Richard," said Yoel, when I got the line, "I need you to get in your car right now and meet me at the Jerusalem District Court. Judge Hornik's courtroom is on the second floor. We have a hearing at twelve o'clock. The hospital leeches have actually brought an action against Daniel."

"But why the short notice? I can't really get away right now."

"Well, you have to. They tried to get an *ex parte* injunction yesterday. The judge threw them out on their ear but agreed to hear the motion today, with us present. They are charging him with everything they can think of, except perhaps stealing milk from the premature babies' ward."

"But, they will surely not get into patent issues now, and I will be of no use over there. On the other hand, I have so much work to do here ..." I made a feeble attempt, but I didn't really sound convincing.

"Yeah? Don't go on telling me, or you'll make me cry. I need you here with me, so get into that nice car of yours and be here on time," he said, and hung up.

Yoel was right; I had to be there. I gave hurried instructions to a terrified Oz and, hoping for the best, left the office heading for Jerusalem. I was less worried about what my raging clients would do when their appointments got canceled again and much more by what Becky would say if she found out. She was not to find out, I decided.

Finding Judge's Hornik's courtroom was not an easy task, but when I finally found it and got in, Yoel was already sitting on the right-hand side of the room, wearing his robe. Daniel and Paula were in the room, sitting behind him. The judge heard some other case and paid no attention to the various people who were continually entering and leaving the room.

"You're late," Yoel complained.

"They haven't started yet, so what do you mean I'm late? I'm not late."

"Here," said Yoel, "take a look at their motion." He handed me a voluminous document titled "Motion for Interlocutory Relief." The motion was fifteen pages long. Many documents were attached to it, including an affidavit bearing Professor Abramov's signature. It would have taken me the best part of two hours to figure out what it said, so I put it aside and concentrated on what was going on in the courtroom. "All right," said the judge. "What do we have here?"

The court clerk handed him a massive file, which the judge inspected with open discontent. He then turned to the stenographer sitting at the far end of the bench.

"Ah, yes. This is in the matter of Holy Mount Medical Center versus Doctor Daniel Vargo. Who is here on behalf of the plaintiff?"

"Advocate Saul Feldman," said Feldman, rising briefly and then sitting again.

"And who represents the defendant?"

"Advocate Yoel Dayan," said Yoel, rising an imperceptible fraction of an inch.

"Okay, Mr. Feldman," said the judge, "let's have it."

"Yes, Your Honor," said Feldman, rising to address the judge. "We have here a motion for interlocutory relief brought by the Holy Mount Medical Center against Doctor Daniel Vargo. The motion is supported by an affidavit of Professor Abramov, the Medical Director of Holy Mount. I would like to explain the facts of the case to Your Honor if it pleases the court. I will try to be brief."

"Yes, Mr. Feldman. Please do just that. It is getting late, and this court will appreciate concision."

The lawyer embarked on a lengthy exposition, but the judge

appeared to be losing patience after a while.

"What is the relief that you are asking for?" he asked.

"We are not asking for much, Your Honor," said Feldman, making a dismissive motion with his hand. "We ask the court to order Doctor Vargo to deliver up all his results, laboratory samples, and data, and to cease and desist from taking any action connected with the research. We further ask the court to enjoin him from entering the laboratory at the medical center. All this, I should add, only until the medical center has had an opportunity to review the data and to assess the damage caused to it by Doctor Vargo's doings."

"I am not sure that I agree with you that you are not asking for much, Mr. Feldman," said the judge. "Nevertheless, I'm not saying that the requested relief is not commensurate with the danger and damage caused to your client. But, of course, you'll have to prove that first. Okay, Mr. Feldman. Now, Mr. Dayan, please."

Yoel rose, stared for some time at Feldman and at his client, and then, with a pained look, turned again to the judge. I had seen him doing that before, and I wasn't sure what it was meant to accomplish, but I liked it nonetheless. When the silence in the courtroom became almost tangible, Yoel finally spoke.

"I have listened attentively to what my learned friend has explained to the court right now, Your Honor. Very attentively." He managed an even more pained look than before and continued.

"The Holy Mount Medical Center is a very respectable institution. We are all very grateful to it for its outstanding efforts in medicine. I also think that very few people in Israel and in the medical world at large have not heard of Professor Abramov's outstanding achievements in cardiovascular medicine."

Yoel stopped and gazed straight at Abramov, who could not but bow a little in response to this flattery. Then Yoel went back to looking the judge in the face.

"I am also aware that Advocate Feldman is an outstanding representative of the legal profession. Nevertheless, Your Honor, I am afraid that my learned friend has been somewhat economical with the truth in his exposition of this case. He has omitted to present to the court some essential details that must be told if we wish all the facts to be before Your Honor. He has also made some inferences that I believe we will show without difficulty, are based on erroneous factual premises.

"I would like to submit to the court an affidavit by Doctor Vargo, which sets forth a few of the salient facts of the case. My friend, Advocate Feldman, has received copies of the affidavit one hour before the hearing."

"Now, Mr. Dayan, do you plan to cross-examine Professor Abramov on his affidavit?"

"I most certainly do, Your Honor."

"Then, we'll take a fifteen-minute break."

"All rise," shouted the court clerk, and the judge was gone. We ran to the coffee shop and managed to grab a sandwich and bottled water before running back.

After the break Judge Hornik walked in and sat quickly, motioning us to sit down. He looked at the file and then at us, as if in disbelief that we hadn't gone away. Then, with a marked sigh, he started running the show.

"Professor Abramov, kindly approach the witness stand. I remind you that you are giving testimony and that you are still under the obligations taken when signing your affidavit. You are warned that you must tell the truth and that you shall be subject to the penalties under the law if you do not do so. Do you understand that?"

"Yes, I do."

"All right. Mr. Dayan, please proceed."

I had seen Yoel at work before, and I knew where he was going. After a few background questions, he closed in for the kill.

"Professor, could you please explain to the court what exactly Doctor Vargo is doing?"

"Well, I know that he is taking fetal biological material and studying it. And I know that his results have to do with cancer."

"With all due respect, we knew that without your help. I would like you to be a little more specific if you don't mind."

"I'm not sure that I understand what you want. I am really trying to help here, but we are talking about matters that you cannot understand, and I find it very difficult to satisfy you."

"Let's be simple, then. You claim that Doctor Vargo stole something that belongs to you—to the medical center, to be precise. Before making this accusation, I am sure you have ascertained a) that you know what he has taken away from you and b) that it was taken from the medical center. So I am asking you, what is it that he has taken away?"

"But, of course, the results of the research. It's obvious."

"The results being ... ?"

"Data, conclusions, discoveries."

Yoel gazed at the high ceiling, then looked at his shoes, and kept silent. He went on being silent for a whole minute. The silence began to be oppressive, and I wondered for how long the judge would remain patient. Then Yoel lifted his eyes and turned again to Abramov, asking him in a low, sweet voice: "You really don't have a clue, Professor Abramov, do you?"

Abramov looked back, opened his mouth as if to speak, then closed it again, and lowered his gaze.

"You have no idea whatsoever of what Doctor Vargo has been doing. You don't know that it has been taken from the medical center. In fact, you positively know that it cannot belong to the institute because whatever it is, it was done on somebody else's money, premises, and time. Was it not?"

Abramov didn't answer. He shot a desperate look at Feldman, who looked away, then returned his gaze to the bench in front of him.

The judge sat there, looking from right to left and switching his eyes from Yoel to Abramov, Feldman, and back. Finally, he spoke, and it was clear that he was fuming.

"Mr. Feldman! I strongly recommend that you withdraw your motion and spare this court the need to rule on it. I am tempted to find your client guilty of perjury, and I am not doing so only because of his position in the medical profession. But this case smells very strongly of bad faith, and I want it off the table. And I mean now."

"I understand that the appearances may give the court a negative impression, but I am sure that as you hear on, you will form a different opinion."

"Hear on? What gives you the impression that I am going to hear any more of this? No, I am ready to rule on your motion. I am charitable by suggesting that you withdraw it, along with your ridiculous and libelous claim, before I go on record with my opinion of it."

"I am grateful for your patience, Your Honor, but if I withdraw the motion and claim, I will not have an opportunity to appeal against your ruling, which, I understand, may be somewhat in my client's disfavor."

"Somewhat? Are you dense, or are you trying to be funny, Mr. Feldman? I won't ask you again. Are you going on with this motion?"

"Yes, Your Honor."

"All right. You asked for it."

Throughout these exchanges, Yoel merely stood there, looking respectful. Now he whispered, "Yes!" loud enough to extract a pained look from Feldman.

Judge Hornik dictated to the protocol. "Having heard the arguments of the parties, and the testimony of the Plaintiff's witness, the motion for an interlocutory injunction is denied. A reasoned decision will be made available to the parties in writing at the Court Secretariat no later than Wednesday, ten a.m. A date for a hearing on the main case will be set at a later time."

I looked at my watch: it was ten minutes past four, and I had to rush back to my office. God, I prayed, make it that Becky has been busy and has not tried to call me. Otherwise, I am done for.

With a hurried goodbye to everybody, I ran away. They were too busy celebrating, anyway, and nobody paid attention to me.

CHAPTER 6

Things were starting to shape up well, at last. The court's victory had infused a lot more confidence in us and given us the feeling that we were doing the right thing. Even Paula seemed more bearable to me now.

And that day, after court, I had made it back to the office in time to deal with a few urgent matters and to pick up the phone for Becky's call. All pretty smooth and working out well. But I had never been able to keep anything from Becky, and so that evening, I told her about our success in court. Well, perhaps I made it seem a rather quicker affair, but still, she got the salient facts.

"So, you see, it is all going well. The judge also thought that Daniel was being persecuted by the hospital without any reason. Now, I guess they are stuck without any good reason to stop Daniel's research."

"Yes," she said, sounding dangerously calm, "but you have done it again."

"Done what?"

"You ran to help that woman instead of doing your job as you promised me," she said.

Right on the spot, I couldn't think of anything to say that would placate her, but before I managed to say anything, she got up.

"I'm going to bed," she said, and left without looking at me. When I finally managed the courage to go up to our room, she was asleep or was pretending to be.

The next morning I got up early, feeling restless. Becky was still asleep, and she would get up in half an hour to get the kids ready for school, so I managed to brush my teeth, shave, grab a cup of coffee, and leave for the office before she woke up. The perfect husband doing his bread-winning duty—at least that's how I hoped that she would look at it. Also, I didn't want to speak with her before she had had the time to cool off during the day. This was not our first tiff, although we didn't fight a lot, and I knew that she needed a couple of days to get it out of her system. There was also an upside to being cold-shouldered by her for a while: the make-up stage of it was always great, and my hormones already started to warm up for the night.

In the office, I got down to work at a furious pace, making up for the lost time, and was doing well when the phone rang. It was Becky.

"Have you seen the newspapers?" she asked, speaking dryly.

I never have the time for more than a quick glance at the morning paper that we get on our doorstep. I hadn't even looked at the front page that morning, so much I was in a hurry.

"No, why? What's in them?"

"Your friends are. Pick one up and take a good look," she said, and hung up.

I yelled for Lia, but it turned out that there was no evening paper in the office, so I sent her out for one. She was back in no time and put the paper neatly on my desk. I looked at it in disbelief. The headline went:

"DOCTOR DISCOVERS CURE FOR CANCER AND IS PROSECUTED"

and the subtitle read:

"In a groundbreaking ruling, the court found that Dr. Daniel Vargo's revolutionary research belongs to him and not to his employer."

The article occupied two-thirds of the front page, and I read through it quickly. About half of what it said had any meaning or relation to reality. The rest was a mixture of disinformation and stupidity. Mercifully, my name was not mentioned. Yoel's was.

I grabbed the paper and left without bothering to tell Lia where I was going. I didn't bother to let the Vargos know that I was coming and that I was pissed. They'd know that soon enough. In the car, driving to Jerusalem, I tried to make up my mind as to whether I should resign from the case immediately or give them an opportunity to explain first. But there was also Yoel to be reckoned with. I dialed his number, and he answered immediately.

"Dayan."

"Yoel, this is Richard."

"Hi, Richard. I was about to call you."

"I assume that you have seen the papers, then."

"Yes, indeed. They did us proud, didn't they? Quite a boost to our practice, ah?"

"So, you aren't annoyed?"

"Annoyed?" Yoel asked, sounding surprised. "Why should I be annoyed? The paper says that I tore that idiot Abramov to pieces, which I did. It says that Daniel was maliciously accused of wrongdoing and painted him as a modern Dreyfus. I'd like to see them now trying to bring charges before the ethics committee. No, I loved the article."

"Yeah? Well, I didn't. I thought that we were supposed to keep quiet until after we filed a patent application."

"Well, that was before they went to court. Now it's out in the open. I guess that you should get busy, Richard. This is getting hot. Well, talk to you later. Must rush."

Yoel had taken much of the wind out of me, but I still didn't like it, and I still meant to tell the Vargos a few home truths. This was clearly their doing. I could see Paula's hand behind the article, and I didn't like being made a fool of.

When I got to their house, it was almost dark. I knocked on the door, and Paula came quickly to open it.

"Richard! What a nice surprise. I wasn't expecting you. Hey, I think you were great yesterday in court. You did a lot for us."

"I did nothing, really, except sit there. Yoel did all the work."

"You're just being modest. I know that Yoel wasn't prepared to go to court without you. But I didn't know that you had planned to meet with Daniel today. He is resting ..."

"I wasn't. I came here to talk to you about this," I said, handing her the newspaper.

"This is good, isn't it? At last, the world is starting to pay attention to what Daniel is doing. And it was all the hospital's doing. You know, there was this reporter there in court. I think they brought him with them, anticipating a victory. After you and Yoel left, he came to us, asked us a few questions, and went away. I didn't think that he would publish such a high-profile article. We didn't have to do anything, really."

I didn't recall having seen anyone who could have been a reporter, but I couldn't swear to it. I had the feeling, nay, the certainty that she was lying to me, but there was nothing I could do about it. I wasn't going to let her off lightly, though.

"We had an agreement that you wouldn't talk to anybody without my permission before we filed the patent application, and you shouldn't have talked to this reporter."

"But, really, Richard, this was nothing we had control over ... wait a second."

The telephone was ringing, and she ran to answer it. I listened to her side of the conversation.

"Yes," she said, "this is the residence of Doctor Daniel Vargo. No, sir, it is not possible to speak with him. Doctor Vargo does not answer phone calls right now. I understand that you are calling from Australia, but all the same, I can't put you through to him." She listened in silence for a minute, and then she went on. "I am very sorry to hear about your wife's illness, sir, but Doctor Vargo's findings are preliminary. A long time will be needed before a commercial drug is made available. Yes, I understand that your wife can't wait. I am really sorry, but ... No, no amount of money could make the drug available to you right now. Perhaps in a few months ... I understand that a few months may be too late for your wife, but there is really nothing I can do. I really must hang up now. I'm sorry," she said, and hung up.

"Do you realize what you've done?" I asked. I was angry at the irresponsible behavior that was now causing desperate people to hope again, only to plunge them back into despair.

"You don't need to tell me. This has been going on since morning." For the first time, she wasn't looking self-centered, as if other people's troubles had touched her. "Daniel spoke to a couple of callers, early today, and it broke his heart, having to disillusion them. I don't know how all these people got hold of our phone number, which isn't listed under our name. After a while, I sent him to his room to lie down, and I have been answering the phone all day."

"What is this? Who's here?" Daniel's voice came from the corridor.

"It's okay, honey. It's Richard. Come here."

Daniel walked into the room, a worn-out look on his face. He came to shake hands in silence with me as if this were a funeral.

"Hi, Daniel," I said, trying to get us back to a normal atmosphere. "I hear you have had a difficult day."

"Difficult? Horrible, you might say. Look here, Richard. We must finish this patent application quickly. I must be able to talk to some biotech company and get them to work on the project immediately. You see, while we sit and do nothing, people out there die. And I could save them all if I only had the support of a pharmaceutical company. But I can't get that until we file a patent application. It's hell."

"I agree, Daniel, but we are doing our very best. We need at least some preliminary data."

"I've got data. Here, look," Daniel said, handing me a sheaf of paper. "Last night, after the hearing, I started to worry. I said to myself that this time we made it, and they couldn't stop me. But next time, they may get lucky. They may get a more sympathetic judge, and then we are done for. So I sat down all night and went through every single piece of paper I have and organized all the data for you. I went on today, and I have just finished. I think that what we have here is enough, at least as a start. What do you think?"

I sat down with the material and started going through it. Daniel had prepared tables in neat handwriting that summarized the protein activity and a couple of graphs showing a concentration dependency. He had also summarized all the experimental conditions and had identified the cell lines and the materials used.

It really started to look like a much better set of results.

"Why, it looks good, Daniel. I wish you had given this to me from the beginning."

"I know, I'm sorry. It took me a great effort to organize all this. At first, I thought that generating a new set of experiments could be the better option, but now I realize that we may not have the time. So, do you think that this will suffice?"

"Well ...," I said, doubtfully, "this is a start, but we still need to characterize the protein. How are we doing there?"

"I have got some biological material from which I can prepare the extracts for your friend to work on. It's here in the freezer."

"Here? You keep fetuses in your freezer?"

"I don't have a choice. If I leave it at the hospital, they may take it away from me, and then we won't have anything. I am no longer allowed into the operating room, and these may be the last samples I can get. A friend gave them to me, at grave risk for himself. If they ever find out that he has helped me, he is doomed."

"All right. Then I suggest that you start working on them in Tel Aviv tomorrow. My friend at the university will get you access to his equipment, and the moment you give him samples, he will work on their characterization."

"But, Richard," Paula said, looking worried, "Daniel can't just go to Tel Aviv and stay at a hotel. It may be dangerous. I won't let him."

"He can stay with us for a couple of days," I said, immediately regretting the suggestion. Our house is not big, and Becky hates guests who spoil the intimacy of the family.

"Thank you very much, Richard. I appreciate it," said Daniel. "But are you sure that this will be okay with your wife?"

"Quite okay, don't worry. She will love having you," I lied.

"Then, please take the material with you. It will be safer in your place."

"Wait a minute. Do you want me to take fetuses into my home?"

"It's nothing, really. Just a small container that looks like an ice-cream box. You don't have to open it. I'll do it when I get to the lab. Wait a second," Daniel said, rushing to the kitchen. He came back holding what, in fact, probably *was* an ice-cream box, with its lid tightly held by an elastic band. "Here it is. Just put it into your deep freezer, and it won't spoil."

I got up and walked quickly to the door, holding the specimen box in my hands. Paula and Daniel walked with me and, when we got to the door, Daniel put his hand on my shoulder, looking past me. I could tell that something was on his mind.

"Richard ... this is very embarrassing, but, you see, with all these problems at the medical center, well ... I may need to borrow some money from you. Not a lot. For transportation, you know. I am not used to asking for money, but ..."

"Don't say another word, Daniel. Here, this should be enough to get you by for a few days," I opened my wallet and gave him all I had, probably feeling more embarrassed than he was. "You'll repay me ten times over when you are rich. Don't worry."

I opened the door and left hurriedly.

CHAPTER 7

Becky took it better than I had anticipated. She wasn't happy but didn't throw a fit either. I guess she was starting to get curious about these people that had been absorbing so much of my attention lately. And the newspaper article suddenly had made the story seem very real.

"We'll have to put him in Elan's room, and Elan will sleep in Dana's bed."

"He is tall," I remarked, "and Elan's bed is short."

"Well, I'm not going to give him *our* bed. Why don't you send him to the Hilton?"

"He's scared of being out there alone. I guess that all his problems with the hospital have made him a bit paranoid and perhaps with good reason."

"Well ... yeah. Okay," Becky said, unenthusiastically. And that was it.

The time was almost eight p.m. when the bell announced that

Daniel was at the door. I had started to worry that he might have lost his way, but here he was, wearing a light raincoat over a gray turtle-necked sweater and mismatching mustard-colored jacket. He held a small suitcase in one hand and a gift-wrapped package in the other.

"Come in, Daniel. Welcome. Make yourself at home," I said as if this could ever happen. "Becky!" I yelled, and she emerged from the kitchen.

Becky is a marvel at dealing with situations. She has the feminine instinct needed to understand and interpret relationships in a flash and react correctly. In this case, she also seemed to have instantly developed a motherly instinct toward Daniel, and she did her very best to make him feel at ease. And when Becky does her very best, you feel at ease if you know what's good for you.

"Hi, Daniel. It's so nice to have you here," she cooed to him. "Richard has told me so much about you and your wife that I couldn't wait to meet you. Such a pity that you couldn't bring her with you."

"Thank you very much. I hope I won't be in the way ..."

"Nonsense. You? In the way?"

"That is very kind. I am sorry that Paula is tied up with work and couldn't come for a couple of days, but someone has to be a breadwinner in the house," he said, with an attempt at a faint smile. "And, oh," he continued, looking at the gift-wrapped package as if surprised to see it there, "she gave me this to bring to you. She knows how much you and Richard love antique Japanese lacquers, and she sends this, hoping that you will like it."

Becky had already unwrapped the box, which she now opened to reveal a small rectangular lacquered tray. It had birds of some sort painted on it. It was ugly. Becky, nevertheless, managed to look positively ecstatic.

"Why, Daniel, you shouldn't have! Please tell Paula how much we love it. It's beautiful. I'll put it away now, to make sure that the kids don't scratch it." That was our private joke when a particularly ugly present was brought into the house. "Be careful that the kids don't scratch it," Becky would say, and when out of earshot, she would add, "Make sure they break it."

"Come here," I said to Daniel, who was still standing near the door, "I'll show you your room."

We climbed the short stairway to the second floor. I am not very tall, and I never felt conscious of the ceiling, but Daniel had to lower his head to pass through the door at the top of the stairs. Elan's room was the farthest from ours, and Becky had prepared it for Daniel. It contained a small writing table, where even I couldn't sit for more than a minute without getting cramps, and a small bed, hardly the right size for Daniel.

"I am sorry that the bed is not going to be very comfortable," I said, apologetically, "but it's the best we have available."

"Don't worry, Richard. This is just fine. I don't know how to thank you for all you're doing for me. I can't think what I would do without you."

I left, closing the door behind me and went into the kitchen. Becky was stirring the soup but stopped as I came in and turned to me.

"What is all this about us loving Japanese lacquers? Since when can you tell a Japanese lacquer from a melamine plate?"

"First of all, I do know something about Japanese lacquers, and I like them as a rule—not this one, to be sure—but I didn't mention Japanese lacquers to them. They probably confused us with somebody else."

"Now, when was the last time you went to the supermarket?"

"I can't remember. Maybe two or three weeks. Why?"

"Because the chain that we have here—the one I buy groceries from—are having a countrywide 'Japanese Week.' They sell everything that is Japanese. If you buy their sushi, they give you a loathsome tray to go with it. The very same tray that your friend right now presented us with. Antique lacquer, my foot! This is 'Japanese Week lacquer.' Your friends are phonies. Fakes. That's what they are."

I saw that Becky's temper was getting out of control and started to worry that she might become dangerous.

"Keep your voice down," I admonished her; "he may hear you."

That was a wrong move. Becky hates being shushed.

"I don't care," she shouted at the top of her voice, "let him hear me. He's the one who's making fools of us, not the other way around."

"Listen," I said, desperately, "it's not his fault. I am sure that he knows nothing about this Japanese tray. He buys whatever Paula tells him. He, himself, doesn't have a clue. Besides," I continued, lowering my voice to a barely audible level, "they've been left with no money. I guess this is all they had to give, and Daniel didn't want to come empty-handed. The value of the gift doesn't count," I recited, to keep talking, "what counts is the spirit with which it is brought to you. You see," I added——another wrong move in retrospective——"they are so hard up that I had to lend them some money to eat and for travel."

"You did what?"

"I lent them some money. Not much, just a few hundred to see them through the week."

"That's it. Now you're officially crazy. You should be certified. And what will you do when they have no more food next week? I'll tell you what you'll do: you'll give them more money.

And more again the week after. Are you out of your mind? You know what, don't answer that. Just don't give them any more money, understood?"

"Yeah, yeah. Okay," I said, sighing contritely. I did feel sort of stupid, but I knew that in my place, Becky would have done the same.

"Now go and see to it that Elan and Dana shower and wear decent pajamas. Dinner will be ready soon."

Dinner turned out to be a surprisingly pleasant affair that evening, despite everything. Becky chatted away pleasantly with Daniel as if she didn't have a thing on her mind. Women are really amazing at masking what they think.

Daniel and Elan also seemed to hit it off. Dana fell asleep into her plate at an early stage and contributed nothing to the conversation. When it became clear that she was a spent force, I lifted her up and tucked her into bed.

Back in the living room, I was happy to leave Elan and Daniel watching TV together and to get busy helping Becky to do away with the dishes. She seemed to be in a good mood.

"He's a nice guy," she said, at last.

"I told you so. He is not perfect, but he is basically okay. I like him."

"Yeah, I can understand it. He seems so fragile."

"I'll make coffee, then," I said, to change the subject.

I am very proud of my espresso machine, which makes excellent coffee if you know how to handle it. By the time Becky had removed her apron, I had three hot cups on a tray—not the Japanese one. We sat down with Daniel, who seemed happy at the opportunity to stop watching the sitcom that was absorbing Elan's attention.

"This is a great coffee, Becky. It reminds me of the ones we used to have in Paris."

"It was actually Richard who made it. The espresso machine is his baby."

"Richard ... you have hidden depths that I didn't suspect. Not only a patent attorney but also a coffee maker. I wonder what else ..."

"That's all he knows, Daniel," said Becky, sounding a bit too smug for my liking. "Don't get too excited."

"Thank you very much," I said. "If you don't mind, now Daniel and I have to sit down and do some work—men's work, you know? Patents."

"Go ahead, but put Elan to bed first."

Elan attempted a half-hearted protest, and I sent him up to brush his teeth, promising to come to say goodnight to him in a minute.

When I went up, Elan was already in bed, seemingly asleep. Dana slept beside him, and she was so tiny that she barely took any part of the bed at all. Elan, by contrast, looked strong for his age. I liked to watch him sleep because I realized that those were my last glimpses of him as a baby, undergoing his metamorphosis into a grown-up boy. It was all taking place too quickly for my taste.

I sat on the bed, looking at him, and he opened a sleepy eye.

"Hi, Daddy. I'm tired."

"I can see that."

"No, *really* tired."

"Okay, really tired. So go to sleep now."

"I like him."

"Who?"

"Whom."

"Who is 'Whom'?"

"No, *you* should've said 'whom.' I like Daniel."

"We all do."

"I thought his fangs are awesome."

"His what?"

"Fangs."

"You talk nonsense; you're asleep already."

"No, I'm wide awake," said Elan sleepily and turned to one side—his usual sleeping position—with a snore.

I got up, took a last good look at Dana, and left the room. Outside, Daniel was standing in the corridor.

"I wanted to say 'good night' to Elan, can I?"

"He's fast asleep now."

"Then I won't disturb him. He is a hell of a boy. Bright. Very bright."

Becky grumbled a little about my taking work into the house—a mortal sin in her view—but then decided to go over to a neighbor for coffee and gossip. Daniel and I were left in the sitting room, going through our respective copies of the draft; the silence was broken only by turning the pages and the scratching of Daniel's pen and mine, marking up comments and changes.

Daniel was very easy to work with. He quickly accepted my views and abandoned his suggestions for improvements if I didn't like them. We worked quickly through the draft, resolving all the problems in no time, and a half-hour later, I realized that there were no more questions left.

"This is great work, Richard," said Daniel.

"Well ... it is not a great patent application, you know. We need to file an improved one as soon as possible, but this will do for a start. I might be able to file it tomorrow, or the next morning at the very latest."

"Great! This is great. I must tell Paula. Can I use your phone?"

I nodded, thinking how dependent on his wife this man was. He might turn out to be the greatest scientist of his generation, but he still had to report his every move to Paula. But then, to be honest, was I any better? Didn't I tell Becky everything and abide by her every wish?

"Time to go to bed," I said to Daniel when he got off the phone. I felt wasted.

I went to Dana's room for a last look at her and Elan. They slept peacefully and, reassured, I climbed into bed.

CHAPTER 8

Something was interfering with my sleep, and I was trying to resist it. God, I needed my rest so badly.

"Richard, Richard. Wake up!"

It was Becky, shaking my shoulder forcefully and calling to me. But there was also another sound that penetrated through the mist of sleep.

"Daddy! D-a-d-d-y!"

It was Elan, calling, and crying at the same time. I jumped out of bed and ran to Dana's room. Daniel was there, standing by the bed. I ran over and hugged Elan, talking to him reassuringly at the same time. At his age, "night terrors" were common, and we had grown accustomed to them. The first night it happened, it scared us witless. Elan was sitting in bed, calling out to us, looking at us while we stood beside him, talking to him. He looked at us but kept calling as if we weren't there. We had learned since that a child who experiences "night terrors" acts awake but is not really awake. We also knew that we shouldn't try to wake him up but only comfort him in his sleep. I believe that Becky and I read all the books on the subject before we were finally convinced that we knew what to do. Some books tell you that the "night terrors" are more frightening to the parents than the child. I can't say that we are buying it, although it is definitely quite scary for us every time.

As always, I held Elan in my arms, murmuring soothing words to him. But this time, there was something different: he was hot.

"Daniel ..." I said, looking at him inquiringly.

"Yes, he has a fever. It's high. We must lower it immediately."

By then, Becky was standing beside us and had heard Daniel's words.

"I'll fill the bathtub with lukewarm water. Undress him and bring him to the bathroom," she said, looking efficient and in control.

Elan had calmed down by now and was no longer in the grip of the night terror. He was sweating profusely, and his pajamas were wet. Daniel and I undressed him gently and carried him over to the bathroom. When we immersed him slowly into the water, he opened his eyes.

"Daddy ...," he said feebly, "I don't feel well."

"I know, I know. You have a fever. But don't worry; we are taking care of it."

"Do you have any paracetamol?" Daniel asked, talking to nobody in particular.

"Yes," said Becky, "syrup or tablets?"

"Better syrup, it will be easier to give it to him."

Becky ran down and was back in no time with a bottle and a spoon.

"This is good," said Daniel, appreciatively, after inspecting the bottle. "We need to give him two and a half spoons for his body weight."

I was holding Elan in the tub, wetting his body gently by squeezing a sponge over him. His eyes were closed, and he was breathing quickly. There was no sign that the temperature had gone down. Becky filled up a spoon, and I offered it to Elan, who firmly closed his mouth.

"I'll pinch his nose," said Daniel. "That will make him open his mouth, and then you can pour the syrup in. We have no choice," he added, looking at my unhappy expression, "we must lower the temperature, and the bath alone is not doing it."

Working together, we finally succeeded in making Elan swallow the medicine. It took some doing, a lot of crying, and we spilled a spoonful or two in the bath, but we finally made it. Becky kept the water running, and after a while, Elan started to tremble like a leaf. I looked at Daniel, worried.

"Don't worry," he said calmly. "It means that the temperature is going down."

And in fact, after a few more minutes, Elan's temperature was back to normal. We took him out, dried him gently, and dressed him in fresh pajamas. He was still shivering. Becky and I took him into our bed. There was no question of letting him out of our sight that night. Becky chose to stay with him for a while, and Daniel and I went to the kitchen for a well-earned cup of tea. On the way, I took another look at Dana. She was sleeping with a smile on her face.

"It's all right now, Richard," said Daniel with a tired smile. "The crisis is over, and the fever is gone. You should keep him at home tomorrow, but I don't expect that there will be anything to worry about."

Later, Becky came into the kitchen, looking calm.

"Elan is sleeping well now and is breathing regularly. Thanks to you, Daniel. I'm really grateful."

"It was nothing, really. You didn't need me. I'm sure that you would have managed just the same without me, but I'm glad I was here to help."

"Why don't we all try to get some sleep now?" I suggested. I was annoyed. It was true that Daniel had helped, but I was the one who had done all the hard work, and it seemed as if Becky didn't notice that I was there. Women! Only a few hours before, she was ready to throw him to the wolves, and now he was her hero. I got up markedly and walked to the door. I don't think that they noticed me, though. Becky was pouring herself a cup of tea and going again through how wonderful Daniel had been. I was sick of it and went to bed.

The next morning we decided to take it easy. We got up late and let Dana oversleep as well. She could stay home and keep company with her brother. Elan was feeling well but tired and chose to stay in bed for a while longer. He turned on the TV set in our bedroom and soon got absorbed in it.

We had a light breakfast in the kitchen and, mercifully, Becky didn't start harping again on how wonderful Daniel had been that night.

"As soon as you're ready," I told him, "we'll go to Yair's lab and get you started on the preparations. Here, I'll fetch the samples," I said, fishing the box out of the freezer and immediately regretting it.

"What's in that box, Richard?" asked Becky. "I meant to ask you."

"Oh, it's nothing. Just stuff."

"What kind of stuff?"

"Stuff we need for Daniel's work. Sealed stuff."

"Do you mean aborted babies?" she asked menacingly.

"Now, really," I said, trying to pass lightly over it, "it's not like that. Just a few samples for laboratory work."

"And you've kept them in my freezer?" she went on, mercilessly, "with the rack of lamb I'm preparing to cook when your parents come over next week?"

"Don't be worried," said Daniel, coming to the rescue, "it is merely a sealed box containing sealed packages of perfectly innocuous material. I keep them in my freezer also. Nothing to be concerned about."

And such was the power of Daniel's charm after last night that she merely said, "Oh, okay," and there the matter rested.

Daniel and I drove to the university. I had called Yair earlier that morning to let him know that we were coming as planned. The most challenging part of the journey was, as usual, finding a parking spot, but eventually, we managed to park not too far from the laboratory. Yair was waiting for us in his office.

"Yair, this is Daniel," I said, making the introduction.

"Hi, Daniel. I've heard a lot about you. And read a lot too."

Daniel blushed. I had thought, I don't know how many times, that he should learn to behave a little more manly. Instead, he thrived on his spinelessness.

"I hope that you didn't get the wrong impression from the newspapers."

"I never believe what's in the papers. They never know what they are talking about."

"I appreciate your help. I really do. Everybody is so wonderful to me. It repays me for all I've been through."

Yair took Daniel by the arm and motioned him into a laboratory, explaining all the while.

"I have reserved this laboratory for you for today and tomorrow. It's yours. Feel free to use it as you need. Here is the ultracentrifuge, and here are the filters ..."

He guided Daniel through the equipment in the laboratory, and I listened passively. All I wanted was to see Daniel getting started and then to run to my office for a day's work.

After a while, Yair showed us the coffee machine and left us to ourselves, with a few words of admonition:

"If anybody comes along and starts asking questions, tell them that you are carrying out a project for me and that they should ask me about it. Then, call me immediately. Okay?"

"I understand."

"You okay?" I asked. I was worried lest Daniel might break down in the face of all the potential problems we were cautioning him against. Perhaps we had overdone it.

"Yes, yes. No problem. I have all I need, and Yair left me his extension number, in case I should need anything else. I'll get going on this if you don't mind. I have a lot of work to do."

"All right. When you are finished, give me a ring at the office, and I'll come to pick you up."

The day at the office was uneventful, and, for once, I saw smiling faces around me as the work got checked and distributed, like in the old days. I called home a couple of times to check on Elan, who felt fine. Daniel called a couple of times, too, to tell me that he was making progress.

"Have you had anything to eat?" I asked, suddenly remembering that we hadn't taken care of that.

"No time. Too busy. I'll eat when I'm through."

"Do you want me to bring you a sandwich?"

"I won't be able to find the time to eat it, anyway. Save it for when you pick me up. I'm never hungry at work. Well, I must go," he said, and hung up without further ceremony.

As the day wore on, I found myself becoming more and more optimistic. Daniel was going to finish preparing his samples of protein today. The patent application would be filed tomorrow, and the protein would be characterized in a few weeks, after which a complete patent application would be filed. Yes, we were definitely seeing the end of it and coming out of it unscathed despite all the unusual trouble attached to this case. It was, indeed, not bad.

At six p.m., Daniel called me to say that he had almost finished. The time was nearly seven p.m. when I reached the university. The parking lot in front of the lab was empty, and I parked near the building entrance. Daniel and Yair were having coffee in the laboratory, sitting on high wooden chairs by the working bench. I declined the invitation to join them. Somehow, coffee and fetuses didn't seem to blend well in my mind.

"We are all set," said Yair when I came in. "I've got ten nice samples of fractions that Daniel prepared, from which I can isolate the protein. They are freezing right now over here, and I'll start working on them as soon as I can."

"When do you think that we'll get some results?" I asked. I didn't want to seem pushy—after all, Yair was doing us an unpaid favor—but I didn't want him to think we had all the time in the world, either. We needed the results to file a better patent than the preliminary one we had ready.

"I would normally do it in ten days or so, but with my current workload, I'd say four to six weeks, if everything goes well."

"We appreciate your help very much. Thanks, Yair."

We parted from Yair with a few more expressions of appreciation and drove back to the house. Daniel was quiet, and I guessed that he must have been worn out after a full day on his feet at the lab.

Becky was home and greeted us with another portion of the previous day's hot soup that made my mouth water even from a distance. Her soups are always better the next day. Daniel sat down and wolfed down everything in sight, until coffee was served—instant stuff, not my own espresso—when he unbuttoned his jacket and said:

"Well, I'd better be going now."

"It's getting late; it is almost eight o'clock. Wouldn't you rather stay the night and go home early tomorrow morning?" I asked.

"I don't think so. Paula is at home alone, and I am taking up Elan's bed, which isn't fair to him or, indeed, to you. Besides, I'm already homesick. No, I think that I'll take the ten-thirty bus. It stops at my house, and it is very convenient. I'll take a nap on the way. Do you think that you could get me a taxi?"

"Don't be silly," Becky said, "Richard will be happy to drive you to the bus station, won't you, Richard?"

"Of course," I said, making a mental note to talk to Becky about it. I had thought that calling a taxi was a perfectly admirable suggestion, and why she should feel that she had to volunteer me out of the house at that time of the evening, and after dinner, it was more than I could understand.

Daniel collected his few belongings into his suitcase, made a quick phone call to Paula to let her know that he was on his way, and stood on the doorstep. Elan and Dana came to the door to say goodbye. Dana wasn't really interested, but she gave him a quick hug and a kiss, as she had been told numerous times to do. Elan wasn't hugging in public. "Childish," he labeled it, as if to imply that he was a grown-up already. "Will you be coming back to visit us?" he asked.

"I hope so. And if I don't, then I hope that you will be coming to visit us. You will like Paula—my wife. She bakes wonderful cakes. Tell your mom and dad to bring you one of these days."

"We will, we will," I said, "but if you don't get into that car, you are never going to make it to your bus."

"Goodbye, Becky," he said, looking at her and extending a hand, which she took. "You have been wonderful, much as I had expected of someone married to your wonderful husband. I can't thank you enough."

"Don't mention it. Our pleasure," said Becky, and I was astonished to note that she was blushing. Becky hadn't blushed since that day when I had proposed to her, and even then only because she had drunk too much punch. She was blush-proof—and yet, here she was, undeniably blushing.

"Get in the car, Daniel. Get in the car, or we'll be late," I said, almost pushing him inside.

I kept silent during the short drive to the bus station. Once there, we barely had time to buy a ticket, for which I paid. At the platform, I said a hurried goodbye. I got a few more corny remarks from Daniel, boosting my many qualities as a friend, my intelligence, and my general approach to life. He finally climbed into the bus, which pulled away from the platform and disappeared into the night.

I was happy to see him go.

CHAPTER 9

As the days went by, life started to go back to normal. Hysterical clients calmed down, the work got done, and everything was peaceful again. Elan recovered entirely in twenty-four hours, and the episode of the night fever was forgotten.

Then coming home one evening, about a week later, I was surprised to find Daniel sitting with Becky in my living room. As he saw me, he jumped to his feet.

"Hi, Richard, how are you?"

"I'm good, but what are you doing here? Is there a problem?"

I gazed at Becky, but she turned her head away, looking guilty, or at least that's how it felt to me.

"No. No. Everything is okay. I came because I wanted to get your opinion on something. I have been invited by my foundation—you know, the one that finances my work—to a scientific meeting in California. It will probably keep me away for ten to twelve days, but it may be important for me to meet people in the field, perhaps investors ... What do you think?"

"You didn't come all the way here to ask me that," I said, pointedly, again looking unsuccessfully for a reaction from Becky. "You could have phoned me. Anyway, it sounds like a good idea to me."

"But if I'm gone, will it not delay our work on the protein? Can I afford not to be here?"

"Yair is only starting to work on it at the end of this week or early next week, and he won't have any results to discuss with you for the next three or four weeks. Don't worry."

"So, you think it's okay for me to go?"

"It's okay." I wanted him gone, and the sooner, the better.

"I'll go then."

"Yes, yes. Go. When is your flight leaving?" I asked, hoping the answer was "right now."

"Early tomorrow morning." That was good enough.

"I'll see you when you get back, then."

"Of course. And Paula will know how to get hold of me if you need me."

"All right. Have a safe trip, then."

Daniel thanked me and left. I turned my attention to Becky.

"How long has he been here?" I asked.

"Perhaps a half-hour," she said. She wasn't looking me in the eyes and seemed embarrassed. Something was undeniably wrong. I remained silent for a whole minute, facing her as she stood there in silence.

"Is there anything that you want to tell me?" I asked at last, as calmly as I could manage.

"No, nothing ... I'm tired, and my body aches. I may have gotten the flu. I'll go to bed if you don't mind."

That was wrong. Becky never got the flu. She never ached. I

felt unreasonable anger mounting in me.

"Where are the kids?"

"Out with my sister. They'll be back soon. Please take care of them. I'm going to bed," she said, and left. She hadn't looked at me even once.

I let fifteen minutes pass, and then I went up to our room. Becky was in bed, asleep. I watched her slow breathing for a minute, and then I walked into our bathroom. I sat on the edge of the bath, seething about something that was probably nothing. At last, I got up and went to the sink to wash my hands. A strange smell hit my nostrils; it was a blend of mint and cheese. The smell came from a blob of blueish-greenish goo that sat in the middle of the sink. I dipped a finger into it and brought it close to my nose. At the touch of my finger, it fizzled and then evaporated. The remaining smell was too unpleasant, so I turned the tap, washed it away from my hand, and watched the last traces of goo in the sink disappear. I had meant to ask Becky what that stuff was in the morning, but it slipped my mind.

A vacation from the Vargos, I thought to myself, was an unexpected gift. I'd had all I could take for a few weeks, and I was happy not to hear from them for a while.

But, of course, Paula called me the next day.

"Rich-ard! How are you?"

"I'm fine."

"Daniel is gone, you know."

"Yes, I know. How is he?"

"I haven't heard from him yet. Listen, I have been working on the project's business end, and I have some ideas that I would like to discuss with you. Could you come tomorrow?"

"No, I am afraid that tomorrow is impossible. Tomorrow it's

Dana's birthday."

"Oh, happy birthday to her. Then, maybe the day after?"

Here I was on solid ground. "I am giving a speech that evening, on recent developments of patent law, at a gala dinner of the Industrialists' Association, I'm sorry. Perhaps sometime next week."

"Oh, yes, I read about the dinner in the newspaper. When is your speech? I may want to come too if I can make it."

"My speech is scheduled for eight p.m., but you can't come if you are not a member of the association; I'm sorry."

"But then, you can get me an invitation, can't you?"

"No, I can't. It's a private function."

"So, you'll be there something like seven to ten pm.?"

"Probably until elevenish. But does it matter?"

"Oh, no, it doesn't. I would love to hear you speak and be able to tell everybody: 'Here's my patent attorney.' But never mind. Some other time, perhaps."

That's all I need, I thought, but I said, "Yes, certainly. Some other time."

I hung up, feeling that I had been too optimistic in believing that a vacation from the Vargo family was possible. These people had become a fixture in my life, or so it seemed.

Dana's birthday went well, with lavish gifts and a colorful dinner at her best-loved Chinese restaurant, where you got fortune cookies, umbrellas, and, on your birthday, a special sweet with fireworks on it. So everything was perfect if you didn't count the fact that Becky had acted distant all day. I had come home early to find her sitting by the bedroom window, staring out.

"What's up?" I asked, trying to sound cheerful.

"Okay," was the almost-whispered answer.

Becky got up without gazing directly at me and turned to go into the bathroom.

"What's the matter?" I asked, finally starting to lose my patience.

"Nothing."

"Nothing? You've been acting like I'm not here since Daniel's visit, so I ask again: what's the matter?"

"Nothing, I told you," she answered, speaking tonelessly.

That left me with the option to pick a fight or move on. I opted to move on since Dana was already yelling, "Daddy, Mommy," all excited about her birthday. But once we returned home and the kids went to bed, I had to bring this up again. I sat on the bed and turned to Becky, who had gotten under the sheets quickly and without a word, not even her usual "Good night."

"Do you want to tell me what's the matter?" I asked.

She gazed straight before her, and I saw that she was struggling with an answer.

"All this got me thinking," she said in a low voice.

"All this what?"

"The Vargos. You. Paula. All the work you're putting into it."

"We've talked about this already, haven't we? It's only work."

"Yes, but ... it got me thinking."

"About what?"

"About me, us, our life. What we are doing here."

That really got me worried. Something was going on that I couldn't understand. Something that had to do with the Vargos, but I couldn't figure out what it was and why it had such an influence on Becky.

"What happened the other day, when Daniel was here?"

"Daniel? Nothing."

"What did you two talk about?"

"Oh, things."

"Like what?"

"This is silly. I don't want to have this discussion. Good night," she said, and turned her back to me.

I should have insisted and forced her to air it, but somehow I couldn't bring myself to do it. This was not my Becky, whom I had known forever and loved, and I didn't want to have this talk with her. Stupid of me, I guess. It never pays to run away from problems that will eventually come back to bite you.

The next day was another story. Talking to some two hundred uninterested industrialists on a topic such as "Modern Trends in Patents Law" was not a simple undertaking. Overall, it was the most boring function I had ever attended. I had to sit and listen to a seemingly endless list of VIPs, who delivered meaningless welcome speeches. Becky, who usually accompanied me to public functions, had announced that she had a date with her sister. I didn't insist since I no longer seemed to know how to speak to her and didn't relish a long evening of silence. The speaker before me gave us a lot of information, the nature of which I can't quite recall, on a reasonably interesting topic, which, I think, had to do with high-tech taxation—but I can't be sure.

My speech went well. The audience liked the anecdotes, and those who understood them also enjoyed a few jokes that I sneaked in *impromptu*. After my speech and the concluding remarks of the head of the association, I mingled a bit in the crowd that lingered with coffee and *petit fours* and exchanged pleasantries with people I knew.

By the time I got home, it was almost midnight, and I was falling off my feet. I always find that dinners and cocktails are exhausting functions, particularly those where you are expected to be friendly and smile at everybody. Becky wasn't home yet. I thanked our babysitter, apologizing for the late hour, and paid her lavishly, feigning to miscalculate the number of hours she had been at the house. She didn't seem to mind the tip. Before she left, and as an afterthought, she handed me a note, scribbled in Elan's handwriting. It went:

"Dear Daddy. He called and said you should call him soonest. I told him you were away, and I will tell you. And, Daddy. He said it was urgent, and here is the number. And, Daddy. Never mind if it's late. He wants to speak with you also in the middle of the night. Love, Elan."

The number was one I didn't recognize, with a Jerusalem area code. Of course, Elan hadn't written down the caller's name, which was his maddening way of taking messages. I had spoken to him about it a million times, but here he was, doing it again. I dragged myself up to Elan's room and shook him partly awake.

"Elan, Elan! This note here. Who was the caller?"

"Ah?" Elan mumbled from the mist of sleep.

"Who called? Who left the message that I should call him at any time?"

"Mommy?" he suggested.

"No, not Mommy. Pay attention for a moment, Elan, for God's sake. Someone called and left a message with you. Do you remember his name?"

"Sharan. He said Doctor Sharan." He opened his eyes and asked, "Time to go to school?"

"No, not yet. Go back to sleep," I said, and left the room. I knew no Doctor Sharan, and I couldn't think why he should be calling me at home. I debated whether to call him. It *was* late, indeed, but if Elan got it right, he wanted me to call him at any time, and it could be something really urgent. I lifted the receiver and dialed the number. After two rings and a click, I got a recorded voice.

"You have reached extension ... click vishh ... five-three-seven. The person you are calling is either on the phone or away from his desk and cannot answer your call. Please leave a message at the beep."

I hung up. I wasn't going to leave any messages for a person I didn't know. My secretary would sort this out in the morning.

I debated whether to wait for Becky but was too tired, so I took a quick shower and discounted the idea of making my usual late-night coffee. I believe that I was asleep before my head touched the pillow.

In the morning, I got up fresh and rested and sat in the kitchen for a light breakfast. Becky was up too and a bit more communicative than she had been for a few days. Perhaps whatever brand of blues that had possessed her was wearing out. I hoped so. I was tired of having to tiptoe around my own home. I ran through the newspaper quickly, looking for a mention of yesterday's dinner and my speech. I almost missed the item at the bottom of the front page. The paper said:

"SCIENTIST FOUND DEAD IN CLOSED HOSPITAL LABORATORY"

And in smaller letters:

"Dr. Tarun Chandran was found dead by a security guard following an anonymous phone call. The reasons for death are yet uncertain. A special investigative team has been appointed by the Chief of the Jerusalem police."

So that was it! It was Tarun who had called me yesterday evening, it wasn't Sharan, it was Chandran. I should have made the connection, but perhaps I was too tired, or simply I wasn't expecting Tarun to call me at home so late.

I wondered what Tarun could have wanted so late and so urgently. I guessed that I might never be able to find out now. And another thought occurred to me that perhaps I could have saved Tarun's life had I been at home. The paper mentioned a closed laboratory. That could be a hint that Tarun had committed suicide. Perhaps he needed a friendly voice, and with Daniel abroad, he had chosen to call me. We would never know.

"Look at this, Becky," I called. "Do you know who this guy is?"

"Never heard of him."

"He is Daniel's assistant. The post-doc who was working for him on the project. Now Daniel is really in trouble. My God! I don't think that his death is the hospital's doing, but that's really a troubling thought. Paula said that strange things were happening and that Daniel was afraid ... and replacing Tarun is not going to be easy; that's bad because his experiments were supposed to help us strengthen Daniel's patent."

Becky was visibly alarmed. She placed the mug from which she was about to drink back on the table with a furrowed brow. "You don't think that this may have anything to do with Daniel's project, do you?"

I mused for a while. I thought that the medical center was headed by dishonest people, who would bend the truth for their own advantage, to the point of ruining a good doctor's career without a qualm. But I doubted that they would resort to murder to achieve their purposes. The stakes were not high enough. Or weren't they?

"I sincerely hope not. I don't think so. It's inconceivable. These people lied straight-faced in a court of law, trying to destroy Daniel, but murder ... no, there must be another explanation."

"I wish you would get out of this project. You've done enough, and I don't think that you want to be involved in something that has to do with a murder."

"Don't say 'murder.' I'm sure that there is no question of it. Probably Tarun got careless and made a mistake in handling lab equipment, which cost him his life. This is the simplest explanation, and I bet it's the right one."

But I wished I were as convinced as I hoped I sounded. I was shaken and resolved to call Yoel as soon as I got to the office to discuss what we should do. I didn't want to do it from the house, where Becky would overhear our conversation.

I dressed quickly, tried to kiss Becky without getting much encouragement from her, and went to the door. As I was about to leave, the doorbell rang. I opened the door and saw two unknown persons on the mat.

"Mr. Luster?"

"Yes?"

"I am Yosef, of the Jerusalem police. This is my colleague, Uri Fribert. We would like to ask you a few questions."

"Is this about Tarun?"

"How do you know about Tarun?" asked the one called Uri, giving me a suspicious look.

"It's in the papers. I just read about it. I am still shaken by the story. What really happened?"

"We were really hoping, Mr. Luster, that *you* would answer a few of our questions," said the one called Yosef with a pleasant smile, "not the other way around."

"Could we go to my office? I'd rather keep my wife out of it. She's shaken already as it is."

"We were planning to ask you to accompany us to the Jerusalem headquarters if you don't mind," said the one called Yosef, who was doing most of the talking. "There may be other people wanting to talk to you. It's only a forty-five-minute drive," he added with a conciliatory smile, "far quicker than getting into town to your office."

"Oh, all right. If that's necessary ..."

"It is. It is. We appreciate your cooperation, Mr. Luster. Please get into the car."

I realized, too late, that Becky would see my car parked by the house and would wonder what had become of me. I dialed our house from my cell-phone and got her immediately.

"Becky? I just wanted to tell you that I have left the car at the house. Something has come up, and I had to go to Jerusalem. It is regarding Tarun. The police want me to help them a bit. I'll be back in the early afternoon," I said, looking interrogatively at Yosef, who nodded in assent. "No, don't worry," I reassured her, "I won't be long. I'll be in touch as soon as I am through. Bye."

Nobody spoke during the whole trip to Jerusalem. I tried to ask a question or two to better understand what had happened, but all I got in return were silent stares and sad shakes of the head. So I eventually kept quiet too.

The police headquarters were bustling, with uniformed policemen hurrying to and fro. Yosef disappeared immediately into a corridor, promising to be back "soon"—an expression I had learned to fear in governmental agencies because what it really meant was "sometime in the future, don't ask me when, because I don't know." The one called Uri stayed with me, standing by the bench where I sat and surveyed the activity around us with hooded eyes. Every now and then, someone would walk by us and throw him a hurried "Hi," to which he invariably responded with a silent nod. Not a chatty type, this Uri.

After what seemed to me like ten hours but was probably more like twenty minutes, a uniformed policewoman approached Uri and told him that 23D was available. Uri motioned me to follow him along the corridor. We entered a small room with a table, a water pitcher, and four rather unclean glasses. Yosef was sitting there by a tape recorder and greeted us when we came in.

"Sorry you had to wait, Mr. Luster. We are obliged to tape all our interrogations and had to wait for a room with a tape recorder to become available. I hope you were not too uncomfortable. Some water?" he asked, raising the pitcher.

"No, thank you. I'd rather get started with your questions and get back to Tel Aviv as soon as possible. Still, I wish you would tell me a little about what happened to Tarun."

"We will, we will, Mr. Luster—or may I call you Richard?" I nodded mechanically, and he continued: "We will, Richard, but first things first. I'm turning on the tape recorder. This is a recording of the interview with Mr. Richard Luster. Richard, could you please confirm, for the purpose of the tape, that you are aware that this conversation is being taped?"

I nodded, and Yosef continued with a smile: "The tape recorder doesn't record nods. Please speak up."

"I do."

"Then, Richard, please tell us where you were yesterday night, the twenty-third, at eight-thirty p.m."

A chill ran along my spine. Now I understood. I was a suspect.

CHAPTER 10

"Why did Tarun call you?" This was Uri, suddenly turned loquacious.

"I told you, I don't know. How could I? I didn't talk to him."

"But his phone record shows a conversation of over four minutes with your house, at seven-fifteen. What did you talk about?"

"We didn't talk. I wasn't at home, at seven-fifteen. He spoke with my son, who took a message."

"What did the message say?"

"It said, 'please call.'"

"So, what did you talk about when you called?"

"I didn't call."

"But your phone records show that you called his lab at five minutes to twelve."

"But I didn't know it was him. My son got the name wrong. And the records will also show that the call lasted only for a few seconds."

"And what did you say to each other during those few seconds?"

We had been at this dance for a couple of hours by now. They, trying to confuse me into saying God knows what, and I, trying to keep my patience. But I was out of patience.

"Look here, this isn't getting us anywhere. From your questions, I gather that Tarun was killed around eight-thirty ..."

"How did you know he was killed? Maybe he died of natural causes."

"Give me a break, will you? Would we be here wasting everybody's time if he had died of a heart attack? So why ask me questions about what we said to each other at midnight? If he was dead at midnight, then obviously you know that we didn't speak."

"Do you have anybody who can confirm your whereabouts at eight-thirty?" This was a new genius that had come into the room half an hour ago, and I hadn't caught his name.

"Only about five hundred people," I said, losing my patience. "Look, if you plan to go on asking me stupid questions, you'll have to find new ones. I have answered these three times already, and I'm not going to answer any more."

"Yes, you are," said the new one.

"Yeah? Then make me," I said, defiantly. They had all gotten on my nerves, and I had had about enough. "Until you do, no more questions. And if you don't have any more questions, I'll be going."

"You can't go," said Uri, seeming surprised at the notion.

"Why not? I'm not under arrest, am I?" Their faces said that I wasn't, but that they would have loved me to be. "Then watch me," I said, getting up.

It was then that Yosef came into the room. He had been gone for a while, after the first round of questions. The first round hadn't been so bad. Yosef had asked reasonable questions and got honest answers in return. But then these jerks had all tried their hands at me, hoping, I guess, to be the one to crack the case.

I hadn't quite figured out yet who was what here, but by how they treated him with respect, it was pretty clear that Yosef was higher ranking than the others. He now addressed me civilly.

"Richard, the boss would like to have a word with you in private before you go. You can go," he said, talking to the others, "we are done here."

The geniuses turned to the door with, I thought, a murmur of discontent but left the room without arguing.

"And who would the boss be?" I asked.

"The captain. He's in charge of this special investigation. Here he is," he said when the door opened.

I looked up at the captain's face, and my surprise was complete. The "captain" was no other than my old buddy, Eitan Akerman. Eitan and I went back a long way. We had been in school together since fourth grade when his family had moved into my neighborhood. I hadn't seen him for a good five years now, but before my marriage, we used to meet regularly with other friends for a game of cards or for a barbecue.

"Eitan! You a captain?" I asked in disbelief.

"Yeah, you see how they make me dress up," he said, extending a friendly hand for me to shake and pulling at his uniform with the other.

"I thought you were in the highway patrol."

"No, not the highway patrol. Homicide. Not very different these days, though, the way people drive out there."

"It's a small world," I remarked, without trying to be particularly original.

"Oh, yeah, a tiny one," he answered, with the matching cliché.

An embarrassing silence ensued, as often happens with old friends who unexpectedly meet at a distance of time.

"Ehmm ... if you don't need me, boss, I'll be gone," said Yosef.

"No, thank you. I won't be needing you."

Yosef left the room, and Eitan took a chair and sat down. I dragged my own chair closer to his.

"So, what is this little mess you have gotten yourself into, Richard?"

"No mess that I know of. Guy I met only once signed off. So what does that have to do with me?"

"It looks like someone wants you to be involved, and I'd like to find out why."

"What do you mean?" I wasn't following him at all.

"Perhaps I should tell you the story as we know it, from the beginning."

"That would help. I've been trying all day to get some information out of your baboons—sorry, I shouldn't call them that, I should say 'officers,' shouldn't I? In any case, I have tried to ask them what this was all about, but they only kept asking me the same silly questions all over again. It was all very frustrating."

"You shouldn't blame them. They are not allowed to give any information to a suspect."

"So that's what I am? A suspect?"

"Were. No longer. You are cleared. But you should light a candle to your protecting angel that made me be the one who runs the show, because the way it looked at the beginning, anybody else would have put you in custody for a few days for starters, just to let you know that he meant business. But I know you well enough to be ready to assume that you are no murderer—perhaps you are a cheat at poker, but not a killer."

"I'll pass lightly over the slanderous statements about my

extremely honest game of poker, only because I understand that you just saved my life. But I still don't have the faintest idea of what you are talking about."

"Well, it's like this." He stopped, as if to collect his thoughts, and then went on. "What we know is that this guy, Tarun, was working with a client of yours, Doctor Vargo. Doctor Vargo is currently abroad, and we can't get in touch with him. We tried to speak with his wife, but she got hysterical, and I don't know when we will get anything useful from her. In any case, she doesn't seem to know anything about Tarun's doings, and she doesn't really know what was being done in the laboratory.

"In any case, what we know is that Tarun went to work yesterday as usual. We don't know the exact time of his arrival, but we have a witness who is positive that he saw him in the corridor, coming from the men's room, at about five p.m., so we know that he had been at work at least since then.

"We then have him placing a call to Doctor Vargo's house, at around five forty-five. From what my men have been able to understand from the Vargo woman, there was nothing special about the call. He asked about Doctor Vargo and how he was doing in the U.S., and they chatted for a minute or so. She said that he sounded quite normal, although she doesn't know him well enough to judge whether he might have been in a state of mind any different from usual.

"Then we have him calling your house at seven-thirty, for about four minutes. We now know from you that he spoke with your kid and left an urgent message for you to call him—a message which, if I understand it correctly, you didn't receive until you got home, around midnight."

"Well, to be precise, I didn't get it even then, because my son didn't write the name down and, when I woke him up and tried to ask him who called, he was too sleepy to concentrate and gave me a wrong name."

"Okay. Then we know that you called the lab."

"I got curious because I didn't recognize the phone number that was on the message. So I dialed it, but a machine answered, and I hung up."

"This is what we know on phone calls. He made no other call that we could trace, and nobody else called his number. Then around one o'clock last night, we got an anonymous call telling us that there was a dead man in a laboratory at the medical center. The person calling gave us the room number of the lab but refused to identify himself. He said, however, that if we questioned a Mister Richard Luster, we would learn interesting details about the death of that man, whose identity at the time we didn't know. He also said that, if we asked around, we would be able to confirm that Mr. Luster was in the building sometime between seven and nine of that night. Then, he hung up, and we weren't able to trace the call, although all calls to our police station are monitored. He must be a fucking wizard or something to do that. I have a team checking how we screwed up in locating the origin of this one, and you can bet I'll find out.

"Oh, and by the way, the officer who took the call couldn't say whether it was a man or a woman calling because the voice was masked. And the call hasn't been taped either. Good work, ah?" said Eitan bitterly.

Throughout this last part of the tale, I had sat there, petrified. I could see where this was leading, but it felt unreal as if all that was about someone else.

"You know that this is all nonsense, don't you?" I said, quickly, to make sure that no misconception about my alleged involvement still existed. "At the time that your caller said I was in the building in Jerusalem, I was in fact lecturing to a few hundred people in Tel Aviv. I was at the Industrialists' Association gala dinner all evening, and I never moved from there."

"I know that now. We have questioned a few people who were at the dinner, and they all confirmed having seen you and having heard your lecture. No, you're off the hook for all that concerns this murder. Still, there must be a reason why someone is trying to implicate you."

"But what happened then? What did you find?"

"We had one of our patrol cars go to the lab immediately. When they got there and knocked on the door, they got no answer. The door was locked from the inside, and light filtered from within. Because of the information they had, they forced the lock and got into the lab. Tarun was lying on the floor in the middle of the room, plainly dead. The medical examiner who saw him on the spot said that it seemed to him that he had been electrocuted."

"That sounds to me more like an accident than anything else. He may have gotten careless and touched an exposed wire—perhaps an electric cord of some equipment—and may have died because of that."

"Excellent theory, Richard. We thought of it also. There is a little problem, though: where Tarun was, there is no electric equipment, nor any electrical wire, for a radius of at least ten meters. Besides, we had all the electrical equipment checked, and none has a defective cable or connection. Plus, all the electrical appliances were switched off, and none showed any sign of a short-circuit or of an abnormal heating or any other reason why someone would have gotten an electric shock from them."

"You must have overlooked something, obviously."

"Believe me, we didn't. We fine-combed that lab and went through every single possible appliance, but we drew a blank. And even had we found a defective appliance, what would that have meant, given that he was nowhere near any of them? A man doesn't get himself electrocuted and then walks away to die in a more convenient place. When you get electrocuted, you drop on the spot."

"It is bizarre, but there must be an explanation."

"You think this is strange? You haven't heard the half of it. The medical examiner called me just a few minutes ago. He has completed the autopsy on Tarun, and he tells me that the internal injuries he found couldn't have been caused by simple electrocution. They are consistent with injuries inflicted on someone who has been struck by lightning."

"There you are. Here's the solution to your mystery. You didn't find any appliances near Tarun because he has been killed by lightning. It's an uncommon occurrence, but it happens."

"Yeah? And how do you think that the lightning got in, seeing that the lab is in the basement and has no windows?"

I hadn't thought of that. I was too happy to have found a simple solution to Tarun's death, one that didn't imply malicious intervention, that I had overlooked that simple fact.

"I hadn't thought of that," I said, mortified.

"That's why they didn't make you a captain," said Eitan. "Besides, yesterday was a beautiful night, without a cloud in the sky. The weather has been sunny for the last three days."

"Then it's a mystery," I said, at a loss to offer any more useful suggestions.

"Yes," said Eitan with a sigh, "isn't it? And what's worse, it's mine."

"I'm sorry. I wish I could help."

"Perhaps you can. Tell me about this Tarun. What do you know about him?"

"I know very little, actually. I met him only once, ten days ago, to discuss some experiments that Daniel Vargo wanted him to carry out. We met in the lab briefly and talked shop, and that was it. I never saw him or spoke with him again."

"Do you have any idea why he should be calling your house?"

"Not really … except maybe he got some important result and was excited about it and wanted to tell me. He seemed to be a very motivated person, and he took his work seriously and very much to heart. Also, he seemed to worship Daniel Vargo, and I assume that he would have called me if he had good and exciting news."

"Any other possible reason?"

"Well,…" I hesitated to share my suspicions about Abramov and his gang, but eventually, I decided that I had to be candid with Eitan. "This may be nothing, really. It probably is, and I don't want anybody to say that I have gone around making baseless accusations …"

"Don't worry about that. You tell me anything that comes to your mind, and we will check it thoroughly before mentioning it to anybody."

"Okay, then. You may have seen in the newspapers last week that there had been a brawl between Daniel Vargo and the medical center, particularly the medical director, Professor Abramov. That is what Yosef was referring to."

"Yes, I'm aware of it."

"Abramov and his colleagues became wild because the discovery was made by Daniel on his own time, and with the money of a grant he got and was not the property of the medical center. The laboratory in which you found Tarun has been rented by Daniel from the medical center."

"That could be a motive for murder. I have seen people being killed for much less than that."

"Yes, but why Tarun? I could understand it if they had killed Daniel, but Tarun ... doesn't make sense."

"Perhaps they wanted to stop the research."

"But this is not gonna stop it, and they know it. At most, they are delaying it a bit. You don't kill a man for that."

"Perhaps you're right, but there may be timing considerations of which we are not aware. They may be running parallel research, and time may be an important factor. A delay may be all they need to get to the result first."

I nodded but was not convinced.

"Even if this were a reasonable theory, you still have to find out how they did it. They are not minor gods throwing lightning bolts. There must be a better explanation."

"I hope you are right. In any case, I will have to ask you to let us take your prints. We want to go through those lifted from the lab and concentrate only on the ones we can't account for."

He took my prints, and then Eitan and I parted company, with me promising to call him if anything came to my mind, which I thought might have any significance whatsoever.

Eitan walked me to a car that had been assigned to take me home. The driver was one I hadn't seen before, and his conversation didn't go beyond a learned but quick discussion about my address and the best way to get there. It was okay with me, though. I had been given much food for thought.

PART TWO
Facing Facts

CHAPTER 11

It was dark by the time I got home. Becky was waiting for me on the porch. I hadn't called her on my way back because I didn't want to be pressed to tell her what was going on, with that police officer driving me and hearing everything I said. She walked quickly toward me as I got out of the car and clutched my arm.

"Don't say 'I told you so,' please," I begged.

"What happened?" she asked simply.

"Let's go inside and get us a cup of coffee, and I'll tell you all about it."

"No. Why do you think that I have been waiting for you outside? I don't want the children to hear anything that may worry them. Tell me quickly, then we'll go inside."

I sat with a sigh on one of the plastic chairs that we keep on the porch. I really needed a cup of coffee, but I could see her point, so I sat there and told her all I knew. She listened attentively, interested but distant. Once again, I felt like a gap had opened between us, and

I couldn't figure out why or how to close it. All I could do was give it time because I knew instinctively that confronting her with it could lead us down a road and a place I didn't want to go. So I gave her a quick summary of the day, and she listened in silence and without asking questions, then she got up, and I followed her inside.

My cell-phone rang as I was pouring coffee. I had forgotten to turn it off, which I usually do as soon as I get home. It was Yoel.

"Where the hell have you been?" he asked. "I've been looking for you all day after I read the news this morning. Didn't your office tell you?"

"I haven't been in touch with the office, sorry."

"And your cell-phone was turned off," he added accusingly.

"Yes, I apologize," I said, sounding and feeling annoyed, "but they make you turn these things off when they grill you for murder at the police station. It is considered bad form in police circles to talk on the telephone while they ask you questions on your whereabouts at the time of death."

The silence at the other end of the line told me that my message had gotten home.

"You've gone to the police?" Yoel asked.

"Well, not really 'gone,' you know. More sort of 'picked up and taken there,' as it happens. I got an invitation I couldn't refuse, in the form of two plainclothes policemen standing on my doormat."

"And ... ?"

"Oh, everything's fine, as you hear. I'm back home and no longer on the suspects' list. All the same, I think I may need some good legal advice. And maybe we need to rethink our involvement in the Vargo project. Are you free tomorrow?"

"I'm tied up in court until noon, but if you come to my office around two o'clock, we will have time to talk."

"I'll be there at two," I said and hung up.

That night I slept deeply as I hadn't slept for months. I simply got into bed and, before I closed my eyes, it was morning already. Apparently, the day's commotion had taken its toll, but now I felt much better. I dressed quickly and got out in time to take the children to school—a rare occurrence lately.

At the office, Lia and Oz didn't ask questions, and I didn't volunteer any information regarding the circumstances of my disappearance on the previous day. I got cold-stared at by Lia a few times during the day, but I didn't let this change my decision to leave her out of it.

After a frugal lunch consisting of sandwiches delivered from a nearby deli, I jumped in a taxi that brought me to Yoel's office at five past two. Yoel was there, looking somber.

"Hi," I said, trying hard to sound joyous, "why the funeral face?"

"I've done some serious thinking, yesterday and today, and I'm not certain that I like the result. By the way, talking of funerals, shouldn't we be going to Tarun's?"

"Uhm, I haven't given much thought to it, to be honest. But ... no, I mean, I didn't really *know* him, and you haven't even met him. And besides, the funeral is probably already over."

"Good," said Yoel, getting up to close the door and sitting down again, "then let's talk."

I looked at him inquisitively, waiting for him to start the conversation. I had some questions that I wanted to take up with him, but seeing Yoel act so seriously made me wonder.

"Talk, I'm curious," I said.

"Yeah? Well, *I* was curious after you told me about your visit with the police. They told you that an anonymous caller advised them that you might have pertinent information relative to Tarun's death. Now, let's see who the son of a bitch might be."

"I have no idea, but I think that I will have to look within the medical center people for that."

"But they don't know that you exist or that you knew Tarun."

"I guess they do, after that day in court."

"That was my first reaction too. Then, I started to go through my memory of that day, step by step, and I realized that I never introduced you to the court or to anybody else. When the judge asked who Daniel's representative was, I just called out my own name, omitting yours—a gross omission on my part, of course, but justified by the great pressure of time in which I was at the moment, having to fight this motion that had been dropped on me out of the blue. So they didn't hear your name there."

"And my name wasn't in the paper!"

"Exactly. So, who knows that you have met with Tarun?"

"I guess that it's only us, Daniel and Paula—and, of course, Becky."

"Okay, we are making progress. Becky and I are out by definition, and Daniel is in California. So who are we left with?"

"Paula? I don't believe it. The person who made the call is very likely also the killer. Paula didn't have any reason to kill Tarun."

"Was it a man or a woman calling?"

"The police don't know. The voice was altered. Could've been either."

"Then it could have been Paula."

"In theory ... but it doesn't make sense: she and Daniel may be in deep trouble now, with Tarun gone and nobody to make any progress on the research work."

"You are talking sense, and that's the problem. What if she is a psycho? Then reasonable rules don't apply anymore. Crazy people do crazy things, even if it hurts them eventually."

"Look, I dislike Paula intensely, but I don't think she is crazy. In fact, I rather think she is the more balanced of the two."

"Do you think so? Well, as I told you, I gave some thought to it, and I didn't feel so generous toward her after I realized that she might be the killer, so I started thinking about other matters. Do you remember that she told us about this lawyer, Aaron Dworsky-Ehrenfeld, where she did her internship in Jerusalem?"

"Right."

"Well, then take this book," he said, sliding the official list of the members of the bar association toward me on the table, "and look under the entry for Vargo."

I did so and found three Vargos. They all were males, and of course, none was named Paula.

"But, I don't understand ..."

"No? Then look in the Jerusalem section and find an advocate called Aaron Dworsky-Ehrenfeld—no, don't waste your time. There is no such name in the list, in Jerusalem or elsewhere. I checked the whole list."

"Do you mean that she has made all that up?"

"I don't see any other explanation. And she gave us this story looking us in the eyes, lying straight-faced. She even made up this most improbable name, Aaron Dworsky-Ehrenfeld, knowing very well that we could check on her and try to contact him, but gambling that we wouldn't. She is either very clever or completely nuts."

"Then, perhaps the whole story is something they made up ..."

"No, there I think you are going too far. I believe that Daniel is genuine. He behaves genuinely, and he is a scientist. But perhaps even he doesn't know how crazy Paula is, or maybe he knows but is somehow dominated by her. Take your pick."

"Oh my gosh," I said, suddenly starting to panic, "and we have become involved with them, and maybe ... we could be cooperating with a murderess. What shall we do?"

"You realize that we are in a spot. We represent her and her husband and can't do anything that may harm them unless we have solid reasons to suspect criminal acts. We must try to find out who she really is and learn about her background as much as possible. Then, we must try to establish what Daniel does and does not know about her. If it turns out that he is an accomplice in her crazy scheme, whatever that is, then we shall have to go to the police. In any case, if anything comes up that may tie her in with the murder in any way, we will have to report it. But we must first find out all we can. I don't want to go out there making wild accusations, only to discover that it was all a misunderstanding, and she is perfectly innocent of everything. Who knows. Maybe that Aaron Dworsky-Ehrenfeld existed and is dead or retired now, and that's why he's not on the list."

"So, what are we going to do?"

"You remember that she told us about her studies in Paris? I think that Paris is a good place to start. She must have met people and made friends there, and the university certainly has a file on her."

"Do you know any good investigator in Paris?"

"Investigator? No. We can't have an investigator do a job on one of our clients. It's unethical. Besides, what would the investigator do? We can't tell him exactly what we are after, and if we start giving him a partial picture of the job, it won't get us anywhere. Even if he stumbles on an important clue, he won't be able to recognize it. No, my friend, this is a job for us."

"You seem to have given a lot of thought to all this."

"I've done much more than that."

"What do you mean?"

"I mean that Air France has a beautiful flight to Charles de Gaulle Airport tomorrow morning at ten, and you and I are booked on it. Don't forget your toothbrush."

"You're joking."

"Do I look to you like someone who is joking? Do you *think* that I'm in the mood? Then think again. No joke. We put ourselves into this mess, and we must pull ourselves out of it."

I appreciated Amonon's chivalrous reference to "we." I know how easy it is to blame all our trouble on somebody else, particularly since, in this case, I was the one who had brought this particular Pandora's Box to him.

"For how long do you expect us to be gone?"

"I have booked our return for Thursday morning, which makes roughly three days in Paris."

"But what shall I tell Becky? I don't want her to worry."

"Tell her that I have asked you to accompany me to Paris for an important matter of a client of mine, the nature of which you can't disclose."

"You know I'm a bad liar. She'll find me out in no time."

"You're not lying here. She is a client of mine, it is an important matter, and you can't disclose its nature, otherwise, Becky will freak out. All perfectly true."

"Mmm ..."

"You tell her what you want, okay? But let me know what your story is so that I can back you up. Now please go and let me do some work. I'll see you at the airport at eight sharp tomorrow morning. I'll bring the tickets. Get out!"

I knew that I should have talked to Becky immediately, but there was something that I wanted to get done first. I found a supermarket, one of those that had the promotional offers for the Japanese month going on, and walked in. The first thing that hit me as I got in was a massive pile of Japanese dishes of all kinds, shapes, and sizes. I selected a soup bowl that seemed to be less repugnant than the others, paid the equivalent of five dollars for it, and took it back to the office.

In the office, I looked for a small box to fit the bowl and was lucky to find a white one without any particular markings. Then I fetched a roll of toilet paper, two small plastic bags, and some white tissue paper that I had picked up at the supermarket and locked my door. I didn't dare to think of what Lia might be making of all this since I never lock my door, but I didn't have the time to do this elsewhere.

Wearing the plastic bags on my hands as if they were gloves, I took the toilet paper and started rubbing the bowl gently but firmly. Two minutes later, the bowl was so shiny that you could have used it as a shaving mirror. I had no doubt that it was now thoroughly and completely clean, inside and out.

I then took the wrapping tissue paper and wrapped the bowl gently in it, after which I placed it carefully into the box and closed the lid. Only then did I take off my "gloves" and dispose of them, together with all the spent paper, in my wastepaper basket. Then I lifted the receiver and dialed a familiar number.

"Vargo," Paula's voice answered.

"Paula, this is Richard."

"Hi, Richard, nice to hear from you. How are you doing?"

"I'm well. What about Daniel?"

"Daniel ..." she sighed, "I just got off the phone with him. He is devastated. You have heard about Tarun, of course."

"Yes, this is why I was calling you. I wanted to hear how you are, and Daniel ..." I was starting to become a natural liar, after all, out of necessity.

"Daniel is very sad. He loved Tarun, and he can't figure out what may have happened. He wanted to come back right away, but he has these important meetings with potential investors in California, and I convinced him to stay. There is nothing he can do, anyway. The funeral is over—you know, I didn't have the strength to go. Poor Tarun! And there is nothing that Daniel can do now, so he's staying abroad for the time being."

"I see. It was a wise decision, I think. Now something else, Paula. If you feel up to it, I would like your advice on something. Are you going to be at home for the next couple of hours?"

"Yes," she sounded surprised by my sudden desire to socialize, "of course, you're welcome. I thought of buying some groceries but don't feel like going out after all this."

"Okay. Then I'll be there in an hour or so. See you then," I said, and waited for her to hang up before I did.

The trip to Jerusalem seemed shorter than usual. Perhaps I was getting used to it. When I reached the door, no light showed from inside the house, but the living room light went on immediately as I pushed the bell. Paula came to open the door.

"Sorry to keep you waiting," she said. "I think I dozed off."

"It's okay. You didn't keep me waiting at all."

She led me into the living room, and I sat on the sofa, holding the box in both hands. It felt strange—surreal, in fact—to sit with a woman whom I suspected of being a dangerous psychopath and to behave as if nothing were out of the ordinary.

"So, what did you want to talk to me about?"

"Well, I'm sorry to disturb you on a day like this, but tomorrow is my father's birthday, and I was planning to bring him a present. He likes Japanese lacquers very much, and I understand from Daniel that you are something of an expert. Now, I have this antique dealer I know, who is offering me this bowl," I said, handing her the box, "and I would like to have your opinion of it before I actually buy it. He wants five hundred dollars."

She took the box and opened it, taking out the bowl.

"Careful," I cautioned her, faking concern, "he says it is very delicate."

Paula turned the bowl in her hands, examining it intently from all sides, turning it upside down and back again

"It's a nice bowl," she said when her examination was completed, "and I'm sure that your father will love it if he likes Japanese lacquers. But I think that five hundred dollars may be a bit too much. I've seen bowls as nice as this one sell for half that much in Paris. I would haggle if I were you and try to lower the price to no more than three-fifty."

She put the bowl carefully back in the box and closed the lid. I thanked her profusely and left hurriedly, allegedly to meet with my imaginary antique dealer. Instead, I drove further into Jerusalem and parked outside the police headquarters.

"I'd like to speak with Captain Akerman," I told the receptionist.

"Not in," he answered laconically, without lifting his gaze.

"Then, with Yosef, please."

"Yosef who?"

"Yosef who works under Captain Akerman."

He raised his head from the diary and gave me a long, dirty look.

"Do you know how many Yosefs work here? Don't you have a surname?"

"I'm afraid I don't."

"Then I'm afraid that I don't have a Yosef for you," said the receptionist, brightly.

"When is Captain Akerman expected back?"

"How would I know? I bet *he* doesn't know."

"All right. Can I leave this with you for him?"

"Can do that," said the receptionist, as if making a significant concession.

"Okay, then I'll leave it with you with a note for him. But you must be careful with it. It may become evidence in a murder case. And I want a receipt." I wasn't at all sure that the receptionist would remember to give Eitan the package if I only left it with him. A receipt might do the trick, though. Or so I hoped.

I took a piece of paper and wrote, "Dear Eitan, I was here, but you were out. I'm leaving this box with the receptionist for you. It contains a lacquered bowl. The bowl has been thoroughly cleaned before being handled by a person who might be a suspect in the Tarun murder. Please have the fingerprints taken from the bowl and checked against those found in the lab. Talk to you soon. Richard."

I had promised Eitan to help him, and he couldn't complain that I wasn't getting busy. In truth, I was rather pleased with my little work of detection and the cunning that I had brought to the job of obtaining Paula's fingerprints.

Not bad for a novice, I congratulated myself. Not bad at all.

CHAPTER 12

The café in which we were sitting in *Place Saint-Germain des Prés* was packed, the air thick with the smoke of too many cigarettes. The customers were noisy and altogether, much too cheerful for my taste. I hated everybody that morning, and with good cause. The previous day had been a complete washout. We had hit the road early and had a simple plan: we wanted to reach the university as the offices opened, get in, copy the documents we needed, get out, and hop on the plane on our way back home: a simple plan, and a naive one.

It took us a while to find the right office, but we finally stood before a small window that opened into a room marked "Students' Directorate," and began negotiations with a dark little individual with shifty eyes, who appeared to run the place. We had a straightforward request: a copy of a former student's file, Paula Vargo. My French is far from perfect, but still, I am usually able to convey my meaning. This time I could have been speaking Sanskrit for all the results it produced. All we got were clicking noises, puffing sounds, and supercilious looks, intercalated by a few "*Malheuresement ...*" and "*Impossible!*" all mixed together with vigorous shakes of the head. Translated into plain English, our charming interlocutor was telling us to get lost. Yes, they did have a file on Mrs. Vargo. No, they were not going to give a copy to us. No, they were not going to allow us to take a brief look at it. Yes, we might speak with the gentleman's supervisor at his return from vacation in ten days, but these were his express instructions anyway so that talking to him was going to do us a fat lot of good.

"What now?" I asked Yoel after we walked out of the building.

"A small setback. Don't worry. I have friends here in Paris. Let's go and talk to them."

"What kind of friends?"

"Lawyers, of course. There is one, Ambroise Bettencourt, who owes me big time. I'll call him right now."

What I like about Yoel is his optimism. The idea that you could actually *talk* to someone in Paris at a moment's notice was enthralling—but that didn't deter him. And he worked his magic.

"He'll meet with us tomorrow evening at seven," he said, replacing his cell-phone into his pocket.

"So now who tells Becky that I'm not coming back on tomorrow's flight as I had anticipated?" I asked.

"I guess you'll have to, don't you? *It is* nice to be a bachelor," he said with a dreamy smile.

Bettencourt's office was located in a well-kept building and flaunted an expensive reception area. I was impressed to notice his name was the first one on a very long list of firm partners. Being so important, of course, he kept us waiting until a quarter to eight. At that time, we were shooed by a spectacled secretary into a small and stuffy meeting room where we were joined by Bettencourt himself—a tall and lean man with the most enormous beaky nose in France.

Ambroise Bettencourt was easily the most unpleasant person I recall having ever met. His English was good, and his manners patronizing. He seemed to be giving a great deal of thought to inventing new ways of being insulting with every sentence. Yoel didn't seem to notice, or if he did, he didn't mind it. I did.

He told Bettencourt as much of the story as he needed to know, and his so-called friend listened attentively, clicking his tongue and shaking his head the while, as if in disbelief.

"No, no, no," he said finally, like a teacher addressing a particularly stupid pupil, "that won't do. You can't go to the Students' Directorate at the university and simply ask for a file. No, that was a foolish thing to do. Well, come back tomorrow at noon. I will see what I can do."

We had a reasonable dinner and turned in early. I called Becky and gave her the speech I had prepared. I wasn't sure that I had sounded very convincing, but she sounded apathetic as if what I did was no concern of hers, which for once suited me well.

I sat on the bed for a long time, thinking. I was really worried by the turn that things had taken and was having a hard time figuring out how I had let myself become involved in this mess to the extent that I had to jump on a plane and go abroad at a moment's notice. Yoel didn't seem to be worried at all and even appeared to be enjoying himself, and for some reason, that annoyed me even more.

By the time I got up the next morning, breakfast was no longer served in the hotel's restaurant. Yoel was nowhere in sight, and I took a stroll around before getting a brioche and *café-au-lait* at a nearby place. I got back at half-past eleven and found Yoel waiting for me in the lobby.

A taxi took us in good time to Bettencourt's office, where we went again through the drill of waiting for three-quarters of an hour for his majesty, the advocate, to dignify us with his presence. When we were finally admitted to a different but equally small and stuffy meeting room that smelled strongly of French tobacco, Ambroise joined us almost immediately. He had a little folder under his arm, which he threw triumphantly on the table.

"Here is your dossier," he said with a self-satisfied smile. "It's all in there. I've gone through it, though, and I couldn't find anything special. She's just a run-of-the-mill student. No great grades, no particular complaints. It is not clear why she dropped out of school only a few months before graduating."

"Dropped out of school?" Yoel and I exclaimed in unison. We both remembered vividly how she had told us about her graduation and her internship.

"Yes," said Ambroise, giving us a perplexed look. "It's all in here. She never graduated, and the list of her grades ends in the middle of the academic year."

"Gimme," said Yoel simply.

He opened the dossier. It was the student's record of Paula Vargo, née Pristowsky. It had a photograph on it. From the picture, a brunette with sensuous lips and freckles was looking at us. She didn't look anything like Paula.

"Are you sure that there was no mix-up when they copied the file? Could it be that the photograph was switched?" asked Yoel.

"No. This is the original file. They gave the original to me to copy and return to them."

"Wait a minute. Let me see it," said Yoel, who was turning the few pages feverishly. "Look at this, Richard. Paula Pristowsky married Daniel Vargo in her first year, and her name was changed in the file. Here, you see? She got a distinction award in her second year, and this is a picture of the ceremony. And guess who is standing beside her."

I took the picture and looked at it. Paula—the one in the file, not our Paula—was standing with a plaque of some sort in her hands, in a group of four other students holding similar ones—very likely, her fellow winners of that year's award. Beside her, and slightly apart from the group, stood a man whom I immediately recognized as Daniel Vargo.

"I'll go and have a copy made for you," said Ambroise and left, not a moment too soon since we needed to vent our surprise.

"Have you noticed?" asked Yoel, who at last allowed himself to be excited. "*This* Paula is a full head shorter than Daniel. My recollection is *our* Paula is almost as tall as Daniel."

"Yes," I answered, "and the one in the photo is wearing high heels as well."

"Daniel is Daniel, and Paula is not Paula," said Yoel, pensively. "I wonder what this means. Right now, I must confess that I am at a loss to figure out what the scheme of things is."

"Could it be that Daniel remarried, and by chance, his second wife is also called Paula?" I asked, hopefully. Any other explanation, if there was one, was mind-boggling.

"A fat chance," answered Yoel. "The Paula we know is using the biography of this one. No, this is fishier than we thought."

Ambroise came back in a few minutes with a copy of the file. We thanked him profusely and left.

"Let's plan what to do," said Yoel. "The dossier gives this Paula's last known address in Versailles. Why don't we go down there and inquire?"

"I see no reason not to. This is getting weird, isn't it?"

"Weirdest," Yoel agreed.

The trip to Versailles was a short one. The house we were looking for was located in a small and quiet street, not far from the Palace of Versailles. According to the dossier, the Vargos had inhabited Apartment 2B. We pushed the button of the intercom for Apartment 2A, and the door opened with a click. Climbing the stairs, I suddenly realized that we had not discussed what we should do once we got here.

"What are we going to do, Yoel?" I asked.

"Don't worry. I've got a plan," he answered briefly and then knocked on the door of 2A.

The door was opened by a small woman in her late thirties and very much pregnant. She looked at us inquiringly.

"I am sorry to disturb you," Yoel opened in English—a tricky way to start a conversation in Paris. I was relieved when she answered, with a tolerable accent.

"Yes, what can I do for you?"

"I am an attorney," said Yoel, fishing out a business card and handing it to her. "I am handling a matter related to the estate of a deceased person, and I'm trying to contact a Paula Vargo who used to live here, perhaps you know her? I may have pleasant news for her. This is my associate, Mr. Luster," he said, disposing of me quickly.

"Oh, my," she said, "Paula ... would you like to come in? I'm Yvonne."

"Yes, thank you," I said in French, speaking as charmingly as possible.

She led us to a small sitting room and motioned us to a couple of armchairs. She took a high-backed chair.

"I did know Paula. Actually, we were good friends when she was studying law. She lived in 2B, you know, and we were always dropping in on each other for coffee and a chat." She stopped for a moment and then continued. "I'm afraid that I have bad news for you. You see, Paula was involved in a car crash seven years ago. The vehicle caught fire, and she was severely hurt. She suffered multiple burns and was kept in hospital for a month. When she came home, she still had to remain in bed, and her head was entirely bandaged. You could barely see her eyes.

"Her husband, the poor soul, did everything he could to help her recover, but she wasn't improving. She was badly depressed and wouldn't talk to anybody, not even to me, no matter how hard I tried or how many times I visited her. Eventually, her husband decided that what she needed was a change of scene, and they left. I haven't heard from them since. I think about her every now and then, but you know how it is. Life goes on ..."

"Could you tell me the approximate date of the accident?" Yoel asked.

"I can do better," she answered. "I have kept the newspaper that told the story. Let me look for it."

She left the room, and I looked at Yoel inquiringly.

"Later," he whispered. I was glad to see that he was confused too. I didn't know what to think, but perhaps the newspaper would shed some light on this nonsensical story.

She came back with a newspaper, and I read the headlines avidly. Yoel, whose knowledge of French ends more or less at *bonjour*, waited for me to translate.

"It says here in general what Yvonne just told us. No interesting details. Look here, it says that this is Paula Vargo." The photograph showed the Paula from the university file. Another picture showed an indistinct figure leaving a building. The legend identified it as Daniel Vargo coming to the hospital.

"Nothing more for us to do, then, I'm afraid," said Yoel. "But perhaps you could tell us where to find them?"

"I'm afraid I have no idea. They didn't leave a forwarding address. I'm sorry."

"You've been very helpful, Yvonne. Thank you very much," said Yoel.

In the street, we walked silently for a couple of minutes, each trying to organize his own thoughts.

"Do you think it possible that Paula's face as we know it is the result of plastic surgery?" I asked.

"To reconstruct her face after the accident, you mean? No, too good a result. No scars or signs of any kind. It's highly unlikely."

"On second thought," I said, "plastic surgery cannot account for the height difference. No, it's clear that there are two different Paulas."

"I have a guess on the origin of this mess," said Yoel. "Let's say that his wife eventually died, and Daniel came across an illegal immigrant—the one we know as the current Paula. He may have used his deceased wife's papers to give her an identity and make her legal. Probably she convinced him—you know how weak he is—and once they started with it, he was in her power."

I had a different guess.

"I think you're wrong. She probably murdered the real Paula to take her identity. She's the type."

"Whatever they did, it's fishy, and it's illegal."

"Yeah, and we represent them."

"Not for long, Richard. Not for long."

CHAPTER 13

When we got back to our hotel, a message was waiting for Yoel. A client of his was in serious trouble.

"I have to take the next flight back," he said, "and I must leave in fifteen minutes to catch it. I'll see you back home."

Our flight was scheduled for early the next morning. I toyed for a moment with the idea of joining Yoel and flying back immediately, but I was too tired, and I needed to relax a bit and let the new developments sink in. Besides, a few more hours would make no difference. Also, I would have a lot of explaining to do to Becky when I returned, and I wasn't looking forward to it.

I walked Yoel to the taxi that took him to the airport, and then I headed for the hotel bar. The bar was full and smoky, like everywhere else in this city, and after a hurried gin and tonic, I stepped out. I needed some fresh air. The weather was clement that afternoon, and I strolled aimlessly through Paris. For someone with time on his hands, Paris is a pleasant city to walk around in—at least, as long as you don't have to deal with clerks behind glass windows.

My walking took me to *Place Vendôme*, and I stood in front of the Hotel Ritz, looking at the stream of guests going in and out of the front door. It was strangely soothing, merely standing there and watching carefree people passing by. It was late afternoon now and, apparently, a party was on at the hotel. An endless stream of luxury cars disgorged sheiks and girls who all looked like supermodels, at a dazzling rate, and the doorman became richer with every second and every new tip that passed hands. A Jaguar stopped at the door, and a man dressed in dark clothes and a white turban emerged. The car was a beauty, but before I could take a good look at it, it drove away to make room for a Bentley. The driver jumped out and opened the door for a woman in an evening dress, immediately flanked by a young man. I looked at him and saw a tall, broad, military-looking man with an earpiece. He was unmistakably a bodyguard. I stood there and gaped at the woman. It was Paula— our Paula, the current one I knew from Jerusalem. Her hair was done differently, and her demeanor was by far more ladylike than I was used to with her, but there was no doubt. It was she.

She passed through the front door, smiling graciously at the doorman, without looking right or left, and disappeared within. She obviously hadn't seen me, and I ran in pursuit. The doorman gave me a brief look as if to weigh whether I was to be allowed into the hotel but apparently decided that my business suit was decent enough. A crowd had gathered outside a banquet hall in the hotel, and Paula was in the corridor, talking to a young woman. I approached her without stopping to think.

"Paula ..." I called. She paid no attention to me, so I called again, this time louder: "Paula."

"Pardon me," she said, turning around and speaking in

French, "you were saying ... ?"

"What are you doing here, Paula?" I asked.

"I'm sorry, but you must be confusing me with somebody else. I don't think that we have met."

"Is this man bothering you, Miss Vernon?"

The bodyguard put himself between Paula and me as if to shield her. He was looking at me menacingly, flaunting his muscular body, a head taller than I. I decided to ignore him.

"You mean to say that you are not Paula Vargo?"

"Definitely not!" She now was smiling, amused. "I've never heard that name in my life. I am Elise Vernon, and I don't think that you have an invitation to the gala evening," she said, looking at my decent but somewhat worn-out business suit, "and you will have to excuse me now."

Without another word, she turned on her heels and walked into the banquet hall, leaving me free to feel stupid. It felt as if the whole hotel knew of the social blunder I had just committed, and it seemed that everyone was staring at me. The bodyguard stood there, looking at me doubtfully, as if incapable of deciding whether I represented a security hazard or not. I murmured a few indistinct words, looking down at my shoes, and walked in my best-dignified manner to the exit.

Outside, I took some time to collect my wits. This trip was becoming weirder every moment that passed, and I was not yet convinced that I had not been made a fool of by Paula right now in the hotel. As I walked around the hotel building, trying to think of the right thing to do, I saw Paula's ... Elise's car parked among many other luxury cars. The chauffeur was standing with a foot on the bumper, smoking a cigarette. Here was my answer, I thought.

"Hi," I said to him. He looked up, courteously throwing away his cigarette.

"Hello, sir. Can I help you?"

"I saw your car, and I thought it looked like my friend's car. Elise Vernon, I mean. Is this it?"

"Yes, indeed. This is Miss Vernon's car."

"Oh, good. She's around, then? I'd like to see her. I haven't seen her in ages."

"Miss Vernon is at the gala evening at the Hotel Ritz."

"Oh, in that case, I won't disturb her. Unfortunately, I'm in Paris only for tonight, and I won't be able to see her—but perhaps I can make it tomorrow morning. Would you know where she is staying?"

"But, of course, at her father's residence," he answered, sounding somewhat perplexed.

"You see, I never met with her in Paris," I hastened to explain. The last thing I wanted was to raise suspicions with my only source of information. "We only met abroad, and I thought she might be living on her own by now."

"Well, you can't blame her father for keeping her near him after the kidnapping ..."

"Kidnapping?" I couldn't repress my surprise.

"Yes. Didn't you know?"

"No, I didn't know. She never mentioned any kidnapping."

"But everybody knows her story!"

"Well, I don't. I don't live here. But I'm curious now, please tell me what happened."

"Miss Vernon is trying to forget it and never speaks about it. She was kidnapped as a child and lost her memory, and only when she grew up did she regain enough memory to recall her father's name and find him. At least, that's what the newspapers said. I wasn't a Vernon employee at the time."

"Fancy her never telling me! Now I have a good reason to make an effort to pay her a visit tomorrow morning. Could you give me her phone number? I don't want to call unannounced."

"Here, I'll give you a card."

He handed me a card, beautifully engraved in gold on white, high-quality paper. It simply said, "Vernon Residence," with the address and a phone number.

"Thank you. Much obliged," I said, and handed him a bill. In the dark, I couldn't see the value of the bill, but by the way he thanked me, I knew I had parted with a good sum. Still, this could have been my best investment since I got to Paris. I walked quickly away, and, as soon as I was out of sight of the driver, I hailed a taxi and gave him the address of the Vernon residence.

I had not formed a real plan, but I had a distinct feeling of urgency. Something truly fishy was going on, and perhaps this time I could get some help—and information—from this man, Vernon. The taxi dropped me at the door of an impressive building, and I pressed the bell. The door was opened almost immediately by what definitely was a butler. I hadn't seen a butler in real life before, and this one was quite impressive.

"Yes?" he inquired.

"I am here to see Mr. Vernon," I answered, trying to sound natural.

"Mr. Vernon does not receive, save by appointment. I am sorry," he said, starting to close the door.

"No, wait!" I almost shouted. He stopped and looked at me, inquiringly. "I bring information of momentous impact. Mr. Vernon's life may be in danger. I must talk to him. I am an attorney," I said, handing him my business card. Well, a patent attorney is an attorney ... of a sort.

"Wait here," he said, unconvinced, but took the card. He closed the door and was gone for perhaps two minutes when the door opened again.

"Mr. Vernon will see you now," he said, admitting me inside.

Without another word, he turned and guided me along a corridor to a wood-paneled double door at which he stopped. Outside stood a young man who could have been the twin brother of the bodyguard who watched over Paula. The butler opened the doors ceremoniously and motioned me to enter. As soon as I passed through the doors, they closed behind me. A middle-aged man stood in the room by a Louis XV table, slowly turning my business card in his fingers. He didn't offer his hand to me, nor did he ask me to sit down, so I merely stood there before him.

"I am Pascal Vernon," he said. "What is all this about?"

"I don't know how to begin," I said, truthfully, "and I have no way to break this to you gently, so I'll give it to you straight. The woman who poses as your long-lost and newly found daughter is an impostor. Her name is Paula Vargo—or, at least, this is the alias she goes under now, but I know it's not her real name—and a few days ago, she was in Jerusalem. I don't know what she is up to, but it has to be something fishy. And it may be dangerous. I had to warn you so that you can take your precautions. That's it."

He looked at me unsympathetically. He went on looking for a whole minute, without saying a word, turning my card again and again in his hand and working his jaws so that its muscle stood out. Then, he finally spoke.

"Let me tell you a story, Mr. Luster," he said. "Twenty-five years ago, I lived with my wife in a palace not far from here. We had a beautiful girl, Elise. She was six years old when she was kidnapped. The kidnappers asked for a ransom—a very high one. I am a rich man. *Very* rich. And I was willing to pay any price to get my little girl back. So I paid, and the kidnappers disappeared with the money and my daughter, and we never heard from them again. My wife died of a broken heart two years later, and I was left a living dead. Until Elise came back. We believe that the kidnappers did something terrible to her, and she lost her memory. She was raised by foster families in the Balkans, until one day she started to remember things. First, she remembered my face, and then my name. Eventually, she remembered the city she used to live in—Paris. She came to Paris looking for me. I am well known here, and the story of my daughter's kidnapping is not a secret, so she found me easily."

"But ..." I tried to intervene, but he went on.

"I am a lonely old man, Mr. Luster, but I am no fool. You can trust me that the thought has occurred to me that she might be an impostor, someone who's after my money. You know, when I die she will be very, very rich. So I decided to check her story. That was easy enough. The police had my daughter's fingerprints, which they had lifted from her room and her toys. They were hoping to use them to help find her, and they distributed copies throughout France. Sometimes kidnappers travel with the kids they kidnap, drugged. They dye their hair, change their appearance to make it difficult to find them. But you can't change fingerprints. The police still had my daughter's fingerprints. So we took Elise's and compared them with those in the police file, and they matched. So you see, she is my daughter after all."

"But ..." I tried again, but he silenced me with a gesture of his hand.

"And then you say that until a few days ago this woman, this ... Paula, was in Jerusalem. Well, let me tell you that my Elise has been living with me for the past five years, and I have never let her out of my sight for more than a few hours, and she only goes out accompanied by a bodyguard. So, you see, she couldn't have been the one you saw in Jerusalem a few days ago."

"Mr. Vernon," I finally managed to say, "I really don't know what's going on here, but I know what I saw. She is Paula, and there can be no mistake about it. I don't know what kind of conspiracy she is taking part in, but it scares me. Someone has died already, under mysterious circumstances. I couldn't stand aside and let you become a victim of God knows what scheme."

"This is very commendable, Mr. Luster," he said cynically, "but totally unnecessary. As you can see, I am perfectly safe here, and the danger, I'm sure, is only in your imagination."

"Have you taken a DNA test?" I asked on an impulse. "No? Then, please, do take a DNA test. Then you will be sure. Will you please do it?"

"Mr. Luster," he said, impatiently, "I don't know what you are seeking to accomplish with these wild allegations. Perhaps you, too, know that I am wealthy and hope to benefit from your 'chivalrous' acts. If that's the idea, I suggest that you think again. Now you will have to excuse me. Alex!"

He had barely raised his voice, but the door opened instantly, and the bodyguard was in the room.

"Alex," said Mr. Vernon, "Would you be so kind as to throw Mr. Luster out?"

"Take the test," I said, moving toward the door, following Alex's nod. "Take the DNA test, please."

"Goodbye, Mr. Luster," said Vernon, and the door closed behind me, as if by magic.

I was back in the street again, not for the first time, feeling stupid. Why did I have to go out on a limb to warn Vernon? I didn't know him, and I owed him nothing. But I knew that this was not about Vernon. This was personal, and it was about Paula and me. I had the feeling that she was playing a game with me and winning all the time. She was winning because I didn't know what the game was, and you can't win if you don't know the game and its rules. So I had to find out what the game was and whether it had rules.

First, I had to prove to myself that I wasn't crazy. I dialed the Vargos' number on my cell-phone and waited while it rang at the other end ten times before hanging up. I hadn't expected Paula to pick up, since she was in Paris, but I would have felt foolish if she had answered the phone. Still, Vernon said that she had never been away from him for more than a few hours, so I wondered how she had managed to pull that off. Everywhere I looked, I only saw strange, weird events that I couldn't make sense of. I stopped a taxi and went straight to my hotel. I packed and got ready for an early start in the morning. That night I barely slept. Suddenly, I felt the urge to get out of there and back home where I belonged.

CHAPTER 14

The next morning I got up early, checked out of the hotel, and took a taxi to the airport, determined to make sure I wouldn't miss the flight home. I reached the airport more than two hours before the appointed flight time, and the check-in counters weren't open yet. A quick brawl with a ground attendant who dressed like a general and behaved like one did nothing toward allowing me to check my suitcase early but helped me pass the time. I wondered whether these Frenchmen were similarly obnoxious to everybody, or perhaps I was getting special treatment. Maybe they sensed that their dislike was reciprocated.

The flight was nothing special, but it got me to Ben-Gurion Airport in time, which was all I needed from it. I had forgotten to arrange for a cab to pick me up at the airport and had to wait in line for one to come along. When we finally reached the house, it was a little after two p.m., and I wondered whether Becky would be waiting for me. I should've called ahead, I realized too late. I paid for the taxi, and then I dragged my suitcase into the house.

"*Becky*!" I called loudly, and I heard her footsteps coming down the stairs.

"Richard!" she said, "Good that you're here."

I had expected a bit more enthusiasm at my return, but before I could say anything, I saw Elan sitting on the couch. He was watching me in silence."

"Hey, big boy, Daddy's home," I said.

"Hi Daddy," he said, mildly, and turned his attention back to the TV.

"Well, that's ..." I started to say, but Becky squeezed my arm.

"It's okay," she said, "leave him alone."

It's a rule that Becky and I have never to argue in front of the children, so I let it pass.

"Let me tell you who called you. First, Eitan called. Twice. He said that you should get in touch with him immediately when you return."

"I'll call him as soon as I've had a cup of coffee."

I got up and started messing with cups and spoons, giving myself the time to reflect on the cold welcome I was receiving while Becky went on.

"Then Paula called. She wanted to know when you would be back, and I told her that I expected you back today. She didn't call again."

"Then," Becky continued, "someone named Yair called. He said he's a friend of yours and that he got some results that you will want to hear. That's all."

"All right, thanks."

"Do you plan to tell me what all these calls are about?"

"Nothing special, usual things, work things," I lied, and went back to the coffee machine that was already letting out steam without looking Becky in the eyes. I put a mug on the table in front of her and took a deep sip from mine. It was good, mainly because it tasted like home. Becky kept silent, merely gazing at me in a detached way. It made me uncomfortable, and I had to move away from her gaze, so I went to the kitchen phone and dialed Yair's number.

"Yes?" Yair's voice answered.

"Yair? It's me, Richard. My wife said you called me."

"I did. I certainly did. Do you have a few minutes to hear about what I've done so far?"

"Certainly, shoot."

"Good. Your friend, Daniel, left ten samples of extracts with me. Five are supposed to be the protein we are interested in, three are the whole extract, with the protein of interest and all other proteins, and two samples are supposed to contain all proteins, except that of interest—or in other words, they are the fraction that didn't pass the filter when the protein of interest was isolated. You follow?"

"Yes, quite simple, so far."

"Okay, then. I tested the first sample supposed to be of a single purified protein. When I tested it, I found that it contains at least three different proteins, maybe more, although others are only present in trace amounts. I thought that this first sample may have become contaminated during its production. In any case, it is useless, so I went on to the next sample."

"And?" I prompted him when he stopped for air.

"And the second sample was the same—only the proteins present in the extract were not exactly the same as in the first sample and not in the same proportions. So I tested all the samples, and the results are more or less constant. There is no isolated single protein. The identity of the major protein in the sample varies from one sample to another. In short, it's a complete mess, and I can't generate any useful data from this material."

"What can be the reason for the problem?" I was flabbergasted. I had made strenuous efforts, hosting Daniel in my house, paying for equipment, travel, and food, to permit this analysis to take place, and we didn't have anything to show for it. It was a real setback for the project.

"I really don't know. It can be that Daniel is not such a hotshot in the lab and made some mistakes that ruined the material. Or perhaps the material was no good to begin with. It is possible that it was taken in an inconsistent manner or contaminated with unrelated tissue. Who knows?"

I recalled that Daniel had told me that a friend of his had provided the material since Daniel himself was no longer allowed into the operating room. Perhaps his friend had screwed up. Or maybe he had provided contaminated material on purpose, in cooperation with Abramov, to delay Daniel's work. These days, when nothing was what it seemed, perhaps friends were really enemies, and Daniel had been too naive.

I thanked Yair and hung up. We could do nothing further until Daniel's return. If we didn't trust the raw material we had, any further analysis of it would be meaningless. Besides, I still had to decide whether I was going on with the project or dropping the Vargos altogether, which I admitted to myself might be inevitable. Caught in the heat of the discussion with Yair, I had forgotten that Paula might be a murderess, an impostor, and who knows what else and that the first item on my list was to disentangle myself from her. But I was still hooked on Daniel's project, which looked too big to simply give up.

I decided to call Paula, regardless of my aversion to speaking with her now that I saw her in a dubious light, but I needed to find out when Daniel was finally going to come home. The phone rang five, ten, fifteen times until I decided that she was out. The Vargos didn't have an answering machine, and I would have to call her again later.

Our home phone rang, and I rose to answer it. It was Eitan.

"Well, thank you for calling me back," he said.

"I just got here," I excused myself, "I was planning to call you soon."

"Would you mind telling me now what kind of prank you thought you were playing on me?"

"Ah?" I answered. I didn't have the foggiest idea what he was talking about.

"The jar. The thing you left me."

"You mean, the Japanese bowl?"

"Whatever."

"That was no prank. Didn't you get my note?"

"I got it. That's why I'm asking. You said that we should lift the prints on it, which may belong to the killer. Well, we did."

"And?"

"And they belong to you."

"I don't believe it!" I exclaimed. "I have gone to no end of pains to clean it thoroughly before using it, but if you found a print of mine, it seems that I haven't done a thorough job. But what about the other prints? Have you identified them?"

"What other prints? There are no other prints, only yours."

"That's not possible. You're pulling my leg."

"I'm doing nothing of the sort. I'm telling you that all the prints on the bowl are yours and beautiful prints too. We have a perfect set of all fingers for both hands, evenly distributed and clearly embedded on the thing. Perfectly matching the ones you were so kind as to leave with us when we met."

"But Eitan, I never touched that bowl. Those prints must've been left by somebody else."

"I don't think that anybody would take the trouble of manufacturing fake prints of yours."

"I thought that you can't fake prints."

"You can, with today's technology, but it's extremely high-tech and complicated. If you have a quarter of a million dollars and the technical know-how to do it, it's a piece of cake. The CIA does it. But I don't think that the CIA would take the trouble to fake your prints just to annoy you. So I'm asking again. What was all this supposed to be?"

"There must have been a mistake. I must have made a mistake. I thought that I was giving you a bowl with the prints of Paula Vargo, but apparently, I messed it up. I'm sorry."

"Paula Vargo? But she never went near that laboratory. She is not a suspect at all, so we never took her prints. She apparently never met Tarun in person, and we have no reason to believe otherwise. Stop playing detective, Richard. Stick to your patents. I'm happy we cleared this bowl thing up. It was driving me crazy."

He hung up, apparently no longer mad at me. I was no longer suspected of being a prankster, but merely of bungling things—apparently a lesser offense.

But I couldn't make heads or tails of it. I stood there, replaying my movements before and during my visit to the Vargos', and I couldn't find any way in which I might have mishandled the bowl. I definitely hadn't touched it. And even if I had touched it, Paula's fingerprints had to be there too. I distinctly saw her holding the bowl with both hands, carefully, which should have left ten beautiful, distinct prints on the bowl. And then she had touched the inside as well. I was at a loss to understand what could have happened.

Later, after we put the kids to bed, I rang Yoel's house.

"Yes?" he answered immediately.

"Yoel, it's me."

"Hi, Richard. You're back?"

"Yes. I need to talk. Can I come over?"

"I'm putting the kettle on," he answered without hesitation.

I told Becky where I was going, and she nodded. She didn't remind me that I had just returned, that I hadn't spent time with the kids yet, or a million other things she could have said, but I was too rattled by the bowl mystery to give too much thought to it.

Yoel lived in a cozy and spacious apartment in the heart of Tel Aviv, within convenient walking distance from his office. When I got there, he greeted me in a T-shirt and shorts, barefooted and with wet hair—which told me that I had probably disturbed him in the shower. He gestured me to the living room, where I seated myself in a low armchair. He brought tea and biscuits and sat down.

"How was your case?" I asked.

"It stank, really, but I'm glad I came back to deal with it. So what's up?"

"I don't know where to start."

"The beginning would be a good place," he said, making me feel stupid because that was what I used to say to other people.

"There is quite a lot of it. First, there was this woman in Paris ..." I told him about Elise Vernon and my visit to Pascal Vernon's house. I stopped and looked at him, half expecting to hear him come up with a perfectly clear explanation, instead of which he looked at me doubtfully.

"Are you sure that she really looked like Paula? You could've been mistaken. You were excited."

"She not only *looked* like her. She *was* her. She moved like her. She talked like her, only in French. I can't explain, but meeting her leaves no doubt."

"Perhaps Paula has a twin sister, and that's who you met."

"Perhaps. But then she is not Vernon's daughter. You can't have it both ways. Vernon didn't have twin daughters that were abducted. Only one."

"Weird," said Yoel. "That means that these twin sisters if that's what they are, have been busy. Paula impersonates David's wife, and Elise impersonates Vernon's daughter."

"And you haven't heard the half of it." I told him about Yair's results.

"Why do I have the feeling that we've been screwed?" asked Yoel when I finished my report.

"I don't know. We may have, but I don't know by whom. It could be Abramov, or Daniel's friend, or Daniel, who can't handle a test tube properly, or who knows what."

"The only one who can help us with this is Daniel," said Yoel, "and there is no point in worrying about it until he returns from his trip."

"I agree. Additionally, until Daniel returns, we have no way to continue the experiments, so we shouldn't waste time worrying. But now, let's get to the reason why I wanted to come and talk to you."

"I thought that what you just told me was an excellent reason. Is there more?"

"Much more." I told him about the Japanese bowl and the fingerprints. I also told him about the Japanese lacquer that Daniel had brought to us as a present and how that had given me the idea.

"*The mystery of the Japanese bowl*. That could be a good title for a Nero Wolfe story. She outsmarted you," said Yoel, when I finished explaining, "no doubt about that. But how did she do that now ..."

"That's what is driving me crazy. I was hoping that you might have an idea."

"Well, one possibility is that she knocked you out cold—perhaps she drugged your drink—and then she wiped the bowl of her own fingerprints and put your fingers to it."

"Nice theory, but I wasn't there for more than ten minutes, and she wouldn't have had the time. Besides, I didn't drink anything."

"I've got it! Then the only explanation is that she hypnotized you. That would have taken only a minute, and you wouldn't have remembered anything. How do you like that?"

"Very colorful, really, but I don't believe that we are dealing with a hypnotist. There must be a perfectly simple explanation, but it eludes me."

I was a little disappointed. I had expected Yoel to pull the answer out of his hat. Suddenly, Yoel's face lit up.

"In fact, there is a straightforward explanation. I should have thought of it immediately." He looked at me with a smug expression of self-satisfaction on his face.

"What?" I almost yelled.

"The police are the ones who screwed up. They do it all the time. They mix up blood tests, DNA tests, urine tests, speed control machine photos, and everything else they can put their hands on. They probably mixed up the prints in the lab and returned a wrong report."

I was relieved. This was undoubtedly the simplest explanation, but, of course, the police would never admit to having made a mistake. This meant that I had to devise a new way to take a set of Paula's prints. But this time, I resolved, I wouldn't let them out of my sight and would go to the lab with them.

I thanked Yoel warmly and drove back home, relieved that my honor had been saved. I was yearning to tell Becky all about it, but she was fast asleep when I got home. That would have to wait.

I got into bed and then remembered that I hadn't talked to Paula. The time was eleven-thirty p.m.—still early enough to call her, and if I woke her up, that was okay with me. I got out of bed and to the phone and dialed the number I already knew by heart. The phone at the other end rang twenty times before I gave up and went back to bed. That, too, would have to wait for the morrow.

CHAPTER 15

"The number you have dialed is temporarily disconnected. Please try again later."

This was the telephone company's recorded message that greeted me when, the next morning, I tried again to call the Vargos' house. I knew they were hard up, but I couldn't believe that they hadn't paid their phone bill. I dialed again, hoping to have reached a wrong number, but only got the same recorded message again.

I felt stuck. I needed to talk to Daniel, and I wanted to know when he planned to return from his trip. I had no choice: I had to drive to Jerusalem again.

I got into the car, trying not to think of the work waiting for me at the office and got on the busy highway heading for Jerusalem. Becky had left early to take the kids to school, so she wouldn't know that I was skipping work again in favor of the Vargos. Thank God for small mercies, I thought.

The drive to the Vargos' house took almost one hour and a half because of the heavy morning traffic, but when I reached their street, parking space was plentiful, and I parked right in front of the house. I walked down the stairs leading to the door and looked at the building. I didn't have to ring the bell to know that the house was empty. And I don't mean that Paula was out. I mean, the place was deserted—a lifeless shell. I can't say what it was that showed its emptiness, but I had no doubt. The Vargos were gone.

I rang the bell for good measure but didn't expect an answer, and none came. I circled the house, trying to peep in through the windows, but the shutters were closed, and I could see nothing in the dark interior. I pushed my body against the shrubbery that grew unkempt under the kitchen window, but all I got for it were scratches on my hands and bruises on my shin.

I decided to continue circling toward the living room's windows, and I reached the kitchen door. On an impulse, I put my hand to the handle, and the door turned open with a high-pitched squeak. I walked hesitantly into the kitchen, wondering what I would say if I was found out. I could always say that I got worried that something might have happened to Paula because she hadn't been answering the phone for two days, and since the door was open, I had walked in to check on her. I was her attorney, after all.

In spite of the shutters, enough sunshine filtered through the cracks, and it let me see the surroundings without the need to turn on a light. I stood in the middle of the kitchen. It all looked like I had seen it the last time. The sink was immaculate, and the teacups were laid upside down in a neat row.

I walked into the living room. Here, again, everything was hauntingly neat and orderly. I started walking toward the bedroom area. I had never been in that part of the house, but I knew where it was from having seen Daniel emerge from it. It felt really wrong to invade the privacy of their bedroom, but I had gone too far and couldn't stop now. The first bedroom was large and had an adjoining bathroom. This was obviously the Vargos' bedroom. I opened a closet and saw a line of what I assumed were Paula's dresses that filled it as if she had left without taking anything with her. Another door of the closet opened to show men's clothing, obviously Daniel's. Here, like everywhere else throughout the house, the items were neatly stacked and in perfect order.

I went into the bathroom. It contained the usual items—toothbrush, hairbrush, towels, soaps, but it was strange: it was so neat and orderly that it looked as if it had never been used. Two brand new toothbrushes kept company with a new tube of toothpaste. I opened the small cabinet above the sink and was surprised to see how little was in there. It contained a razor, shaving gel, and after-shave and a bottle of perfume, but nothing else—no creams, files, miscellaneous bottles, and items that you usually find in cabinets. On the middle shelf, I saw a blob of blueish goo and touched it instinctively. It was similar to the one that I had found in my sink. It fizzled at the touch and changed into hot vapor. Startled, I retracted my hand from the cabinet. The goo was gone, leaving a slightly minty and cheesy smell on my finger. I ran the water in the sink and washed my finger thoroughly until the smell was gone, chasing the thoughts about its strange nature from my mind for the time being.

I took some toilet paper, lifted the perfume bottle, opened the lid, and sniffed it. It was the scent that I remembered smelling when Paula was around. No doubt, this bottle had to have Paula's fingerprints on it, and sure as hell, I would not touch it with my fingers this time. I went back to the kitchen and fetched a plastic sandwich wrap in which I bundled the bottle that went into my pocket. I would deal with it later.

I walked back into the bedroom and looked around again,

trying to define the strangeness of the house. Then I got it: the bedroom felt more like a display in a department store than a place where people actually lived. There was no trace of the little things that make a house alive; no piece of paper with a phone number scribbled on it, no grocery bill lying around, no book waiting to be picked up again. The clothes hung neatly as clothes do in department stores like they had never been worn.

I looked around some more without finding anything of interest and had just reached the conclusion that there was nothing more for me to see when my cell-phone rang. In the stillness of the empty house, it sounded like a bombshell, and it sent my heart leaping toward my teeth. I answered it, speaking in a low undertone as if speaking loudly in this house were improper for some reason.

"Yes," I whispered.

"Is it you, Richard?" Yoel's voice asked.

"Yes, wait a second," I said. I was done with my inspection of the house, and I suddenly felt the urge to get out. I walked quickly to the kitchen door and out, muttering "one moment" at brief intervals into the microphone, to make sure that Yoel would not hang up. When I reached the top of the stairs leading to the street, I felt better and walked a few paces quickly to one side. Then I stopped and spoke into the microphone.

"Sorry, Yoel. I couldn't speak. I'll tell you later. What's up?"

"I got a phone call from Simon Finkel. Do you know him?"

"Never heard of him."

"He is a well-known lawyer. Mostly civil stuff. He called me on behalf of his clients. Guess who their clients are?"

"How could I know? I told you I've never heard of him."

"Well, he is acting for Daniel and Paula Vargo *and their investors*, the sons of bitches."

"What!" I ejaculated. I wasn't expecting this.

"What you just heard. They have gone and closed some sort of shady deal, and they now have a big-shot lawyer representing them, who is calling on us on their behalf."

"But we represent them as well," I argued.

"No longer, apparently. Simon specifically informed me that he holds in his hands a revocation of our powers of attorney. Cute, isn't it?"

"But what does he want?"

"I don't know. He wants to meet with us both, and now is not soon enough for him. I told him to come to my office at four p.m., but I have to confirm it with him after talking to you. Can you get here before then? We may need to talk after we have had time to collect our wits, talk this development over, and see what we make of it before he gets here."

"I'll meet you at three-thirty. Sooner, if I can make it."

"Good," said Yoel, gloomily, and hung up.

I wanted to get to Yoel's office as soon as possible, but I had something to do first. I drove to the police station and walked up to the receptionist—not the same one as last time.

"I need to talk to Captain Akerman," I announced.

"Who are you?" he asked. His tone made it plain that he doubted that a dubious character like me had business talking to a captain. I gave him my name, and he pushed a few buttons on the switchboard, shaking his head at the same time as if to show his disbelief at my gall. He then spoke into the microphone of his headset.

"Tell the captain that one Lunitz is here to see him."

"Luster," I tried in vain to correct him.

"Laenz, he alleges now," the receptionist corrected, and then turning to me, he added: "Sit," nodding toward the bench on which I had already spent too much time on my first visit to this station.

Eitan joined me five minutes later.

"Hi, Rich," he greeted me. "I only have a few minutes. I must go to a budget meeting. But let's go into my office." I looked triumphantly at the receptionist, hoping that Eitan's friendliness toward me would make him feel pretty silly, but he was looking away and showed no sign of noticing.

We walked along a corridor and stopped at a door that led into the cubicle that Eitan called his office. He motioned me to the only chair in the room and sat behind his desk.

"So, what's new?" he asked.

I fished the perfume bottle from my pocket and put it on the table. Eitan looked at it and then interrogatively at me.

"You remember the Japanese bowl that I left with you? The one on which your splendid lab found my fingerprints? Well," I continued, when Eitan nodded, "I have reached the inevitable conclusion that the lab somehow bungled it. There is no way that the bowl could have had my fingerprints on it. Nevertheless, that is water under the bridge."

"Listen, Richard," Eitan interrupted me, "we have rigorous and precise routines concerning the chain-of-possession of lab samples, and there is no way that our lab could have made a mistake."

"That is not what I've heard," I said smartly. "However, this is neither here nor there. Forget the Japanese bowl. We will probably never know what happened and why the report you got listed the wrong fingerprints. In any case, this bottle here is another story. This is a bottle that I never touched and that only Paula Vargo may have touched. You will have a sample of her fingerprints compared with the ones you found in Tarun's lab. The ones you couldn't identify. Okay?"

"I see. You have this fixation with Paula Vargo, don't you? I told you that she's not a suspect."

"But will you please humor me and check? Please?"

"Yeah, all right. I can see no harm in it. I'll have the damn bottle checked for fingerprints if this makes you happy."

"It makes me ecstatic. Thank you. But I have another small request."

"What is it?" asked Eitan with a resigned sigh.

"Could you take the bottle personally to the lab and witness the lifting of the prints to make sure that they don't make another mistake? This is very important to me."

"Oh, okay. I'll do it. Only because it's you. But this is really unnecessary, you know."

"It may be, but all the same …"

I thanked Eitan and ran to my car. I was eager to get to Yoel's office.

"So, what do you think he wants?" I asked Yoel when we finally sat down in his office at a quarter to four.

"I've no idea. I tried to get him to tell me, but he said that he would only speak to us both together and that those were his instructions."

"Then all we can do is wait and see?"

"We only have to wait for fifteen minutes," Yoel pointed out, looking at his watch, "but let's try to think of a few possible scenarios."

After we realized that our attempt to guess what was expected was futile, we sat there in silence, Yoel purporting to look through some papers that were scattered on his desk, but I could tell that his heart was not in it. At last, Yoel's secretary announced our guest, and presently he was admitted.

"Hi, Yoel," he said cordially, extending a hand. "Long time no see."

"Yes," Yoel agreed, "it must be a good three years since we spoke. Let me introduce you to Richard Luster."

Finkel turned toward me, and we shook hands.

"Nice to meet you, Richard. I can call you Richard, can't I? I've heard so much about you."

He was so nice and charming that you would have thought that I had made his day just by existing. We all sat down. Finkel occupied the second armchair beside me and held a voluminous file on his lap. Yoel started making small talk—a maddening habit of many lawyers, of which I have had occasion to complain before.

"Can we get to the point of our meeting?" I asked after a while, not minding my sounding impatient. "I have an important conference later this afternoon in my office, and I will have to leave early."

"Yes, yes, I apologize," said Finkel, looking really apologetic. "I'll tell you why we are here." He stopped for a moment, as if to collect his thoughts, and then continued. "My clients, Doctor and Mrs. Vargo, have asked me to hold this joint meeting with you two, to formally sever their professional connections with you and to end your services to them. I have been instructed to ensure that all aspects of your engagement are fully and completely terminated. I have here a power of attorney signed by both my clients," he continued, fishing a document from his file and handing it to me, "which empowers me to do so."

I perused the power of attorney. It seemed quite in order to me, and I passed it on to Yoel, who barely glanced at it.

"You make this sound like an easy proposition, Simon," he said serenely, "but in reality, this is not so simple. When Doctor and Mrs. Vargo engaged our services, we agreed to represent them on the basis of a contract that irrevocably grants us equity rights in the project that Doctor Vargo is developing. So, you see, it is not a matter of saying, 'Thank you for your help, but it's no longer needed.' There is a contractual obligation on Doctor Vargo's part, and the parties are bound by valid legal commitments."

"Well, Yoel," said Finkel, looking sad, "I was rather hoping that you would not bring up this point." He fished again into his file and lifted a copy of the agreement that I knew too well. "Doctor and Mrs. Vargo are quite enraged by this contract, which, they feel, has been imposed upon them at a time when they were in a vulnerable position. I have looked at it and, to tell you the truth, it is quite improper. I don't think that it would bear scrutiny were we compelled to bring it to the attention of a court. I fear that a court would look askance at the practice of taking advantage of your clients in a moment of weakness."

"Hey, look here," I started, half rising from my chair. I had no plan to punch Finkel on the nose, much as I would have liked to, but I needed to move to vent my anger. Yoel touched my arm, and I looked at him.

"Sit down, Richard, please," he said calmly. "Now, Simon," he continued when I did as requested, "as Richard mentioned before, we are pretty busy today, and you have come at short notice, so Richard and I will postpone getting scared by your threats to a more convenient time. Now let's talk sense."

"I wasn't threatening, Yoel. Nothing farther from my thoughts," Finkel said unctuously. "On the contrary, as an old friend, I was just pointing out to you how some people, who don't know you as well as I do, might look at it."

"I'm overwhelmed with gratitude, Simon. But you see, the fact is that the contract was not our idea. We were approached by the Vargos with it, and it was written before we even met them. Furthermore, it was prepared by a qualified advocate, Mrs. Vargo, acting on behalf of her husband. They can't very well play the part of the naive people who have been tricked by these shark lawyers. You will have to find a better way to extricate your clients from their obligations. As far as we are concerned, we have a valid contract, and we plan to enforce it."

"You have always been a good bluffer, Yoel, but you know that I know you well enough to call your bluffs. Paula Vargo is no more a lawyer than I am a tap dancer. She never took her bar exams, and she had no internship. The fact that she studied law doesn't make her a lawyer."

Yoel and I exchanged meaningful glances. I started to get the choking feeling that Paula had planned all this from the start and that lying to us about her being a qualified lawyer was part of the scheme and not, as we had thought, part of her madness.

"Whether she lied to us or not about her being a lawyer is not the important point. The point is that she thought of the idea that is behind the contract, and she drafted it. We merely accepted it, and we did not apply any pressure of any kind on the Vargos. So you can cut the crap."

"I'm not here to give you crap," said Finkel, "but rather to make you an offer."

"Now, you're talking. If you have a reasonable offer for us, shoot."

"My clients and their investors are ready to pay, jointly to you, the sum of three hundred thousand dollars, to be apportioned among you as you wish. Two hundred thousand dollars to be paid in cash at the time of the signature of the appropriate agreement, and the rest in five monthly installments."

"And what do they want in return?" I asked. I hadn't anticipated such an offer, and I wanted to hear more.

"Very simple. You will sign an agreement that releases my

clients from the earlier contract, which will be terminated. You will deliver to me all and every document, samples, and materials pertaining to Dr. Vargo's project and confirm that you have kept no copies. You will keep all information on the project and my clients' secret, with no time limitation."

"Anything else?" I asked.

"One more thing: You will not deal with any project that has a bearing on Doctor Vargo's, or that is in conflict or in competition with it, for two years. That's all."

"If you don't mind, Simon, I would like to have a word in private with Richard."

"By all means, do. Shall I wait elsewhere?"

"No. You stay right here. Richard and I will go to the meeting room."

Once there, Yoel closed the door quickly; I could see that he was excited.

"It's a lot of money, Richard. I say that we take his offer."

"I agree that it is a lot of money. But let's think about it, first. These guys didn't have change for the bus fare last week, and I had to lend them money to eat. Now, all of a sudden, they scatter around magnificent sums. They must've gotten on to something really big to be able to raise that kind of money so quickly. We may be selling away our rights for a plate of lentils."

"Yes, yes. But this is hi-tech, remember? I concede that they must have found big investors, but this doesn't mean that the project will make money. It may lose all the money that these investors are putting into the company. If we manage to keep our equity position, we may be left with nothing. On the other hand, we now get a most respectable sum. If we wait too long, next week, they may not give you a dime for it. I say let's grab it before it's too late."

"Wait a minute. You forget that all this started out as an adventure. We always knew that we would never see any money in all likelihood, but we agreed that the small chance to get into a big thing was worth the risk. So what's the difference now?"

"Do I have to spell it out for you? The difference is that when we started out with the Vargos, nobody was offering you three hundred thousand dollars. Now they are. It's real money, not dream money. Not at all the same thing. And to tell you the truth, I feel that one hundred fifty thousand dollars are an adequate payment for the services that I have rendered to the Vargos—plus, I'm quite fed up with them in general and the idea of getting rid of them and the trouble they bring is too appealing for words."

"Yes, but ..."

"Besides, now you know the Vargos, and then you didn't. We know that Daniel may be brilliant, but he is weak and messy, and we know that his wife is nuts. They are not material that makes a successful start-up."

"Yes, but ..."

"And furthermore, rightly or wrongly, you suspect the Vargo woman to be a murderess. Now, look me in the eyes and tell me if you want to remain a partner in a dubious enterprise with a potential murderess who is positively nuts, and to pay three hundred thousand dollars for the pleasure."

I had always known that Yoel was a fine lawyer. His speech had completely convinced me. But then, I desperately wanted him to convince me. I knew that Becky would be the happiest woman in the world when I told her that our episode with the Vargos was over forever. And the money was right, I agreed.

"Let's go and get the money," I said.

When we got back to Yoel's room, Finkel was sitting precisely as we had left him and hadn't moved an inch. He conjured up to me a picture of a stuffed lawyer in a glass case, but I fought a smile that was finding its way to my lips. We were here on serious business, and I didn't want to look frivolous. Yoel sat down behind his desk and spoke quietly.

"Simon," he said, "Richard and I have consulted. We take great exception to what you have said on behalf of your clients, who, until this moment, were also our clients. We do feel that we don't want to have anything more to do with them, and we find the idea of continuing to be their business partners repulsive. Accordingly, we lean toward accepting your offer, but on conditions."

"What conditions?" Finkel asked, listening attentively.

"First of all, we do not accept any of the allegations put forward by your clients, and the agreement that we will sign will have to reflect that, as well as the fact that we are terminating the earlier agreement of our own free will."

Finkel nodded in consent, and Yoel continued.

"Secondly, I want the remaining hundred thousand dollars, those payable in installments, to be kept in escrow in an account opened by you for this purpose, from day one, so that you can guarantee the payment."

"I am sure that this can be arranged," said Finkel, peering into a document he had fished from his file—one that I guessed contained his instructions. "Anything else?"

Yoel looked inquiringly at me, and I shook my head.

"Nothing else," he answered.

"Then, can we say that we have reached an agreement?"

"Go and draft the papers," Yoel said, "and if they are drafted right, we have a deal."

We got up. For some reason, I didn't feel like shaking hands again with Finkel. I moved to the window and faked interest in the view, merely acknowledging his "goodbye" with a nod of my head.

So that was it, I thought. My adventure with the cure for cancer had ended. I knew that I was supposed to be happy, but I couldn't bring myself to cheer up for some reason.

I left Yoel's office, promising to make myself available to collect and deliver the papers and complete the deal, and got home in time to pick up the phone that was ringing insistently. Eitan Akerman was at the other end.

"I thought you had grown up," he growled without a preamble.

"What's up?" I asked puzzled.

"That bottle you gave me."

"Didn't you find prints on it?"

"Oh yes, we found prints on it. *Your prints*."

So I had left a print on the bottle, after all, no matter how carefully I had handled it. So what?

"But what about the other fingerprints?"

"There were many others. Beautiful and clear ones, all of them. And all of them yours. This is no longer funny, Richard," I could hear the anger mounting in his voice. "I don't know why you think that we have time to waste running after your stupid little pranks: no more bottles, Richard. Bring me no more bottles. And while you are at it, keep out of my way too."

The line went dead. He had hung up. I looked at the telephone, almost hoping to hear it ringing again. It would be Eitan, I expected, calling back to say that this time it was he who had played a joke on me and laughing at my reaction. "No," he would say, "we have a beautiful set of prints for Paula Vargo from the bottle you brought us. Thank you very much, Richard. We will work on it." This was what Eitan should have said once the phone rang again.

But the phone kept silent. The house was empty and silent too. Only my head felt like a beehive. It was as if Paula was laughing at me, playing with me in a way that I couldn't understand. I realized that I was shaking—I couldn't tell if it was more from fear or anger. I walked slowly up the stairs and into my room. Ignoring the late afternoon hour, I stretched on the bed with my clothes and shoes on and fell asleep immediately, completely exhausted.

PART THREE
The Chase

CHAPTER 16

I had expected Becky to be happy at the news that the Vargos were out of our life, and she must have been, but she wasn't showing it. We were still quite frigid to one another, each apparently waiting for the other to mend things. I didn't really know how to do it, though, given that Becky was uncommunicative, but I decided to give her time. Meanwhile, when she was around, I felt like I was walking on eggshells. All she had said that evening after I had given her the news that we were "Vargos-free" was, "Very good," and nothing more. I felt relieved, too, as if a heavy burden had been lifted from my shoulders, but I was still sour at the thought of having been used and then discarded. Although I wouldn't admit it to myself, what hurt me most was that clause in the agreement that Finkel had drafted, explicitly stating that all connections between the Vargos and us were severed and that we should not communicate with them in any way and for any reason. I couldn't understand it. I certainly had done nothing wrong to them. Quite the contrary, I had done my best to help them, professionally and personally, and I thought that Daniel and I had become friends. Still, here they were, dictating that we should not speak to each other ever again. Perhaps it was their conscience that made it hard to meet me in person and look me in the eyes, and they preferred to keep their distance and avoid embarrassment.

But my relief was short-lasting. Two weeks later, my world started to change again. I was sitting in my kitchen, working on a document. It was a Friday morning, and I decided not to go to the office and work at home instead. I had been watching TV earlier, and CNN was still playing in the living room. Voices reached me in the kitchen, but I felt too lazy to get up and turn it off.

"... leaving the immense fortune he has amassed through his diamond mines in Africa to his only daughter," a reporter was saying. "Elise Vernon was kidnapped as a child and only reunited with her father five years ago ..."

I jumped up and practically ran to the TV set. I gaped at it, petrified, and listened to the rest of the story.

"... after his wife's death of a broken heart at the loss of their only child. The French police and Interpol had done extensive searches throughout Europe, but the little girl was not found. Elise Vernon, who had lost her memory because of the traumatic event of her kidnapping at such an early age, only started to regain her memory about six years ago. Her search for her family ultimately resulted in her reunion with the late Pascal Vernon five years ago, with whom she has lived since. Miss Vernon is the heir of a fortune estimated at about a hundred and fifty million dollars, although much of it is invested in precarious African mines.

"Pascal Vernon was electrocuted when he tried to turn a faulty light bulb in his living room. The incident reportedly took place while he and his daughter were having a quiet evening at home, and

Miss Vernon is in shock and unable to talk to the press."

If someone was in shock, it was me. Electrocuted! It sounded dreadfully familiar, particularly where Paula was concerned. But I had to remind myself that no real connection existed between Elise Vernon and Paula Vargo, save in my imagination. As far as I knew, Paula was in California with Daniel, probably living off expedients, while Elise Vernon was in Paris, the heir of millions.

I paced the room back and forth, trying to tell myself that this was none of my business and that the fact that both Tarun and Vernon had been electrocuted was probably only a meaningless coincidence, anyway. But I couldn't shake the feeling that something was the matter. I picked up the phone and dialed Yoel's number.

"Hi, Richard. How are you?" he greeted me.

"I thought I was fine until this morning. Have you heard the news about Vernon?"

"No. What happened?"

I gave him a quick outline of the news.

"So what?" he asked when I was done.

"What do you mean, so what? Tarun died of electrocution—lightning-like, they said. Vernon dies electrocuted. And both are somehow connected with Paula. Doesn't that seem meaningful to you?"

"I don't know, and I don't care. We are done with Paula, and as far as we know, she is in America now. And we have nothing to do with this Vernon guy. That concerns the French police. Why should we lose sleep over it? I don't follow you, Richard."

"Because," I explained patiently, "if it turns out that there is a connection between Elise Vernon and Paula Vargo—and I am sure there is—then it will be clear that Paula must have had something to do with Tarun's death."

"Assuming you're right, why is this any business of ours? Let the police take care of it. We are through with the Vargos, we are not connected with Tarun's death, and we have been paid off to stay away from the project. So I don't see why you should be so worked up about it."

"But, Yoel, we may be talking murder," I appealed to him.

"So?"

"So, don't you think that we should do something about it?"

"No."

"No?"

"No."

"You are planning to sit back and do nothing?"

"You've got it right, this time."

"And if they kill somebody else?"

"No skin off my nose. I have no specific knowledge of a person who is in danger, and it's not my mission in life to fix the world."

"Well, if you feel that way ..."

"That's how I feel."

"Oh, okay then. Talk to you."

"Take care."

I hung up. Yoel was probably being sensible. So why couldn't I leave the Vargos alone? But I knew I couldn't and wouldn't forget them. My conscience wouldn't let me, so I waited for the kids to go to bed and then told Becky what had happened and that I would be looking for ways to do something about it.

"You can't let go," she commented in a quiet, low voice that scared me.

"You know I can't. It's crazy, I know, but I'm the only one who has a clue. I must do something."

"What?"

"Something. I don't know what yet."

Becky didn't argue or start a fight. She just got up and went to bed. We had been like that since the night of Daniel's surprise visit. We no longer acted as husband and wife but like two strangers who shared a house. And the worst part of it was that the kids had become apathetic too. It was as if a mantle of gloom had enveloped what used to be a happy house. I had tried to improve the atmosphere but had no success and eventually decided that I had to let time take its course. It will get better, I thought, but no—it got worse.

The next evening returning home from the office, I found the house dark and deserted. Becky had left a note on the kitchen table. It said: "Call me at my sister's." I ran to the phone, and she answered the third ring.

"What's the matter? What are you doing at your sister's? Where are the kids?" I shot.

"The kids are with me. I'm taking them up north to my parents."

"What do you mean, 'taking them'?"

"I can't stand it any longer, Richard. You are obsessed with that woman, and I've had enough. Call me when you've come to your senses."

"I'm not obsessed with anybody, but I can't just ignore ..."

"I'm done, Richard. You need to make your own decisions, but if you don't give up by the end of the summer break, the kids will go to school up north. Your choice."

"This is crazy, Becky! We need to talk."

"There is nothing to talk about. Don't call me unless you have renounced the Vargos forever. I mean it."

And I knew that she meant it. She had changed since this craziness had started, in a way that made her somebody else entirely, but I still knew her well enough to know that she meant it.

"Just a little longer, I promise. I need to find out what's going on, and then I'll turn all this over to the authorities. I swear," I said, and when that elicited no response from Becky, I added, "I love you."

"Goodbye, Richard," she said, and the line went dead.

CHAPTER 17

The interior of the coffee shop was too heavily air-conditioned and too dark for comfort. Erin sat before me and gazed at me intently, ignoring the coffee that the waiter had put on the table.

Erin Lief was a freelance journalist. I had met her the year before, when she had interviewed me for an article she was writing for a foreign journal. She was Canadian born, and I guessed her age to be around thirty-five. She was petite and energetic, with a nice body and piercing green eyes below auburn hair that she kept almost tom-boyishly short. She had a biology background, and I had been impressed by her easy grasp of complex concepts. I needed an ally in my inquest, and who better than someone with a scientific inquisitive mind and access to the media? I had found her business card in the pile that I kept in my drawer and resolved to call her.

"What do you say?" I asked when I got to the point when Paula Vargo was not Paula.

"I don't know ... I have a feeling that you may be placing a wrong interpretation on the facts."

"It could be. It definitely could. This is either the biggest mystery in modern history or a complex hoax. I may be wasting your time. But I see that you've been giving some thought to what I told you."

"I've done more than that. When you told me that our meeting had to do with Daniel Vargo's cure for cancer, I asked around a bit and came up with some interesting results."

"Like what?" I was suddenly excited. At last, someone was taking an interest in what had become my personal obsession.

"First of all, I visited the Vargos' neighbors, and I talked to a few of Daniel's colleagues at the hospital. I tried to find out as much as possible from their friends about their habits and family life. Here I drew a blank: they simply had no friends."

"No friends? That surprises me."

"None. Then I went to the Ministry of Internal Affairs."

"What for?"

"The MIA keeps a dossier of every person who immigrated to Israel, and the dossier has a photo in it. I was lucky—or so I thought; I found Paula's and got a copy. Here it is," she said, handing a paper to me.

The coffee shop's lighting was so bad that I had to get up and stand by a nearby lamp to inspect the picture. The form on which the small photo was pasted contained standard information on the new immigrant. It was dated some four years before. I looked at the photo. It could have been Paula, but it was a very fuzzy picture, one of those do-it-yourself photos you take in a booth by dropping a few coins, and it was of terrible quality. In fact, it could have been anybody's picture.

"This could be Paula or not. In fact, it could be you just as well," I told Erin.

"Yeah, I noticed. It doesn't help me at all. But that isn't all. You remember telling me about Paula's car accident in Paris?" I nodded. How could I forget? She continued. "Well, I checked the archives of the French newspapers. Browsing through the pages of a newspaper that reported it, look what I found there."

Erin handed me a Xerox copy of a small item. The headline said, "Elise Remembers." I read avidly through it. It was a brief account of how Elise Vernon, who had found her long-lost father two months ago, had now started to regain her memory and was feeling well again. The full story of her reunion with her father after thirty years had been widely covered at the time by the same newspaper, we were reminded.

I looked at Erin, incapable for a moment of understanding the significance of this. My perplexity apparently showed because Erin hastened to explain.

"Don't you see? Your friend Paula is badly burned in a car accident and eventually turns up with a face altogether different from the one she had originally. At about the same time, Elise also turns up, looking—so you say—like Paula's twin. There must be a connection between these events. And if there isn't, then my journalistic instincts have blown a fuse, and I can get a new job knitting."

"Do you mean that ... ?"

"... we have a case," she finished the sentence for me. "We have something definitely worth working on, and I have some ideas too. But ..."

"But?" I asked, suddenly concerned. I was too happy at her interest in my story to be able to bear any "buts."

"But I won't be able to pursue it unless you work on it with me. You know Paula and her face, and you have all the details in your head. I concede that there is something weird behind all this, and it may turn out to be a huge story, cure for cancer and all. But

I won't even look at it unless you help me."

"I'll be glad to help, although I don't know what I can do that I haven't done already."

"For one, you will have to come to Paris with me."

"Sorry. No can do. I am a professional, and I have a firm to run."

"Then I'll have to find another story. I'm sorry, though, because I think that this may be a good one, but I won't work on it without you."

She got up, thanked me for the coffee, and left.

I sat there for five more minutes, feeling helpless. This was a no-win situation. Either I got involved again, which I didn't want to do, or Erin wouldn't look at my story—and she was the only one I knew who could.

I drove home and sat outside in the car, thinking. The house was empty, cold, and dark anyway. It had been almost two weeks since Becky had left me. I found it hard to think of it in those terms, but I had to look the truth in the eyes. I had called her parents' home several times, and she had refused to speak with me. At least, she wasn't keeping the children from me, and I had spoken with them a couple of times, keeping up the pretense that they were away for the summer break and that they would come back before school resumed. "I had to work so I couldn't join you," was the excuse I was giving them for not coming up north to see them, and mercifully Becky was not contradicting me. I guess that she wanted to keep the children out of our fight. But things would never go back to normal until I renounced looking for the truth about the Vargos. Becky had made that unequivocally clear, and I wasn't ready to do that yet. I had convinced myself that once I was through with it, Becky and I would be able to go back to our lives and that everything would be as before, but deep down, I doubted that completely healing the breach would ever be possible. Still, I would settle for whatever I would be able to get.

But not yet.

I had to seize the opportunity that Erin had offered. I could hire someone to look after the office for a couple of weeks—I'd done so before when I traveled to Australia, and I could do it again. And I didn't have to get Becky's approval since she wasn't talking to me anyway. I had planned to place the burden of the Vargos' story on Erin's shoulders, hoping that turning it over to a serious journalist would free me and allow me to forget about it and resume my life. So, was I mad, getting involved like this? Wouldn't I do better to put all my energy into rebuilding my relations with my wife and my family?

Slowly, heavily, I picked up the phone and pushed Erin's number on my speed dial.

"I'm on board," I said when she answered. "Give me a week to get organized."

CHAPTER 18

Erin and I were sitting in the living room of Prof. Mackowski's house in Paris, waiting. The maid who had admitted us had disappeared, and we sat quietly, unwilling to disturb the silence that seemed to reign throughout the house.

She was a uniformed maid, such as I hadn't seen for many years. She wore a dark blue skirt and a light blue blouse and walked around with a white crest and a white apron, precisely as I remembered that maids from my childhood days used to do. This professor had to be an old-fashioned type.

We had reached Paris that morning, and it still felt unreal. Only the week before, we were in a poorly lit café in Tel Aviv, discussing the strange Vargo story. Preparations had taken a week, with Erin getting in touch with friends and colleagues to find useful names and leads. Professor Mackowski was one of them. He was a linguist, a phonetician, and an expert in Slavic languages. Erin had been introduced to him through an acquaintance of hers, and we had spoken with him over the telephone. He had agreed to help us, provided it didn't take up too much of his time. So here we were.

The door opened, and a small man of about fifty-five walked in. He was lean and wore a neat goatee that made him look pretty much what he was: a university professor.

"Good afternoon," he said in perfect English, extending a hand. I let Erin go first.

"Good afternoon, Professor," she said, shaking his hand. He then took my hand and shook it, nodding in acknowledgment, and I did likewise.

"We appreciate your kindness in helping us very much," I said. "We know that you are very busy, and we don't wish to impose on your time more than necessary."

"Oh, don't worry," answered the professor. "I am glad to be of assistance if I can."

"Then, perhaps, you could tell us how you can help?" Erin asked in that direct way of hers. "My friend, who said that we should talk to you, told me that you are a 'wonder linguist,' but I'm afraid that I don't know enough about your specialty to be able to appreciate what this means for us."

"I'll tell you a little personal anecdote, then," said the professor, smiling as if remembering something particularly pleasing, "that I believe will illustrate what I do. It is the story of how I met my wife. It was almost twenty years ago. As I was waiting for a train at the station in Pristina, Kosovo, I saw the most beautiful girl ever, standing at the newsstand, obviously also whiling away the time since the next train out of Pristina was not due for almost two hours. She was talking pleasantly with the lady behind the counter, and I stood behind her, listening to their conversation. When she turned to go away, I addressed her: 'Pardon me, mademoiselle,' I said, touching my hat, 'I hope that you will not think me impudent for asking, but I wonder whether you could tell me what the weather was like in Kraljevo, since I was rather thinking of going there in the next few days.'

"'How did you know that I just came from Kraljevo?' she said.

"'Oh, that's simple,' I answered, 'exactly as I know that you have lived in Belgrade for the past five years, but you were born in Loznica and lived there until you were at least twelve years old.' I watched for the results and wasn't disappointed. She opened her two beautiful eyes and her mouth in amazement.

"'But, but ... how do you know all that? You are right, but how could you know? Have we met before?'

"'Most regrettably, not, mademoiselle. But your speech gave you away. Perhaps we could sit on that bench over there, and I'll explain to you? Here,' I said, when we were seated, handing her my visiting card. 'I am a linguist, and my ears are the tool of my trade. I can tell with no difficulty the origin of every inflection and accent in how people speak. In your case, the place where you grew up, and your current city of residence are strongly given away by your speech.'

"'But how did you know about Kraljevo? I've been there only for five weeks.'

"'When we stay for any appreciable length of time in a different place, we pick up something of the way people there speak. Whatever influence it has, it's not here to stay, and in a few weeks, it will be gone. Even now, it is very faint, but I can detect it. That's how I knew that you were in Kraljevo a short while ago.'

"So you see," the professor continued, "my wife was so amazed by my ability that she forgot that we hadn't been properly introduced, and a year later, we were married. Does that answer your question about my expertise?"

"It definitely does, Professor," said Erin, obviously impressed.

"So, what can you tell us?"

"I have looked at this video that you sent me," he said, lifting the DVD that we had FedExed to him the week before. It was a very short interview with Elise Vernon, given to an Antenne-2 reporter. In the tape, Elise only spoke a few words, stating her devastation at her father's tragic death, before her bodyguard pushed the reporter aside and helped her into her car.

"The audio is low quality, and I had to work on it to clean away the background noise. Another problem is that she only spoke a few words, and she was under a strong emotion when she spoke. And then, she was speaking French, not a Slavic language, and I had to infer from the French speech what the Slavic speech would sound like. All this made my job extremely difficult."

Here, I thought, he is going to tell us that he couldn't use the video. We have come all this way for nothing.

"And?" Erin prompted him tensely.

"But I am the best, as you know, and I know where she came from."

"You do?" I asked, a weight lifting from my shoulders.

"I do. She obviously grew up in a small village, Srapatsko, near Negotin, on the triple border with Romania and Bulgaria."

"How can you be sure?" I asked in disbelief. "You can't know all the small villages in the Balkans."

"Perhaps not, although I probably know most of them, and I have been almost everywhere. But I know Srapatsko well because it is a particularly interesting part of the country. You have linguistic influences from Romania and Bulgaria, which causes a peculiar distortion in how certain vowels are pronounced. People from that area also have a very distinctive way of pausing between certain words. There is no way I could be mistaken. Elise Vernon has lived a substantial number of years in the Srapatsko area, and she was there as a young girl, not lately."

"This is amazing, Professor," Erin said. I could tell that she was genuinely awed. "I think I must write an article on you someday. Most people will think this uncanny, and, to be quite frank, I wouldn't have believed it if I hadn't heard it from your own lips. Is there anything else that you can tell us?"

"Well, I'm not sure ..."

"Tell us anyway," I said. "We won't hold it against you."

"There is something in the baseline of her speech that puzzles me. It is an inflection that I haven't ever heard before. I can't attribute it to any language I know and most certainly not to any European language. It bothers me."

"What does this mean?"

"I don't know. That's why it bothers me. I tried to establish whether this may be due to the limited amount of data available to me, but all my tests were inconclusive. You see, I have improved since I met my wife. Now I don't rely only on my ears, which are still my main instrument, but I also get some help from computer analyses of speech patterns. I have run Elise Vernon's speech pattern through the software I use for my everyday work. It has come up with the same answer as my ears. There is an influence in the baseline that neither I nor the computer can attribute to any spoken language."

"Could this influence your conclusion on the place where she grew up?" asked Erin.

"Not likely. No. I'm quite positive about that. But still, understanding where that strange influence comes from might give us some more insight."

"What do you suggest?" I asked.

"I was thinking that, perhaps, you could get hold of some more recordings of Elise Vernon speaking. A longer sample would help."

"Not from public records," said Erin. "I have asked virtually everywhere, and it seems that there are no recordings of her voice at all. The Vernons have always been very private people, and the press was not let in when the daughter-and-father reunion took place five years ago."

"Then perhaps you could try to talk to her and record her voice. If you do, I am positive that I will be able to find out what this anomaly in her speech means."

"If you think that this is important," said Erin, "we can try."

"It could be quite important," said the professor, gravely.

We thanked Professor Mackowski and left.

"I don't know what to make of all this," I told Erin. "We know where Elise comes from, and we can go there, and perhaps we will find out whether she is an impostor or really Vernon's kidnapped girl. And perhaps we should. But what does this linguistic charade mean?"

"It means I need a drink," said Erin with a sigh.

It was almost six p.m., I noted with surprise. We had sat with the professor for nearly two hours and hadn't been offered even a glass of water. I, too, needed a drink. A taxi took us through the traffic to our hotel, where we took a small table at a corner of the lobby that also doubled as a bar.

"He's quite something, isn't he?" said Erin, with a tired smile.

"The professor, you mean? Yes, he is. Do you believe his story about his wife?"

"Why not? He is hailed as the best phonetician in Europe, and he is certainly an outstanding expert in Slavic languages. I don't believe that he would waste his time bullshitting us."

"Then what do we do next?"

"We talk to Elise Vernon—and record her."

"Now?"

"No. I need to think a bit about the best way to go about it."

Having been left without much to do, we decided to call it a day and get some food. We had a light dinner, after which Erin went for a walk, and I went to bed early. I was tired after the day's flight and fell asleep quickly.

Erin meant business. The next morning found us by the phone in her room. Over breakfast, we had discussed briefly how to approach the problem, and now Erin was on the phone. She spoke French fluently, but with the strange Canadian accent that, at times, made it difficult for me to understand her. However, I could follow what she was saying now since I knew exactly where she was going. She had a second phone in her room that I used to listen in to the conversation, with my hand on the microphone and trying not to breathe. Erin's small tape recorder was recording the conversation through a mike attached to the receiver. During her preparations, I had asked her whether she wouldn't get in trouble recording the call without the other party's consent, but she had brushed it aside by saying, "I'm a journalist," without leaving much room for discussion.

"My name is Erin Lief," she said, "and I am a journalist. I would like to talk to Miss Vernon."

"Miss Vernon is not speaking to the press," said a coarse female voice.

"I understand that Miss Vernon is unwilling to talk about her recent tragedy, and I don't intend to bother her with it. I wrote an article two years ago on Africa's diamonds, and I am now planning a follow-up story. I think it is only fair of me to allow Miss Vernon to state her perspective. In my earlier article, her father's activities didn't come out in a good light."

"Wait a second, please," said the voice, following which we were put on hold with a nice Vivaldi background music. After a while, a masculine voice manifested itself.

"Miss Lief?"

"Yes, it's me."

"I am Alain, Miss Vernon's press agent. What can I do for you?"

"I would like to interview Miss Vernon very briefly for my follow-up article on diamonds in Africa."

"I don't think that this will be possible, I'm sorry. Under the tragic circumstances ..."

"Five minutes. I promise."

"I'm sorry ..."

"Not more than five minutes. And I swear I won't ask her about her father's death."

"I don't know ..."

"Please?"

"Well ... Come here at noon, and I'll see what I can do." He hung up.

"What do you think?" asked Erin.

"I think the guy liked you, but he's not the boss. The only way to find out what will happen is to go there. Do you want me to come with you?"

"As long as you don't show your face. If Elise sees you and recognizes you, we are done for."

At five minutes to twelve, I was sitting in a rented car parked outside the Vernon residence, in what I hoped was a good watching position. Erin was on the doorstep, waiting for the door to open, which it eventually did, and she walked in. Time passed—five, ten, fifteen minutes. That gave me hope that Erin had been successful in getting to Elise. After almost twenty minutes, the door opened again, and Erin came out. Walking quickly, she reached the car, climbed in, and said:

"Drive!"

I did as instructed, and as the car started moving, I asked, "What happened?"

"They did quite a number on me. First, I was taken to the office of this Alain character, who apologized for being unable to bring me into The Presence. But, hey, he told me, don't be sad, because I have this wonderful replacement. Then an old man came in, who identified himself as the Supervisor of Mining Affairs. He gave me a ten-minute tirade on the Vernon philosophy according to which the workers' welfare comes before everything else. He complained bitterly that my earlier article had done gross injustice to their enterprises, and he hoped that I would mend my ways in the follow-up article."

"And Elise?"

"Not a glimpse of her did I get. I asked repeatedly for her, but I was told that she wasn't actively involved in the mining business. I was reassured that I had spoken with the appropriate person. Then this Alain tried to convince me that the Vernon Estate was a worthy establishment that spent a sizable percentage of its income for mankind's welfare, financing basic research through the V-M Research Fund that Elise has been chairing for two years now. And I had to sit there and take notes as if it interested me."

"The V-M Research Fund, you said?"

"Yes."

"Are you sure?"

"Of course, I'm sure. Why are you so worked up about it?"

"Because the V-M Research Fund is the one that financed Daniel Vargo's research. Its name was on the lease of the laboratory."

"Well, I don't know if this means anything. They probably fund hundreds of projects."

"Still ..."

"Okay. I'll keep it in mind for future investigation. But right now, I don't think that I want to worry about that detail."

"So now what?"

"Now I could use a drink."

That seemed to be Erin's panacea for all situations. However, I couldn't think of a better idea myself, so I drove toward our hotel.

CHAPTER 19

The trip from Bucharest to Jimbolia, where we planned to cross the border into Serbia, is not one I remember with pleasure. To begin with, I had never been to an ex-communist country, and I didn't know what to expect. I got off the plane with the strange feeling of being watched by Securitate agents—a feeling that accompanied me until we left Bucharest.

When planning our trip to Srapatsko, we soon understood that the easiest way to get to the Negotin area was via the Romanian border. The alternative was to land in Belgrade and cross half the country to get to the Romanian border, and we didn't relish the idea. However, Romania wasn't very appealing either. To me, at least. Erin seemed to be at ease everywhere and beamed happily at the Romanian policeman who went through our luggage, probably looking for smuggled illegal goods. She smiled at him and thanked him as if he was making her day by turning her bag inside out. I couldn't share her sunny disposition. To me, the policemen were all part of a large net spread by the authorities for the sole purpose of catching me bending—perhaps dropping the wrapper of my chewing gum—so as to send me to the dungeon for life. I knew I was being paranoid, but the atmosphere called for it.

"Let's take a taxi," Erin said when we finally got through the airport bureaucracy.

Five or six taxis were standing outside the terminal. Their drivers approached us all at once and all speaking quickly and equally unintelligibly. Erin selected one, I don't know by which criterion, and presently we were on board an old and battered Fiat.

"Hotel Inter-Continental, please," said Erin. I was happy to leave the leading role to her, and she was probably much more competent than me to deal with these people. I guess it comes from getting around a lot, and a girl who is used to interviewing slaves in African mines takes Bucharest in her stride.

After a trip of about twenty minutes, we found ourselves in *Boulevard Nicolae Balcescu*, a rather Western-looking part of town. The hotel was a pleasant surprise, too, as it looked pretty decent. My low spirits started to soar again.

The rooms were also okay. As agreed beforehand, we organized quickly and met in the lounge.

"I have asked the concierge to arrange transportation for us," said Erin. "Let's see what he's got."

The concierge sounded both cooperative and knowledgeable.

"I have arranged for an English-speaking guide to take you to your destination," he said. "His name is Iuliu. He will drive you as far as the border, but then you will have to take a local taxi."

"Can we arrange for a drive across the border from here?"

"I don't know anybody who can take you. Jimbolia is not really an important place, but I am sure that you will be able to find a local guide for a moderate fee."

"How about Iuliu? How much do we pay him?"

"It depends. Can you pay in American dollars?"

"Yes, of course."

"Then give him two hundred dollars, but pay him only when you reach the border, not a moment earlier."

"Why? Don't you trust him?"

"I trust God, and even Him only part of the time," said the concierge, smiling. "If you pay Iuliu too soon, you may find that his car breaks down and he can't go on, or you may have to pay extravagant sums to get it fixed. If money awaits at the end of the trip, on the other hand, you will be amazed to see how smoothly the car runs."

The concierge also booked a table at a restaurant where we had a decent dinner. Back at the hotel, we got out of the taxi, paid the driver, and stopped before the entrance.

"What about a nightcap?" I asked.

"I'm game," she said with a sigh, turning around and walking quickly into the hotel, but as it turned out, the bar was closed.

"We can raid the minibar in my room," she said.

It had been a long time since a woman had invited me up to her room, and I was a married man, I reminded myself, even if with an estranged wife. But Erin's invite was probably innocent. We were partners in a strange quest, alone in a foreign country, and a bit of camaraderie was unavoidable. I gazed at her, trying to gauge her mood, and couldn't help feeling guilty about the impure thoughts that rushed into my head. After all, she was a beautiful, independent, and strong woman who wanted a drink with her partner. Nothing wrong with that.

"Yeah, what the hell. It's still early," I said, making an effort to sound casual.

In her room, Erin mixed us drinks from the small minibar

bottles, and then we sat in the two tiny armchairs to drink them. Erin was silent and drank slowly, looking at the night through the window.

"What's up, kid?" I asked, sensing that something was the matter.

"Think about it," she said, tapping my arm with her free hand. She was always patting my arm or my leg when speaking, a mannerism that I attributed to her warm, enthusiastic attitude to everything, but I wished she would do that less frequently because it got me thinking in the wrong direction. "Aren't we embarking on a wild goose chase? I was wondering, earlier tonight at dinner if you hadn't managed to infect me with your enthusiasm against my better judgment."

"I'm not usually that contagious. I don't have that effect on people."

"Oh, yes, you do. On me, at least."

I couldn't think of a good repartee, so I kept silent. Erin kept gazing straight out of the window, sipping her drink in what I thought was a moody way. We drank in silence for a few minutes, and then she put her empty glass down.

"It's late, and we should go to bed," she said, rising from her armchair. "*Noapte Buna.*"

I got up and clumsily moved toward the door, brushing against Erin in the narrow space between her and the window.

"What did you say?" I asked.

"*Noapte Buna.* Good night in Romanian. You should learn a few words."

"I don't think so," I said, looking straight into her face. She had a strange, almost angry expression as if something I had said had angered her. That expression invited inquiry, but I was too tired for that. And also scared about the answers I might get.

CHAPTER 20

Eight o'clock in the next morning saw us checked out of the hotel, with self in a bad mood after a restless night on a hard and unfriendly mattress, some of it spent trying to figure out if I had made an ass of myself the night before in Erin's room. In contrast, Erin looked rested and fresh, and for perhaps the tenth time, I was amazed by her adaptable disposition. Breakfast had consisted of a hard-boiled egg, some tasteless vegetables, and a gorgeous-looking cottage cheese that let you down by tasting sour. The bread could have been the twin brother of the stale loaf that had been served to us the night before.

Iuliu was at the door, as promised. He was a sleek character with a hunting cap, a large gold ring on his little finger, and a black leather jacket. I realized immediately that the concierge's notion of an English-speaking driver differed diametrically from mine.

"*Buña dimeneata*," he said, which I guessed meant "good morning" or something along those lines. "Me Iuliu," he continued, informatively, "you mister and miss."

We admitted to being mister and miss and gave him our minimal luggage to load in the trunk. Encouraged by our friendliness, he became loquacious.

"We, you, I go Jimbolia on car," he explained, probably wishing to relieve us of any anxiety about the ability of the car to get us there.

The car was indeed a Mercedes that didn't inspire much confidence. To my untrained eye, it looked at least twelve to fifteen years old, and the upholstery was greasy and torn. The floor in the seat beside the driver had partly rusted away, and I could see the road through holes in it. In the back, a little pool of water rested on the floor, awaiting its turn to convert it to rust.

"Good car. Strong," he added, patting the wheel with the palm of his hand, when we finally seated ourselves inside, with me in front and Erin in the back. "Iuliu good driver, you worry not. I Iuliu," he explained triumphantly, apparently to make sure that we understood how lucky we were.

"What road are you planning to take?" I asked, trying to get on a more practical level.

"Scuse me. *Nu int'eleg engleza.* Thank you. I, Iuliu, good driver. Now go." He threw in the clutch, and the car moved.

"He said that he doesn't understand English," Erin said in amazement.

"I can believe that. I hope he knows where we are going."

"We'd better follow the road on the map."

Our first stop was a town called Pitesti. A reasonably good road took us there uneventfully. However, when we got there, Iuliu stopped the car near a mechanic's shop and turned to me.

"Car tired," he said with a smile.

"What do you mean?" I asked. I didn't trust him at all,

particularly after the warnings offered by the concierge.

"See?" he said, pointing at the heat level. It was deep in the red. "Wait," he added, getting out and walking quickly toward a mechanic who stood nearby. They talked for a while, with Iuliu gesticulating emphatically every now and then. Eventually, he walked back to the car, still with a broad smile on his face.

"No worry. He car fix. We food," he added, pointing to a nearby place that I would never have guessed to be an eatery. At first glance, it looked more like a garage, but I now saw that it had small tables near the window.

"Iuliu," asked Erin, "how long will it take for them to fix the car?"

"Eh?"

"The car," Erin repeated patiently. "How much time for the mechanic to fix it?"

"Ah!" exclaimed Iuliu with understanding, "Soon," he said reassuringly.

We sat in there for almost three hours before the mechanic came to fetch us. He knocked on the window to attract our attention. Iuliu got up and went out. He listened to the explanations of the mechanic for a while, and then a heated argument ensued. They both stood out there, shouting at the top of their voices and gesticulating vehemently. After five minutes of this, they suddenly shut up, turned around, and walked toward the shop. Ten minutes later, Iuliu was back, informative as ever.

"Car good," he said with a broad smile. "Car fixed. We go," he added, making a sweeping motion with his hands, inviting us to get up.

We continued our trip through a town called Craiova, and by dusk, we hit the outskirts of what I identified as Drobeta. My map showed it to be very near our destination—Jimbolia.

"We go hotel," Iuliu said.

We had stopped in a narrow street, in front of a two-story building painted white that nestled between two other, darker buildings. On the narrow door, a sign said, "Hotel," and a smaller one said, "*Nu avem camere libere.*" Iuliu got out of the car and knocked on the door. An old woman dressed in black answered it, and negotiations began. The woman pointed twice at the small sign, and Iuliu nodded and continued to argue.

"I don't know what he's arguing about," wondered Erin. "The sign says 'no vacancies.'"

I looked at Iuliu. The argument was apparently concluded because the woman turned around and went inside, and so did we. She wore a black shawl over her black dress—a sure sign that she was a widow. We stood there and looked at each other. She inspected us as if to gauge what kind of clients we were.

"Do you speak English?" Erin asked.

"No English," answered the woman, shaking her head.

"*Français?*"

"*Oui, je parle français.* Yes, I speak French," she said.

The relief was immense. Here we had some means of communication. As it turned out, her French was quite good, and she was a genial soul. Her name was Mrs. Antonescu. We never learned her first name. She directed us to an empty, dark dining room. It was cold, and we kept our coats on. Mrs. Antonescu turned on a light and soon brought a steaming bowl of chicken soup for each of us. I wolfed it down with several slices of brown bread. It was delicious and helped us to forget the cold.

As soon as we finished eating, we dragged our luggage upstairs to the third floor, which occupied part of the roof. Three rooms opened along a small corridor. Mine was the first one near the stairs, and Erin's the last. I helped Erin with her bag and sat on her bed to rest. The room was small and Spartan, with a short bed, a little table with a lamp, and a cupboard. The window looked out into the street. We said good night, and I retired to my room. I got into bed and opened my book. I read no more than half a page before I fell asleep. My mattress was hard too, and I sincerely suspected that someone had inserted spikes in it to make it impossible to sleep on. But apparently, I was tired enough to ignore them.

I don't know how long I slept. I had a dream. In it, Daniel was in the hotel with me and stood by my bed. He was talking to me, but I couldn't understand a word of what he was saying. The sounds that came from his lips were unintelligible and guttural. And something else was wrong: Daniel was turning green. He was doing so slowly and gracefully, but his shade was definitely turning a beautiful green. And his face was scaly too. He looked like a green halibut, and, for some reason, the scariest thing was that he kept on smiling.

Someone was screaming. I checked my mouth to see whether it was me, but it wasn't. In the dream, I could not turn my head to see who was screaming, which annoyed me immensely, but then I realized that the screams were not in my dream. They were real and came from the corridor.

This realization woke me up instantaneously. I sat on the bed and then ran out into the corridor. The screaming was coming from Erin's room. It now stopped as an indistinct figure came running out of her doorway. I was in the dark corridor, which was narrow, and I was in the way. The figure didn't stop and rammed into me as if I wasn't there, catapulting me on my back. My head hit the corner of the corridor, and I fell, hitting the hard floor. The figure jumped over me and down the stairs at an incredible speed, and I managed to sit, trying to collect my wits.

The middle door opened, revealing a startling sight: Mrs.

Antonescu in a nightgown. She had a candle in her hand, which added little to the light that came through the open door of my room.

"*Que se passe-t-il?*—What's going on?" she inquired in French.

"*Je ne sais pas*—I don't know. There was someone in Erin's room, and she screamed. I opened the door, and he charged into me and sent me flying to the floor."

"Did you see who it was?"

"No. I didn't have the time to see anything. And it's dark here. Let's check on Erin."

At that moment, Erin emerged from her room. She looked lovely wearing pink pajamas, and she seemed to be all right. I was too relieved for words.

"Did you catch him?" she asked in English.

"No, he ran over me and got away. What happened?"

"My bag. He was trying to steal it." Erin's voice was shaking. It was the first time I had seen her lose her composure. I gripped her arm and gently steered her toward her room. "Go get something strong to drink, please," I told Mrs. Antonescu, switching to French, and she went down the stairs without a word, returning soon with a glass of a yellowish liquid.

I had managed to get Erin to sit on her bed, and she took the glass from Mrs. Antonescu with a grateful glance. She took a quick sip and shuddered a little.

"Forceful stuff, this is," she said, coughing a little.

The noise of a car broke the silence. I ran to the window in time to see Iuliu's Mercedes disappear in the darkness.

"It was Iuliu!" I said, and Erin nodded.

"He got into my room, I guess, looking for money. I always keep my bag with documents and money under the pillow when I am in unfamiliar surroundings—a habit I got in Africa," she added apologetically, looking at Mrs. Antonescu, who stood there patiently, apparently not minding our speaking English. "I don't know for how long he was in my room, but eventually, he must have tried to take the bag from under the pillow. I woke up, but he gave me a blow on the neck, and I almost fainted. That was when I yelled. The noise must have scared him off, and he let go of the bag and ran out."

"And I caught him coming. Gimme some of that poison, if there is any left. Did he take anything?"

Erin passed the glass to me and opened the bag. She went briefly through its contents and pronounced them full and untouched.

"This is quite a mess," she said, again switching to French. "We have been left without a driver, and I don't know what we'll do tomorrow."

"Don't you worry," said Mrs. Antonescu. "We will find a taxi for you tomorrow morning. Now I think that you need to lie down and rest. I'll go down to see if your driver has stolen anything else, and I'll lock up again."

I couldn't help admiring Mrs. Antonescu for her practical approach to the incident. No hysterics, no accusations—nothing. But perhaps she was accustomed to this kind of thing. Who knows? I looked at Erin. She was still shaking a bit, but she looked fine now.

"Our hostess is right. You be a good girl and go to bed. You need it."

"You don't look too hot yourself, you know."

I looked at myself in the small mirror that hung above Erin's night table. I had a cut on my forehead that had bled a little, and the side of my cheek was scraped. Nothing serious.

"Only a few scratches. And I think they make me look rather manly. But I'm ready to go to bed too. Here, finish up this drink."

"It tastes like vitriol."

"Yeah, but it's good for you."

"Come here," Ann ordered. "Get me the first aid kit from that bag over there, and I'll fix that cut on your face."

That actually made sense, so I complied. She expertly cleaned the cut and applied some iodine paste, and dressed it. She was her composed and efficient self again, and in five minutes, the bandage was done. I kind of liked being fawned upon and was sorry that she had been so quick.

"Thank you, Florence Nightingale," I said, smiling at her. "I can now go back to bed and try to get some sleep."

Erin gazed up at me. "Stay," she said simply.

"Do you want me to sit by you until you go to sleep?"

"No, I don't want to be alone. Get in with me. Hold me," she said as if it were the most natural thing.

Becky's image flashed before my eyes but only for a second. After all, she had pushed me away, and it felt like we were no longer even formally a couple. I didn't know what would happen when I went back to Becky. I could barely remember her face and felt so disconnected from her that I couldn't bring myself to feel shame for acting intimate with another woman. It was a strangely liberating feeling, something that I had never experienced before in my adult life.

I lifted the coverlet and got in. The bed was less than queen size, and I found myself at the edge until Erin took my arm and passed it over her head, guiding me to hold her shoulder. Then she turned on her side and nestled her head in my armpit.

"You're going to fall off the bed," she said. "Come closer."

I obliged and turned on my side too. The sweet scent of Erin's body and the warmth that she emanated sent a shiver along my spine, but in a good way. I felt self-conscious as I had not been for as long as I could remember, lying there gazing into Erin's face and feeling her breath on mine. Her eyes were closed, and she was breathing heavily, which made me realize that I was doing the same. She threw her left arm over me, and her hand came to rest casually on my hip. I had no doubt as to where this was going, and I realized that I was ready. More than ready—aching for it. We lay there, our bodies very close, for what felt like an eternity, but was probably only a minute or two, and then Erin opened her eyes.

"Are you going to kiss me, or what?" she asked in that disarming, direct way of hers that I found so alluring.

I hesitated for only a moment, and then I kissed her gently. At first, she responded with the same gentleness, but then she pushed back, climbed on me, and started to kiss me wildly and to roll up the T-shirt that I was using as a pajama top. Before I could fully realize what was happening, we were both naked, panting, our bodies moving in unison.

It all lasted for a long time, and finally, we fell into each other's arms exhausted, trying to cover our naked bodies with the thin coverlet, now that we were feeling the cold again. The sensation of her silky skin against my body was heavenly, and I never wanted to get dressed again. Erin fell sound asleep almost immediately or faked sleep—I didn't care which. I, on my part, was too busy reliving what had just happened to even consider sleeping. When, at last, my eyes closed, it was into a deep, dreamless sleep.

CHAPTER 21

The morning light, which came in through thin curtains that held almost nothing back, woke me up. I gazed at Erin and delighted in her beauty. I had had time to think last night, lying awake in bed, and was amazed that I felt no remorse. Becky came into my thoughts now for the first time, but it didn't feel like what I had done was a betrayal. She had betrayed me first, if not with another man, in another terrible way, by shutting me out.

I wondered what this would do to Erin and me. Although we had shared tender moments, no love was involved, but I did feel a kind of warmth toward her that was definitely more than just friendship—but not love. It was the almost natural outcome of the setup: two people thrown into an unusual situation, each needing comfort for his and her own reasons, and we had found it in each other. Two adults who were sufficiently attracted to one another to find safety in each other's arms. What could be wrong with that?

Erin stirred, opened her eyes, and saw me sitting on the bed, gazing at her. She sat up and smiled.

"Good morning," she said. "Were you watching me? That's creepy."

"No," I said, smiling back, "I was just thinking how beautiful you look when you sleep."

"Yeah, yeah. Why don't you go and scare up some breakfast while I get ready?"

"Sure. Let me go and brush my teeth, and then I'll do just that," I said. I got up and turned to leave.

"Richard," She called, and I swiveled to face her.

"Yes?"

"You know that what happened yesterday ... we ... doesn't mean more than it was, don't you?"

"Yes, I do, don't worry."

"I just wanted us to be clear about that. I don't want us to ruin our friendship."

"We won't," I said, and left quickly.

Downstairs, Mrs. Antonescu greeted me with a cup of coffee and gentle inquiries about Erin.

"How is she this morning? Quite a shock she's had, poor girl."

"She's fine. She getting ready and will be down in a short while."

Mrs. Antonescu brought bread and butter, along with some marmalade and cheese, just in time for Erin to join me. I was hungry, and the simple meal was delicious. I ate quickly, drinking plenty of coffee, and Erin did the same.

"I hurried down, so I have to go up and pack," she said. "See if we can get wheels."

I went to Reception, and Mrs. Antonescu lifted her head from the papers she was checking and smiled at me.

"Do you think that we will be able to find transportation to

Jimbolia, Mrs. Antonescu?" I said.

"I have spoken to my brother. He can drive you there, if you want, provided you leave soon because he has to be at work by noon. Would you like him to take you?"

"Why, certainly. Thank you very much. I appreciate it," I said gratefully, not realizing that my expressions of thanks could be misunderstood.

"He's not going to do it for free, you know? The gas will cost him money, and he will miss a few hours of work."

"No, no. I didn't mean ... of course he has to charge us. How much should we pay him?"

"He'll do it for fifty American dollars. I'll add them to your bill. Now you should get your girlfriend and hurry."

I didn't correct her notion that Erin was my girlfriend. I think that she liked me better for that. I thanked her again and climbed the stairs, waiting two minutes before knocking on Erin's door to catch my breath first. I wasn't going to have her see me panting.

"Yes?" she answered immediately.

"Mrs. Antonescu has found us a driver to take us to Jimbolia, and we must leave inside half an hour."

"Come in," she said. "Stop yelling in that corridor. You give me a headache. Can't we do this without rushing for once?"

"I'm afraid not. Mrs. Antonescu's brother will drive us if we leave pronto. Otherwise, we will have to look for alternative transportation, and, frankly, I have no idea where to start."

"Oh, shit!" said Erin. "Then I'll be ready and packed in ten minutes. I planned to take a shower now that it's less freezing in here, but I'll have to give up the idea."

"Good. Don't you try to carry your bag down yourself. I'll do it when you're ready."

"Okay. Now get out, or I won't be ready in time."

I spent the time going through the bill with Mrs. Antonescu. It was all very reasonable—less than two hundred dollars—but I felt that she wished me to check all the items with care. I did so lest she be offended by my lack of interest. By the time Erin came down, we had completed all financial transactions, brother-driver included, and were ready to leave.

I climbed the stairs again, happy in the knowledge that it was the last time that I had to do that, and carried Erin's bag down.

At the door, Mrs. Antonescu introduced us to her brother. She cautioned us that he didn't speak a word of any language, apart from Romanian. Then we said goodbye, and she kissed Erin on both cheeks. For a moment, I worried that she might wish to kiss me too, but apparently, I hadn't been considered for the honor. We went out, carrying our bags and waving again to our hostess, and, in a moment, we were on our way.

The car driven by Mrs. Antonescu's brother, whose name I hadn't caught when she had introduced him to us, was not a Mercedes. It appeared to be some sort of Russian car. It was certainly old, but obviously well looked after, and our trip was relatively comfortable.

After less than one hour, we came to a halt at a roadblock near a small building. Judging by the fact that our driver had opened the trunk and taken our luggage out, I assumed that this was the border. I wouldn't have guessed it otherwise since the building had no visible sign that could advertise its function, except perhaps for the Romanian flag.

We picked up our bags and said a quick goodbye to the driver, who climbed in and drove away unceremoniously.

"Now what?" I asked.

"Let's go and talk to the policeman," suggested Erin, pointing at a uniformed individual who stood at the door and seemed to be the only person around.

We walked the fifty meters to the door, and the policeman extended his hand.

"*Pas'aport,*" he commanded. We handed him our passports, and he inspected them meticulously, looking at the pictures and at us as if to make sure that we matched. After a while, he handed them back to us, moved aside, and gestured us to pass through the door. It opened into a narrow corridor, at the end of which we found a bench and another uniformed officer. Judging by the flag and uniform of different aspect from those seen previously, we were now in Serbia.

"*Dobro jutro. Pasosx,*" he said, extending his hand. We guessed that passports were what he wanted and handed them to him. He went through a routine very similar to that of his Romanian friend and then looked at us inquisitively.

"*Kuda idete?*"

"Sorry," I said, reverting instinctively to Pidgin English. "No speak Serbian."

"Tourists?"

"Yes. Tourists."

"Where are you going?"

This questioning started to make me nervous. I was used to passport controls, but in most countries, you showed your papers, and that was it. Where I planned to go, as long as my intentions were legal, was none of the police's bloody business. But here, a wrong word could mean expulsion from the country and perhaps incarceration for a day or two—or maybe forever, who knows. Yet, the question had to be answered, no matter what the outcome.

"To Srapatsko," I said, bracing myself for the reaction.

"Then maybe you need taxi?"

"Yes, yes," I answered eagerly. "We certainly need a taxi."

"My brother has taxi," he explained. "*Drago!*" he bellowed.

A young man dressed in a decent black jacket with a gray scarf appeared from nowhere and addressed the officer. After a brief exchange in Serbian, in which the only word I understood was Srapatsko, the newcomer addressed us in excellent English.

"Good morning. My name is Drago, and I drive that taxi over there. I understand that you wish to go to Srapatsko. Is that right?"

"That's right." Erin, whose fatigue had slowed her down until then, came suddenly to life and intervened. "But we also need a guide. Can you be a guide?"

"Can I be a guide? Can *I* be a guide? You ask my brother here. I am the best guide you can have. What do you want to see?"

"We need you to take us to Srapatsko and to help us ask local people a few questions. When we are through with that, we need you to take us to the nearest railway station where we can take a train to Belgrade. How much will you charge us for it?"

"I'll tell you, lady. Since I like you—in fact, I like you both—I will give you a real bargain. I'll charge you five hundred dollars flat for the whole day. How do you like that?"

"Two-fifty," said Erin, without batting an eyelid.

"Really ... three-fifty, and I am losing money, but since I like you ..."

"I'll tell you what. We will pay you three hundred dollars. But if you make yourself useful to us and are happy with your services, we will give you a bonus of fifty dollars at the end of the day. Now let's go before I regret my generosity."

"Okay, lady. I accept it because I like you. But I want the three hundred now."

"Aha! You like a good joke, don't you? Not a penny you get from us before you see us to the train station."

Drago lowered his voice and got nearer, speaking almost in a whisper.

"Look here, lady. At least I need you to pay the fifty dollars I owe my brother for introducing me to you. Can you give me that?"

"It's against my principles, but I'll make an exception for once. Give him fifty," she added, looking at me. Sometimes Erin did get a bit too bossy, but this was not a good time to quarrel, so I gave him fifty bucks. He handed them to his brother and then picked up our bags and motioned us to follow him to his car. We ran after him. I was a bit nervous about the bags and didn't plan to let them out of my sight. My views of human nature had become, I'm afraid, quite warped by then.

"I am an English teacher," said Drago. That explained his excellent English. "I bet you are asking yourselves how come I am driving a taxi."

I was doing nothing of the sort. In fact, I would have liked to doze off, but one has to be civil—and Erin didn't seem to be in the market for civilities, so I asked him.

"Tell me then, since you seem to be wanting us to know. Why are you driving a taxi?"

"Well, that's very simple. I drive during school vacations and weekends. To make money, you understand? Schoolteachers don't make much money, and we don't have enough money to buy all we need, with my mother always sick and my sister having her third baby. So I have to work hard."

"When are we going to get to Srapatsko?" Erin asked, unsympathetic to Drago's tribulations.

"Twenty minutes."

We fell back into silence, and a while later, the car stopped. We had been climbing a steep road that wound up a hill between houses. The street ended in a square paved with cobblestones. At the other end of the square, I saw a church with high, closed wooden doors, and in the middle stood a monument that had seen better days. A statue of nondescript form, apparently a mounted soldier, was carved in stone that didn't seem to have been cleaned for centuries. At the near end of the square, a building sported a few signs advertising beers and ice creams—apparently the closest approximation to a bar that these surroundings could offer.

Drago pulled the handbrake with force, leaving the car parked on the slope, and got out.

"Wait here," he ordered, and disappeared into the bar.

I got out of the car. The square was exposed to the wind, and the day was getting quite cold. Still, I'd had enough of Drago's smelly vehicle, and I wanted out.

"Come, let's get a breath of fresh air," I urged Erin, but she shrugged and remained in the car. I walked up to the monument and sat on the ledge that formed a natural seat around it. I looked around. Srapatsko was a tiny village—merely a few houses lined along the main street and a few more scattered about. There was nobody in sight, although it was already late morning. Far away, on the hills surrounding the village, a few more houses were half-hidden by trees, and I thought I could discern a few people and perhaps cattle, moving in the distance against the cloudy sky. I walked back to the car to keep my circulation going.

"Do you know how many people live here?" I asked Erin.

"Nope. But I guess that there should be a few hundred people in this area, judging by the houses I've seen in the village and around. Certainly not more than a couple thousand."

I returned to my monument seat and resumed my pointless watch of the surroundings. After a few minutes, Drago returned and approached me. Erin finally stirred, got out of the car, and joined us.

"I've got what you want."

"Who's he?" I asked impatiently.

"Just as you told me. You wanted someone who has lived in these parts for at least thirty years, and I've found him. He is one of the elders of this village. He's sitting inside. I told him that you are journalists coming to write an article on rural life—so please don't contradict me."

"Does he speak English?"

"No," Drago said with a half-laugh as if the notion were too funny for words. "He only speaks Serbian. I'll translate. Shall we go inside?"

We followed him into the poorly lit room that was the main bar. At a table in a corner sat an old man who looked a hundred and was probably at least seventy. Drago made the introductions. Mirko was his name. He mumbled something.

"He asks whether you will buy him a glass of wine," Drago translated.

"Tell him we'll buy him the whole bottle if he tells us what we need."

Drago translated dutifully, and I saw a light of excitement in Mirko's eyes. He mumbled something else.

"He says you can ask him anything," Drago translated.

"Okay," said Erin, her practical self again. "Ask him if he knows anything about a foreign girl who must have come to live in this area about eighteen to twenty years ago. She would have been five to six years old."

Drago translated Erin's question and Mirko's brief answer.

"You must be talking about the Twin Witches," said Mirko.

"The Twin Witches?" Erin and I almost shouted in unison.

"Who are the Twin Witches?" Erin asked.

And omitting the tedious translation routine, this was the story that old Mirko told us:

"The Twin Witches were two girls who turned up here one day, out of the blue. But you must be talking about somebody else because they weren't five to six years old—more like fifteen or sixteen. I know a lot about them," he explained, pouring himself another glass from the bottle of wine that we had brought to the table and looking first at the bottle and then at us as if to make sure that we were not going to take it away from him.

"The one who took them in was my cousin, who lived in a house up the hill, there," he clarified, pointing at a wall as if it weren't there. I am sure that he knew by heart what was behind it.

"They knocked on her door one evening. It was raining, and they weren't wearing clothing suitable for that weather, so my cousin told me. And they didn't speak a word of our language. My cousin, poor soul, she was a generous Christian. She took them in and fed them and clothed them, and looked after them.

"My cousin was a widow without children—her husband had died in an accident in the local road construction company only a few months after he had started working there, and she lived off a meager pension given her by the state. Her younger brother also lived with her, but he was a loafer who never did an honest day of work in his life. He would get an odd job every now and then when my cousin's money was not enough to buy him the drinks he needed to get stoned. Still, most of the time, he just did nothing, either sitting here at the bar idly or making a pest of himself up at the house.

"My cousin's house is high up the hill there," he explained, pointing again at the stone wall beside him, "and she seldom came to the village. She grew all kinds of vegetables there and kept chickens and pigs so that she only came in to buy sugar, or maybe knitting wool or other items she might need for a special purpose. When the girls grew older, they sometimes came instead, most of the time together, but sometimes only one of them. Nobody could ever tell them apart, so nobody ever tried.

"Then, one day, my cousin died, poor soul. She had suffered from a weak heart for years, and the winter of that year had been too much for her. The girls must've been about twenty by then, and my cousin left them the house, on condition that they would look after her good-for-nothing brother. She said so to the priest who came to administer her the sacraments, so nobody argued with that. The girls and the brother went on living in the house for a while, but there were gossips."

"What kind of gossips?" I inquired, happy to be able to get a word in edgeways.

"Ah! What kind of gossips, do you ask?"

"That's what I'm asking."

"There were indeed gossips. You see, I'm not a gossip. But everybody here knew that her brother was molesting these young girls. Some of the women of the village even went to the priest to complain about the impropriety of two young girls living alone in a house with an unmarried man, but the priest sent them away with a benediction, and that was it. Still, there was gossip—all the time.

"Then, one night—it was the fifteenth of August, the night when in these parts we celebrate the feast of Saint Mary—the whole village saw it. We had music and dances here in the square and a big fire on which we roasted all kinds of meats. Suddenly, one of the girls shouted and slapped the brother, real hard. His face was red because of his anger, and his cheek was red because of the blow. 'Stay away from me,' she yelled at him. 'I've had enough of you,' she said, 'and God will take care of you and will strike you and punish you.' I swear that I was afraid of her when she said that. And I think that the whole village was.

"The brother tried to make a step toward her, but a few young people who knew him grabbed him by his pants and kept him in check. Then he simply turned around and walked away. The feast went on for a while longer, and then everybody went home.

"On the next morning, the brother was found at the edge of the wood, dead. He had been struck by lightning."

"Lightning?" Erin and I shouted together.

"Yes. And you know the funniest thing? That had been a cloudless night. No rain, no thunderstorm. So it was clear to every right-thinking man in the village that the girls were witches and had invoked the powers that release lightning to strike the loafer. There was no other explanation. People often reported strange noises and flashes of light coming from the house, so everybody knew that something weird was going on over there.

"Then, one day—it must've been seven years ago ... no, it was six years ago. I remember it clearly because it was the year when the priest hung himself from the bell chord. It woke everybody up with his body going up and down. Quite an end, that was. In any case, six years ago, they disappeared. They could have been gone for a while before anybody noticed, but the fact remains that once they disappeared, we didn't hear from them anymore. And that was it."

"Didn't anybody institute any inquiry?"

"Why should anybody care? They didn't belong anyway. I went up to the house with my sister, and we took a few belongings that used to be my cousin's, to remember her by, and then we forgot all about them until you came along."

"And while you did that, did you notice anything unusual? Any indication of why the twins should have vanished?"

"No. There was nothing unusual. They just weren't there anymore, and going by the stale odor in the house, they had been gone for at least a few weeks."

"Is anybody living there now?"

"No. People around here don't feel comfortable entering that house. You can feel that there was evil about. People here call it 'the Twin Witches' house.' Nobody goes there, nor have I been there since. Like I told you, the last time I was there, we picked up a few things and left as quickly as possible. They say that the house is now in ruins—which doesn't surprise me since it was in bad repair to begin with."

"Would you like to go there?" I asked Erin, but she simply shook her head and turned to the old man.

"Do you know if there are any pictures of the twins that we can see? Perhaps documents that they had to submit to the authorities?"

"Documents? What documents? The Twin Witches didn't exist. They came from hell and went back to hell, and nobody asks the Devil to fill in papers. No, no documents."

I gave Erin an interrogative look. "No," said her face, "I don't have any more questions." Neither did I.

We were back in civilization, thank God. I sat in the lovely little bar of my most preferred hotel on BannhoffStrasse in Zurich. It was almost 4 p.m., and I felt reasonably well again.

With our interview at Srapatsko over, Drago had taken us to a small, squalid railway station—a drive of perhaps fifty miles. After a reasonably short wait at the station, we had parted company with Drago. We then had boarded an asthmatic train that unwillingly dragged its wheels toward Belgrade.

At Belgrade's airport, we had to wait for a late-night flight to Zurich, on which we were only too lucky to find economy class seats, as our ticket seller patiently explained to us over and over again. Erin had been uncommunicative during the whole trip, and I had left her alone. I guessed that she was entitled to feel a bit worn out after all we had been through.

The train from Zurich's airport landed us at the train station at eight in the morning, and by nine, I was snoring my head off in my hotel room, after a quick but heavenly shower. I was now sitting in the bar, sipping a gin and tonic and feeling alive again, when Erin appeared, also looking fresh and rested.

"Glad to see you," I greeted her. "I have made reservations at this gourmet restaurant at eight o'clock. We will be able to formulate our plans for the future over a most excellent dinner."

"Sorry, Richard, but I'll have to take a rain check."

"What are you talking about? This hotel's restaurant is hailed as one of the best in Zurich by Michelin. Look it up if you don't believe me."

"I trust your judgment on food implicitly, Richard. The problem is that I won't be here. My flight leaves at seven, and I have to go soon. I have already checked out, and my bag is at Reception."

She sat down in the small armchair in front of me, not meeting my eyes, and I looked at her without comprehending.

"But ... what about the story? There are many more angles to verify. There is much work to be done."

"I'm sorry, Richard, but I can't afford it. I have other work to do, and I must leave."

"But how are we going to proceed with the story?"

"There is no story, Richard. At least, not one that I can get printed."

I gazed at her face and realized what was going on. "You're scared!" I threw at her.

"I am," she said flatly. "You didn't read through that university dossier very carefully, did you? Paula Vargo's file that you brought back from Paris I mean."

"I read enough to know that things don't square out."

"That's clear. But on one of the forms in the file, I found an address for Paula's parents, who lived in a small place in the south of France. Before we left for this trip, I asked a French colleague to look them up and find out a little more about Paula. I just got off the phone with him. Paula's parents died in a fire that destroyed their house, only a week after Paula's car accident. She also had a brother who lived in Lyon, but he disappeared around the same time and has never been heard of again. So yes, I'm scared," she admitted.

Her haggard face told the story. She was quitting.

"You never told me that you were following that lead, but that fire may mean nothing; it may just be a coincidence. You're only using it to justify your decision to get out ..."

"I won't deny that I want out. What we heard in Srapatsko was a spooky story. Nothing good can come from it. I can tell evil when I see it, and I am scared out of my wits, okay? That wouldn't have stopped me if I had found something solid to work on, but there's nothing. Nothing, Richard. So do yourself a favor, take that flight back home with me and forget about the whole thing. Besides," she added with a wicked smile, "I would like our friendship to go on. We are good together—or at least we were last night."

I thought about what she had just said. I was undeniably attracted to her as she apparently was to me, and the thought of missing out on that relationship was painful. Still, I had messed up my marriage, which was much more than a fling, to follow the Vargos' trail, so I simply was not going to quit now.

"But you know that strange things are going on," I said. "You can't ignore it." I was desperate and couldn't believe that she would give up so easily.

"Can't I? And what do you want me to do? Do you think that I can find an editor so crazy as to publish an article about facts that

I can't back up? The editor I am working with has just pulled the plug on my expenses for this project and wants me to go immediately to Japan to follow a story that is developing there."

"But you can back them up," I pleaded. "You've seen it for yourself."

"Yeah? Let's see what we have to show for all our efforts. I have your clients who very legitimately fired you and moved to the USA. We have a woman who is a billionaire and who, according to you, must have murdered her father because it is your unsupported belief that she resembles another woman. We then have a fib about twin witches, told us by an old Serbian wino. And, yes, I almost forgot: we have a professor of Slavic languages, probably loopy, who claims that this billionaire must have spent time in a God-forgotten village because his ears say so.

"The only thing I can get out of all this is a nice libel suit, if I am ever able to find someone stupid enough to publish it."

"But, you know that we will find more and more evidence ..."

"Circumstantial evidence."

"Well, circumstantial or not, we will find it if we keep looking for it."

"I wish you the best of luck if you plan to go on but, strange as this may seem to you, a girl has to eat."

Her expression softened, and she sat beside me and took my hand.

"I care about you, I really do, and I hate to see you chasing ghosts and getting hurt."

"I have no choice," I said, and the truth of that statement hit me hard. "I don't know what I'll do without you," I added, and I meant it.

"So, what will you do now?"

"I guess that I'll find a flight tomorrow morning to go back home—or to what is left of it," I said, "and will try to figure out what to do next. What's sure is that I'm not giving up."

"Listen, I'll text you my number as soon as I get to Japan, okay? Keep me informed. If I can help, I'd like to."

I nodded, muttering a "thank you." I felt low, indeed, and Erin must have felt bad about it because she placed a hand on my arm and looked me straight in the eyes.

"Look," she said, "I have a couple of hours before I need to check-in at the airport. Let's go up to your room, and I'll make it up to you."

"For old times' sake?" I said, involuntarily smiling.

"For old times' sake," she said, nodding.

She got up and pulled me out of my chair. I followed her.

One hour later, I sat in my bed, dazzled, looking at Erin's short figure as she dressed quickly.

I have to rush now," she said, picking up her bag. "Take care."
She approached the bed, kissed me lightly on the lips, and was gone.

I was alone again.

CHAPTER 22

Three weeks had passed since my empty-handed return from Europe, and I was starting to forget about the Vargos again. Becky and I had worked out a visitation schedule, and I had seen my kids a couple of times, avoiding their questions about when they would be coming home again. Evenings at home were a dreary affair, and to keep myself busy, I had been working late at the office every day. I liked the late afternoon time when the phone stopped ringing, and the office was empty and silent. Then, Benjamin Richmond had banged on my office door.

At first, I thought he was a hobo asking for a handout and was about to slam the door in his face, but then he called my name. Despite his unkempt appearance, he spoke like an educated man, and when he pleaded with me to give him a few minutes of my time, I let him in.

I have already mentioned Richmond, haven't I? But he is important to the story, so I'll tell you again to make sure I haven't omitted anything and put it in perspective. If it hadn't been for him, I might have given up by then, so disheartened I was about the whole thing. I had been toying with the idea of patching things up with Becky and was planning to call her to try to work things out, but Richmond threw a spanner into my plans.

"I was about to lock up and go home," I said, "I can only spare five minutes."

"Thank you," he said. "That will be enough. I don't have much time left anyway."

I gazed at him. His gray business suit had seen better days, and the tie knot hung lopsided. His shirt, which once was probably spotless, had a yolk stain on it. He was slumped in his chair, breathing heavily, and his complexion stood out pale through a three-day beard. When I offered him water, he merely nodded gratefully. When I returned with a water bottle, I placed it on the desk before him and went back to my seat.

"Do you want to tell me what this is about?" I asked, not unfriendly.

He gazed at me with watery, blue eyes. He seemed to have trouble focusing, but after a moment, he sat up. "It's about the Vargos," he said.

"The Vargos!" I spurted, but I guess I was expecting it. All the weirdness that had come into my life was somehow connected with them. "I am done with the Vargos, and I don't want to hear about them anymore," I lied. Somehow, lying about it felt safer.

"But you have to hear this. You need to know the whole story. Please." His pleading was so intense that I couldn't find it in me to refuse to listen. He took my silence for consent and continued.

"I don't have the time to go into too many details. We must be quick, but I'll give you the important facts. After the Vargos received their first investment, a big one, they set up shop in

California and started hiring. They hired me to look after the business side of things. They want to make a fortune quickly, and looking after other people's money is what I do ... did. That worked well for a while, and then one evening, they revealed themselves to me. You know what I mean."

"I don't, really."

"They let me see them for what they are."

"Do you mean that they let you see that they are bad people with rotten intentions?"

He remained silent for a few moments and then continued, gazing at the floor before him.

"That they are not people. Almost like us, but not human."

"What?" I cried out.

He looked astonished.

"You didn't know?"

"I didn't know what?"

"The Vargos are fake. They are not human. I thought you knew that. I believe they think you know it."

"I'm sorry, but you must leave now," I said, getting up. "I've heard you out, but this is enough." I've had my fair share of crazies coming into my office with wild stories, but this one topped them all.

"No, please, let me finish, and then I'll go. I won't make trouble, but you have to listen."

He didn't look dangerous, merely delusional, so I sat down again and gestured him to go on.

"They chose me well. I am greedy, and they knew that money would buy my fidelity. They needed my help to navigate all the regulatory problems, all the contacts with the investors, and the money transactions. They bought me with the mirage of riches. The fortune they were set to amass was so huge that an infinitesimal part of it would have made me immensely wealthy. But then, to an inside person like me, exposed to many little events and clues, it became clear that something was terribly wrong. I guess they felt that I was thinking of leaving them, so they decided to come clean with me. The mixture of greed and fear that they put in me was such that they had me hooked. I didn't understand their long-term plan at that time, so I went along with it. I didn't mind swindling innocent investors. They had more money than was good for them anyway."

"So, what changed?"

"Their plan started to take shape. I don't know its details even now, but from what they wanted me to do, one thing was clear: they were set to take control of critical Earth resources, which, if misused, could cause catastrophes of epic dimensions. True, it would take time, decades if not longer, but it could mean the end of the human race."

"Why didn't you go to the authorities?"

"You don't really think that I was free to move around as it pleased me. No, I was under constant surveillance, always followed by Paula everywhere; even when I didn't know she was around, she seemed to know everything I was doing. I had become a slave, kept with an invisible chain. And I wasn't the only one. There was another human working with them. One day he disappeared, and then I read in the paper that he had turned up dead. When I told Paula about it, she simply said, 'Yes, he misbehaved,' and smiled. That's who she is." He paused to drink a little water and then continued. "I had to seize the opportunity to get away. They sent me to negotiate with an investor in Austin, Texas, and that was the chance to get away that I had been waiting for. I took a flight but not to Austin, here."

"If what you say is true, by telling me you are putting me in danger too."

"I know, but for some reason, you are special to them. At one time—I must apologize for it, but then I was still their blind servant—I told them that you were dangerous and should be dealt with. I viewed you as a loose end that might create trouble for them. And you know what Daniel said? He said, 'Nobody touches Richard.' I think that Paula disapproved, but your name never came up again."

"But why? What is all this about? What are they about?"

"I don't know, but you must find out. You are the only one who has a chance of exposing them and perhaps staying alive. I know that I am putting you in danger, but what else can I do?"

My head was like a beehive of thoughts. I couldn't decide if this crazy story had any core of truth in it or if the man was out of his mind.

"Honestly, I'll have to think about this. It's a hard story to swallow, and I don't have any proof that there is even a grain of truth in it. You may have misinterpreted everything; who knows."

"Oh, but you will have proof. When I'm dead, you'll know," he said simply, and got up to leave. He threw a brief glance back, and then he left, walking with heavy steps and bent shoulders.

That meeting, and the item in the news two days later, relating the tragic death of one Benjamin Richmond, electrocuted in his hotel room, were what put me at the frontline of a battle that can't be won. True, Richmond had not been hit by lightning, merely electrocuted, but that was close enough for me to connect the dots.

My plan to work things out with Becky would have to wait, I decided. I went to my PC and checked flights for California. The details danced before my eyes while my mind raced through many questions. How soon would I be able to leave? What did I have to do in the office before I would be able to go? What should I tell the kids?

I felt a heavy weight on my shoulders and the immediate need to hear a friendly voice. I picked up the phone and dialed the number that Erin had texted me. Her sleepy voice answered almost immediately.

"Yes?"

"Erin, it's me, Richard."

"Richard ... you know it's three in the morning here in Japan."

"I know, I'm sorry, but something came up, and I'm off to California."

"So, you are telling me this because ... ?"

"I ... someone came to me with an incredible story, but I believe him, and that's why I have to leave."

"You know that you're not making sense," said Erin, her voice now sounding more awake.

"I'm sorry. I guess ..."

"So tell me the story."

"No, not by phone, and ... I just wanted to hear your voice."

"Are you okay?"

"Yes," I said, but I wasn't; far from it. I had just realized that telling her about Richmond could put her also in danger. "I miss you, and I wish you were here."

"That's sweet of you, but can we do this at a more civilized hour? You can call me in six hours or so."

"No. that's fine. When are you coming back?"

"In a week, I hope."

"Let me know when you're back."

"I will."

"Good night."

"Night," she said. I hung up before I said a word too much.

CHAPTER 23

The law firm of Spivak, McCormik, and Appleby, more simply known as "Spivak McCormik," had its head offices in downtown Los Angeles. I had worked with the firm in the past, and that was how I had recognized the SMA red-and-gold logo immediately, that day in Yoel's office, among the papers in the voluminous file that Finkel kept on his knees. I hadn't attached any particular importance to the fact that SMA apparently represented the Vargos' investors and instructing Finkel since I knew that the firm was active in various high-tech areas. I had simply filed away this information in my head, but now it had come in handy.

According to the Martindale-Hubbell lawyers' listing, SMA's main office was home to something like one hundred and seventy-eight lawyers. I knew my way around this kind of firm well, and it was without apprehension that I dialed their number from my hotel room in Beverly Hills.

"Spivak McCormik, good morning. Gill speaking. How can I

direct your call?" was the impersonal answer that I got from the switchboard.

"Good morning," I replied genially. "I have a package for a client of yours that I need to deliver to him. Whom should I speak to?"

"Do you know the name of the attorney in charge? Hold on just a second," she added hurriedly, and a rush of music reached my ears. After a few seconds, she was back.

"Who did you say the attorney was?"

"I have no idea. I think he works with someone from the patents group."

"Then you want to talk to Jayla. She's the secretary of the Intellectual Property Group. I'll transfer you."

Without another word, she gave me more music, and this time I waited for a full two minutes before the line was picked up again. A high-pitched voice was on the other end.

"This is Jayla. How can I help you?"

"Good morning, Jayla. I have a package for a client of yours, a Mr. Daniel Vargo. Could you tell me how to deliver it?"

"Gee, I don't know. We don't normally accept mail for our clients. Who is the attorney with whom he works?"

"I don't know. And it isn't mail. It is a bulky package of personal belongings. Clothing, I think."

"Well, we don't do *that*. This is a law firm, you know? Not a launderette. Wait a second," she added.

I heard the ticking of a computer keyboard being hit quickly, and after a few seconds, she spoke again.

"Is it V-e-r?"

"No, it's V-a-r."

"Oh, all right. I've got it. Professor Daniel Vargo. The attorney who handles his file is Alex Chase. Would you like me to connect you to Alex?"

"Jesus, no. I'd hate to bother him for this. It's just some personal stuff in here. Couldn't I leave it with you to give to Professor Vargo next time he comes in?"

"I can't do that. Sorry. We have no room here for the safekeeping of personal belongings, and I can't take responsibility for anything happening to a client's personal stuff. Why don't you deliver it to him directly instead?"

"Mm ... I could do that. Do you have the address?"

"Yes, I've got it right here. Are you writing it down?"

"Yes, go ahead."

"It is care of DPV-Med, Inc., four-seventy-two Hilltop Drive, Thousand Oaks. It's just off the one-oh-one freeway."

"Yeah, I know where it is," I lied. "Do you have a contact phone? To call ahead, I mean."

"Yes. Here is the number ..." She gave it to me, clearly happy to get rid of me so easily.

I was pretty pleased with myself. Although I had planned this very carefully, I was still amazed that I had gotten all the information I needed for the cost of a phone call. It is scary to think how little privacy we actually enjoy in our life, and how easy it is to get hold of information that you are not supposed to have.

"Thank you very much, Jayla. You have been very helpful. I appreciate it."

"My pleasure. And, oh ... when you call DPV-Med, you should speak with Alicia. My computer says that she is the contact person."

"I'll do just that. Thank you again, Jayla."

"You're welcome."

I hung up. It was almost lunchtime now, and I felt that I deserved a good meal. After lunch, there would be more work to be done, but I had to keep regular eating and sleeping hours if I wanted to quickly get used to the California time zone.

My flight had been quite reasonable. I had found a business class seat on a not-too-crowded plane that had landed at New York's JFK airport at five a.m. on the previous morning. After a longish wait at JFK for the connection, I had gotten on a flight to L.A., which had landed in the early afternoon. A brief negotiation with Hertz got me a nice bottle-green sports car that took me to my hotel by late afternoon. I was exhausted and would have died to take a nap. Instead, I showered, changed, and dragged myself to the bar. I had to keep awake to beat the jet lag.

Finding a reason to come to the U.S. had been easy because I often visited clients, which was the excuse I had given at the office. Not that I needed permission to go, but I didn't want to raise any eyebrows. To remind me why I was there, I kept returning to page three of the daily newspaper that I kept in my briefcase every few hours. A small item at the top of the page related the tragic death of one tourist by the name of Benjamin Richmond. Apparently, he had been careless handling an electric kettle in the motel room where he slept, or that was the only interpretation that the police had been able to put to his death.

Dinner at one of the hotel restaurants had been a sorry function, with me hardly touching any of the three courses I had ordered and with my waitress taking away the almost full plates with a pained look. I had made the mistake of ordering a beer, which had threatened to knock me out. So after lingering over coffee, I wobbled to my room. It was almost 10 p.m., and I decided that it was a decent time to go to bed.

The next morning I felt almost human again. I got up, dressed, and took a long walk near the hotel. It was still early enough and pleasantly cool. Walking had always aided my thought process and walking around, I had planned the Spivak McCormik phone call in detail.

The thorough preparation, as seen, had paid off. I didn't think anybody at Spivak McCormick would pay any attention to my inquiry or even notice it. In fact, I expected that Helpful Jayla had forgotten all about it by now. She didn't seem to be a girl who would spend any effort remembering past conversations with unidentified callers.

As soon as I disposed of a light lunch, I got out through the main door and asked the valet for my car. I drove away and followed the signs for the 405 freeway, and then smartly joined the 101. The map that I had bought at the hotel's newsstand was, for a change, detailed and clear, and I got off the freeway at the right exit. Hilltop Drive is a long and winding road, flanked by high-tech buildings. I was looking for a part of a complex identified by a sign as BioEx Park. It was a small, one-story building that looked exactly like all the others. I drove slowly past it and parked at the other side of the next building. I got out of the car and walked toward the one that was my target.

There was nothing special about the building, and I couldn't have told it from any of the others had it not been for the sign by the door that said "DPV-Med, Inc.," with a logo in the shape of a stylized fetus. So this was it. I wondered what was in there. I walked quickly around the building. It had only four windows, and the farthest one from the door was dark. From the window, I could see what looked like a reception area at the right of the door. A woman was sitting at a desk, and I guessed that she probably was Alicia. I gazed at the remaining two windows. In one room that looked like a laboratory, I saw a man, intent on some task with something that I couldn't see since it was below the window level. The third window opened on what seemed to be a small office, but no one was there.

I circled the building without seeing anything else of interest and walked back to my car. It was getting hot, so I started the engine and turned the air conditioning on. I wanted to watch the building for a while, to get the sense of what kind of activity was going on there, but it was difficult to do it without making myself conspicuous. I was particularly worried lest Daniel might come out of the building and see me. I was sure that he would have recognized me immediately. I stayed there for one hour, and after an uneventful watch, I drove away toward the 101. I had seen what I had come to see, anyway: nobody had gone either in or out of the building. Also, the activity on the other side of the windows seemed to be minimal. Daniel Vargo's laboratory was a rather sleepy place, or so it appeared unless I had hit on an unusually quiet part of the day. And no sign of Daniel himself, which suited me. I was ready to head back.

I had been walking the streets of downtown L.A., looking for a hairdresser. I had peeped into maybe seven or eight places and rejected them all, for one reason or another. Now I stood outside Gabe's Happy Hairdressing, debating whether to go in. From the outside, the place didn't look as filthy as the ones I had rejected before. Inside were three seats, and they were taken. A fat woman was waiting on a couch.

I walked in, and a thin-looking hair artist lifted his gaze from the head on which he was working and eyed me inquisitively.

"I'd like to have my hair cut," I said apologetically, "and something else ..."

He gestured me to the couch with an imperious movement of the comb, and I sat down to wait patiently. I looked at him working. He was moving the comb swiftly through the hair and making apparently random movements with a pair of scissors. Still, the outcome seemed to follow some sort of reasonably planned scheme.

The fat woman was called to a side room to undergo God knows what mysterious procedures. After a while, the hair artist's customer got up, paid, and left. The artist motioned me to the vacated chair, brushing away a few hairs from the seat with a cloth. I sat down and looked at him.

"Well, what will it be today?" he asked.

"I need a haircut, and I was also thinking of dyeing my hair."

"Good idea," said the artist with approval. "Very boring, your hair is. Chestnut kind of color," he added with open disgust, and I almost felt the need to apologize for it.

"Yes, I started to feel the boredom too. I was thinking of a nice blond."

"Okay. Now, what about the haircut? I think that a nice mushroom look would be great on you. Young but conservative. What do you say?"

"I think I would just like you to shorten it, leaving my hairstyle as it is now."

"Boring. Really boring ... but if this is what you want ..."

"Yes. It is. I like it boring. Maybe next time. I'm new to this."

"Oh, all right," said the artist, looking offended by my lack of cooperation.

"By the way," I asked, "are you Gabe?"

"No, I'm not. Why, is that a problem?"

"No, no. No problem. I only wondered."

"I'm not Gabe," he reiterated angrily as if Gabe were a particularly low and demeaning thing to be.

I decided to keep my mouth shut and go through the procedure. Apart from the fact that the stuff he used on me made my scalp sizzle, it was not as bad as I had anticipated. When finally

I looked into the mirror, though, I got a nasty shock. I looked like a silly parody of myself, and my mother wouldn't have recognized me at first sight. Still, that was what I had been doing it for, so I had no reason to complain.

I paid my fifty bucks without a murmur and left. My thoughts went to Erin, who was five thousand miles away and could not see me with my new look. Thank God for small mercies, I thought, not for the first time. And then I realized that it was Erin I was thinking of, not Becky. I should have cared about what Becky thought of my appearance; I always had. But this time, I didn't, and that was a fact.

I shrugged and turned my thoughts to more pressing matters.

CHAPTER 24

The business card that I held in my hand read:

Dr. Karl Heikki
Chief Reviewer
The Vanhanen Foundation
Helsinki

The letters were embossed in beautiful gold and blue. They had been "Printed While-U-Wait," as advertised in the window of the small shop in which I was standing. I looked at the owner with appreciation, trying on him what I hoped was a credible Nordic accent.

"Thank you very much, I'm sure. They look almost exactly like my own cards back home. You can't imagine how embarrassing it was to discover that I had left my visiting cards behind. You have saved me much aggravation. I'm grateful."

"Don't mention it. You have thirty of them in that box. Are you sure they are enough?"

"Oh, yes. I only need them as a temporary replacement for two or three days until mine reach me by Federal Express."

"Well, if it turns out that you need any more, you can give me a call, and I'll print them for you. No need for you to waste your time waiting."

I thanked him again, paid for the business cards, and left. I was making progress, but I still had a lot of preparations to make.

My next stop was at a food shop in Beverly Hills that catered to movie stars and other celebrities. It indeed carried an impressive variety of delicacies, from Belgian chocolate to canned fish from Korea. What I was interested in was the fresh fish section, where different types of caviar, including gray Iranian caviar and caviar from the Volga, were on alluring display. Behind the counter stood a young man in the shop's uniform: a white apron partially covering red-and-white horizontally striped shirt and pants and a funny-looking cook-style hat. His nametag said: "I'm Fred, and I'm here to serve you with a ...," followed by what is technically known as "a smiley"—a round yellow stylized smiling face. Rather childish for a pricey Beverly Hills shop, I thought.

"Good morning," I said, addressing him with a smile.

"Good morning, sir," he answered courteously. "How can I serve you today?"

"I was wondering ... the sign over there," I said, pointing at the one that hung above the cashier's desk, "says that you ship everything, everywhere. Does that include Israel?"

"I believe so, sir, but let me check."

He walked to a phone at the end of the counter, picked up the receiver, and spoke into it, returning to me after a few seconds.

"As I thought, sir. We do ship to Israel. No problem. In fact, I made a shipment only a few weeks ago, but I wanted to make sure that there were no limitations on the type of goods that we are allowed to ship."

"And ...?"

"Well, the only limitation appears to be on shellfish. Were you thinking of shellfish?"

"No. Actually, I was thinking of caviar."

"No problem with caviar, sir."

"Great. A friend of mine is going to have a birthday party in Tel Aviv, and I was thinking of sending him caviar instead of a plant or something."

"Good thinking, sir. Caviar will certainly make a welcome gift. And I have the most perfect jar for a party. Is it going to be a big party?"

"Not at all. Just a family affair. Seven or eight people at most."

"Then may I suggest this little jar over here?" he said, pointing at a jar that could have fed me for a week. "At three-hundred and fifty, it's a bargain."

"Yes. That looks to me like the right size. But something worries me. How can you ensure that it will not spoil on the way? It's a long way, you know. It would be extremely embarrassing for me to send my friend a jar of spoilt caviar."

"You shouldn't worry about that, sir," Fred answered with a little laugh, as if to point out how silly my worries were. "All our goods are shipped with full refrigeration, and we pack them with dry ice for good measure. I am sure that your friend will enjoy his caviar at its best. Shipping for this little jar comes only at two hundred dollars," he added as if to reassure me that it was all a steal.

"I think I'll do it, but I want to inspect the box before it is closed, to see that the packaging is done to my satisfaction."

"No problem with that, sir. If you come before ... um ... eleven a.m.," he said, consulting a chart, "we will be able to get the shipment on the plane in time for your friend to taste the caviar in the afternoon of the next day. I'll pack the jar myself," he added as if nobody could ask for more than that, "and I'm sure that you will be satisfied."

"Okay. Let me think about this a bit more. I'll come by tomorrow morning if I decide that this is the present I want to send. I rather think that I will, but I want to sleep on it."

"Whenever you please. I'm here from nine a.m. on."

"Thank you. I'll come tomorrow."

"We'll look forward to seeing you, sir."

I bet you do, you pirates, I thought. It was the first place I had ever seen where a loaf of bread cost six dollars seventy-five, and I wondered how special a stupid loaf of bread could get.

Next stop, a department store. I forget which one it was. A big one, though. My plan called for a way to keep liquid material safely sealed, so I wandered through the perfumes' department, picking up perfume samples in little vials. By the time I was through, I had seven perfume vials in my pocket, and I was ready to go back to the hotel.

In my room, I checked the vials. Five of them had stoppers that closed tightly. I discarded the others because of size, leaky plug, or other defects. I took the ones I had selected to the sink, where I emptied and washed them with water and liquid soap. Then, I boiled water in the electric kettle provided "courtesy of management and for your convenience." I put the vials and their stoppers in a glass and poured boiling water over them three times until I was sure they were clean enough. I then put the stoppers on, slipped the vials into a small plastic bag with a sealing strip, and sealed it. That tedious task was completed, at least.

I resisted the impulse to go to the hotel restaurant and settled for room service instead. I had gone to too much trouble to remain unnoticed in the hotel, and since dyeing my hair, I felt as if I had a sign on saying, "Hey, look, I'm disguised." I definitely needed a little more time to get used to it.

Lunch brought to me by a moody waiter was quite decent anyway. I lingered over coffee, postponing my next step, which, I knew, was a crucial one. When the clock struck two p.m., I realized that I couldn't afford to put it off any longer. I lifted the receiver and dialed the number of DPV-Med, Inc.

"DPV-Med. How can I help you?"

"Good afternoon, madam," I said, hoping that I was not exaggerating my European accent this time. "I would like to speak with Ms. Alicia, please."

"Speaking," came the puzzled reply.

"Oh, hello. My name is Doctor Heikki. I represent the Vanhanen Foundation from Helsinki, Finland. I am Chief Reviewer for Life Sciences."

"You must be looking for Professor Vargo, but I'm afraid that he's not here. He is in New York City, at headquarters. Would you like me to give you his number?"

"No, no. In fact, I was calling to talk to you, not to him."

"Talk to me? But what about?"

"About Professor Vargo."

"I don't understand."

"Perhaps I should explain. You are familiar with the Vanhanen Foundation, I assume … ?" I left the question in the air. Very few people are armed with the self-confidence needed to deny knowing something that is expected of them to know. Alicia wasn't one of them.

"Oh, yes, of course. *That* Van … Vahna …"

"Precisely. And as you may know, at least as far as Life Sciences are concerned, the Vanhanen Prize is considered in scientific circles far more prestigious than the Nobel Prize."

"Uh ... yes?" I could tell that she was impressed, but I wanted her to be completely captured, so I went on.

"Of course, not for chemistry or physics. The Vanhanen Foundation does not award prizes in those areas, although there are talks that we might do so in the near future. But, definitely, where Life Sciences are concerned, the Vanhanen Foundation is second to none."

"So, what can I do for you?" asked Alicia, obviously entirely bewildered by the flow of my explanations.

"You will undoubtedly be excited to learn that Professor Vargo has been nominated for this year's Vanhanen Prize."

"Wow! You mean it?"

"But, of course, my dear lady, I mean it," I answered, managing to sound offended by the thought that I might not be serious about a subject like that.

"But, who nominated him?"

"I'm not at liberty to say. But the nomination is only part of the story. Five people are nominated, and only one is confirmed, based mainly on my review and the report that I submit to the Board of Trustees. That's why I have called you.

"First of all, it is important to understand that a *sine qua non* requisite to win the nomination is that the nominee must not know of his nomination until it is confirmed. If we suspect that a nominee has gotten wind of our review process, his nomination is scrapped immediately and irrevocably. This is why my review relies so much on employees, like yourself, and on people who have benefited from the nominee's breakthrough—patients and their families. Therefore, I must impress upon you that keeping the fact of our review secret is a must. Between you and me, Professor Vargo has the best chance of being this year's Vanhanen Laureate. It would be a pity to have to award the prize to somebody else because of a leak about the nomination."

"Do you need to talk to the other employees?"

"What are their duties?"

"Well, I am the office manager, and then we have a technician who works in the lab, a biologist who does literature research, and an assistant who cleans the equipment and does odd jobs around. It is a small laboratory, you know."

"Then I think that you are the best person to talk to. You probably know Professor Vargo more intimately than the others."

"I ... I guess so."

"When do you close?"

"Everybody goes at five."

"Could you stay later today and meet with me? I will need to inspect the premises and to ask you some questions."

"Oh, yes. With pleasure."

"Then I'll be at the laboratory around five-fifteen. Would that be all right?"

"That will be fine."

"Okay. But please, remember: you are not to breathe a word to your colleagues or to anybody else. Not to your mother or husband ..."

"I'm not married ..."

"Good. But not a word to anybody, even outside the company. Agreed?"

"I promise."

"All right. I trust you. See you later, then."

I hung up. I felt guilty for not feeling any guilt at all for making a fool of poor, gullible Alicia. She had it coming to her, though.

She's a good employee, I thought, but she is definitely not bright. I had counted on that.

At twenty minutes past five, I knocked on the door of DPV-Med, Inc. I had been standing not far away during the last half-hour and had made sure that everybody else had left the building. Alicia opened the door with a smile. She was slim, with black hair made into a ponytail, and with big brown eyes. She wasn't unattractive, in a way.

"Doctor Heikki?" she asked, obviously knowing the answer since she moved aside with an inviting gesture.

"Good evening, Alicia. It was too kind of you to stay late for me. Your employer is lucky to have you. Here," I said, handing her one of my brand new business cards. "Unfortunately, I must be impolite and ask you to give the card back to me. We cannot risk anybody seeing it in your possession and immediately put two and two together."

She studied the card for a moment, and then she gave it back to me.

"Please take a seat," she said, seating herself behind her desk. "Now, what can I tell you that you need to know?"

"First of all, please tell me about Professor Vargo. How is he? Personally, I mean."

A dreamy look came into Alicia's eyes. I could swear that she had a crush on Daniel.

"He is a great man," she said simply. "Really a great man. It is such an honor to work for him, with all he does for the others. And he is a kind person too. Always smiling, always polite. Where I used to work before, it was a bigger company, and we used to have parties. My boss always invited me to dance at the party. I wonder ..."

"Yes, of course," I said quickly, trying to keep it businesslike. "Now, how would you characterize Professor Vargo's approach to his work?"

"He is married to his work. He thinks of nothing but his work and his patients."

"How many patients does he have?"

"So far, he has received approval to treat three terminally ill patients, and he has cured them all."

"Later, I will ask you to give me the details of a patient that I can approach. I will need to ask him or her a few questions also. But now, do you have any kind of illustrative material that discusses his work?"

"Perhaps you would like to see the movie?"

"What movie?"

"The movie that illustrates the treatment that Abby was given. She was his first patient. Here, let's go into the meeting room."

We moved to the meeting room where I saw a TV set with a large screen. Alicia put a DVD labeled "Abby" into the reader and pushed a button. The DPV-Med logo appeared on the screen, and suddenly, without prior warning, a full-screen shot of Paula replaced it. She looked straight at the camera and produced a twisted smile.

"Did you ever imagine that cancer could be braved?" she asked in her marked accent. "One man has done it. A genius as the world hasn't known before. Professor Daniel Vargo." She concluded her words with a sweeping motion of her hand, and the camera moved on to Daniel.

The movie was a short one, and in it, Daniel showed the X-ray of a brain tumor. Daniel's voice identified it as Abby's X-ray before treatment. It then showed a beautiful young woman lying on a bed in a laboratory, with Daniel explaining, taking out a vial marked

"Abby" and filling a syringe with 50 milliliters of a liquid from the vial, which he then injected intravenously to Abby. All the while, Paula stood by Daniel and every now and then beamed at the camera.

"Two weeks later," Daniel's voice said, while the scene changed again to show another X-ray, "and the tumor is almost gone. Here you can see this little shadow that will be gone by next week. Abby has received three shots of fifty milliliters each and is cured. And the tumor is not coming back. Isn't that great?" Daniel concluded, with a self-satisfied smile, and the screen went blank.

"What do you think?" said Alicia.

"Amazing! Beyond expectation," I said, with much genuine enthusiasm. "Do you think that I could make a copy of the DVD?"

"You can take it."

"Really?"

"Yes. No problem. It's a movie that we prepared for our investors. I have several copies. You can take this one," she added, putting it into its box and handing it to me.

"This is very helpful. Thank you. It will be a good attachment to my report. Very convincing indeed."

"What else can I show you?"

"I will need to see the lab."

"Hm," murmured Alicia, doubtfully. "Daniel ... I mean, Professor Vargo doesn't like to have people in his lab when he's not here."

"I'm afraid that it's a must. I cannot issue a valid report unless I have inspected the premises in person."

"Well, I guess that it is for a good cause."

"Definitely. We wouldn't want Professor Vargo to miss the chance to be awarded the prize because of a technicality. Can we get on?"

"Yes," she said, getting up. "Please follow me."

Alicia took me to a door that opened onto a short corridor. She took a magnetic card that was attached to a key ring and swiped it through a card-reader at the door, and then she turned the knob.

"Wait, please," she said when I stepped toward the door.

Suddenly, the phone on Alicia's desk rang. She walked quickly to her desk, picked up the receiver, but didn't try to speak into it. Instead, she dialed a number, moving her finger carefully along the keypad. I looked at her finger. The number she dialed was 1745. A loud "beep" sound came from the receiver, and she hung up. A security system, obviously, connected with the laboratory. I memorized the number.

"This is Professor Vargo's laboratory," said Alicia, "the one you saw in the movie."

The room was small and bare, without a window. The little bed on which Daniel had treated Abby was the only furniture. At our right-hand side, the wall was occupied by a refrigerator.

"This refrigerator contains the active material used by Daniel to treat his patients," she said, opening one of the doors.

The inside of the refrigerated compartment was almost empty, with only three test tube racks, each containing only one tube. I could read the name "Abby" on the innermost tube and on the closest one the name "John." Alicia closed the door of the refrigerator and walked me out.

"The other laboratory is that in which purification of the material is carried out," she explained.

Alicia went again through the card-swiping-phone-ringing-dialing routine, and we stepped into the second laboratory, which was also windowless. Here I noticed a little more equipment than in Daniel's laboratory. An ultracentrifuge filled a corner, and various staple laboratory equipment was scattered around. I nodded and moved toward the door. We went back to Alicia's desk and stood beside it.

"That's all," she said apologetically. "Except for the search room in which there is nothing but paper and magazines. As you see, this is a very small company, for the time being."

"Small company, but huge achievements," I said appreciatively. "Now, can you tell me which one of the patients I may contact? I need to talk personally with one of them."

"Well," she answered pensively, "I know that Abby—the one in the movie—didn't object to having her identity disclosed. She feels so much in debt to the professor that when he asked her if she would be ready to be in the promotional movie, she didn't hesitate for a second. I know it because I was there. Let me go and fetch her phone number from the file room."

Alicia walked into the other room, and I sat at her desk. The moment she was out of sight, I opened the desk drawers. The first and the second drawers held nothing of importance—merely stuff you expect to see in any secretary's desk. But in the third drawer, I hit the jackpot. At the back of the drawer lay three keyrings, each with a magnetic card and a key. They all looked identical, and I pocketed the first one, closing the drawer quietly and getting up quickly, just in time to see Alicia coming out of the other room.

"Here you are. I have written her address and phone number down for you," she said, handing me a piece of paper. "You can tell her that I sent you if she asks, and she can contact me if she wants."

"This is very kind of you. The Vanhanen Foundation and, of course, Professor Vargo will be much indebted to you for your clear and helpful exposition. Your employer is lucky to have you. Very lucky. Well," I added with a note of regret, "I must be going. I'll wait for you to close up, and I'll walk you to your car."

"Oh, no need for that."

"I insist. It's getting late, and the place is surely deserted. It can't be pleasant for a lady to walk around all alone."

"I'm used to it. Where I used to work before we had shifts, and I often got home late. In any case, if you insist, I won't be a minute. Let me see that everything is in order, and we will be out of here in no time."

Alicia ran around the office, checking the doors and the windows and switching off lights, and two minutes later, we were at the door. She swiped her magnetic card through a nearby card-reader, turned off the main light switch, and closed the door. She locked it using the key attached to her key ring and turned around toward the car park, with me dutifully walking beside her.

"I don't know how to thank you," I said when we reached her car, "but I will certainly mention your cooperation in my report. It shan't go unnoticed."

"Oh, it was nothing," said Alicia, blushing distinctly.

"But please remember: complete secrecy, lest Professor Vargo loses his nomination. So far, there have been no transgressions to the rule, and we aim to keep it that way."

"Don't worry about me. I will keep my mouth shut."

And with those words, she got into her car and drove away. This woman was too naive for words. She hadn't asked me any of the questions that I had anticipated. It had been almost too easy so far, and I had to be careful not to go off guard because of it.

I headed back to my hotel for a light room-service meal and a nap. I still had a lot of work to do that night. But before I turned in, I walked to the concierge's desk and got a stiff DHL envelope. I put the DVD inside and wrote a short note to my personal linguist, Professor Mackowski, which I also included. He had helped Erin and me with the first recording, so I hoped he would be willing to help again. I filled in the airway bill with his address and entrusted it to the concierge to be sent express service to Paris with the next pick-up. I was curious to see what the professor would make of it.

CHAPTER 25

The street was deserted. Little wonder, at two a.m. in an industrial area. I had been sitting in my car for over half an hour now and hadn't seen a soul around. Conditions were perfect, and it was time to move.

I opened the small pouch that I carried on a shoulder strap and took out a pair of surgical rubber gloves that I had bought earlier. They were like the ones that my dentist used, and I had watched him countless times putting them on. They felt uncomfortable, but I had to get used to them.

The pouch also contained a pack of disposable syringes with hypodermic needles and a sealed plastic bag with my vials. I checked that everything was in order and closed the pouch firmly.

I got out of the car and walked to the door of the DPV-Med lab—a distance of a hundred paces that felt like a hundred miles. I had the irrational fear that Daniel might pop up from behind the shrubbery at any moment and catch me, but of course, he didn't, and eventually, I reached the door. Now was the critical moment. I hadn't had a chance to try the key that I had taken from Alicia's drawer, and if it didn't fit, I would be sunk.

Carefully, almost religiously, I inserted the key and started to turn it with a silent prayer. The lock turned with a clicking sound, and the door opened. Inside, I closed and locked the door and immediately swiped the magnetic card through the card reader next to it.

Now I could breathe again. Sufficient light filtered into the room from outside to see the furniture's silhouettes, but not enough to move around easily. I approached Alicia's desk and lit the small table lamp. It had a dimmer, and I turned it to produce a low light, which, I hoped, would not be noticed from the outside. Things were working out right. Then the phone rang.

I looked at it, frozen, not knowing what to do. This was not in my plans. I had expected the phone to ring when I opened the laboratory door, but not now. What was it? Perhaps my magnetic card was not good enough? Or maybe it was too late for the entrance permissions given by the card to work? I had to think quickly. I could only hope to get away with it if the alarm was a stupid one-code system. I picked up the phone and dialed carefully, seventeen-forty-five. A long "beep" sound was followed by silence. Apparently, I had made it ... or else I would be in trouble in a couple of minutes.

I replaced the receiver and walked to the laboratory's door. I swiped the card again, and the lock opened. I waited in the corridor for the phone to ring again, but all was silent. Apparently, one ring was enough for a while ... or maybe the police were on their way here anyway. I shook away the thought and got busy. There was no danger in turning on the lights in the windowless laboratory, and with them on, I felt better.

The cold atmosphere of the room felt hostile, but I ignored it and opened the refrigerator. With a syringe in one hand and a vial taken from the pouch in the other, I lifted the test tube labeled "Abby," removed the stopper, and filled the syringe with the clear liquid. Then, I emptied the syringe contents into the vial, closed it tightly with its stopper, and replaced the stopped test tube into the refrigerator. I repeated the procedure, using two clean syringes and vials, with the other two test tubes from the refrigerator. One sample would have been enough since they all had to contain the same material, but I reasoned that taking more material would be safer. I only took a little from each test tube, and the missing amounts wouldn't be noticed. Then, after having made sure that all the syringes, their wrappings, and the vials were safely back in the pouch and that I had left no signs of my visit in or around the refrigerator, I closed it, turned off the light, and retreated back into the corridor.

The door closed with a click when I pulled the knob, and I made sure that it was locked again. Everything looked pretty much as I had found it. Back at Alicia's desk, my eyes fell on a little stack of business cards that I hadn't noticed before. The card had the DPV-Med logo on it and read:

Prof. Daniel Vargo
Founder, CEO & CTO

It also flaunted a New York address and phone number under "Headquarters." It was amazing how Daniel persevered in bending the truth. Nobody had ever made him a professor, but he didn't hesitate to grant himself the title in print. In any case, finding out the New York address was high in my to-do list, and this made it easier for me. I took one of the cards, knowing that nobody would notice that it was missing.

I searched my pockets for the copy of the main door key that I had made on the previous afternoon and having found it, I opened the third drawer on Alicia's desk. Then, I reached the door, unlocked it with the copied key, swiped the card through the card reader, and ran to Alicia's desk. I restored the keyring with the magnetic card and the key in a position as close as possible to the one I remembered, closed the drawer slowly, and turned off the light on Alicia's desk. I was now ready to leave.

I ran to the door, opened it, closed it from the outside, and locked it with the copied key, which I then put in my pocket. I walked quickly toward my car, looking around me to see if I was being observed by anybody. But, again, nobody was in sight. When I got to my car and switched on the ignition, I felt as if a weight had fallen off my shoulders. Breaking and entering was not something I had trained for during my basic studies, and I thought that I had done quite well for a novice. I looked at my watch and was surprised to see that the time was two forty-five. I could have sworn that I hadn't been in there for more than fifteen minutes.

I drove carefully along the 101, where the traffic was light, reaching my hotel almost at half past three. I parked in the hotel parking lot and got out. I started to push the revolving door at the entrance when I noticed that I was still wearing the rubber gloves. I reared into the street and removed them hastily, and then I stuffed them into my pocket and walked in. The night receptionist didn't even look at me, and soon I was in the safety of my room.

I opened the minibar and placed the three vials inside the tiny ice compartment; I poured myself a portion of whisky from a miniature bottle and sank in the single armchair in my room. I was exhausted, although physically, I had made no special effort. It was the tension that had worn me out.

With my last bit of strength, I ordered a wake-up call from the automated phone system and threw myself onto the bed. My mind was a blank, and I sank into a dreamless sleep.

The phone was ringing, and I was in panic. I couldn't remember the number to dial to make it stop. I knew such a number existed, and I had it on the tip of my tongue, but I couldn't remember it to save my life. And I knew that something horrible was going to happen unless I remembered it and pressed the right digits on the dial.

I sat up, confused, my heart pounding forcefully. I picked up the phone, and soft music reached my ears.

"Good morning. This is your wake-up call. If you wish to receive another call in five minutes, press any digit now," was the annoying announcement that followed. I hung up and got out of bed, my head heavy, and my mouth pasty. The clock on the TV set had the hour as nine-oh-eight—time to get going.

I brushed my teeth, washed my face, and shaved. Then I put on my nicest suit and placed the three vials that I fished out of the minibar in the outer pocket. The liquid was partly frozen, and that was a good enough start.

After a quick breakfast, I drove to the Beverly Hills food shop. Fred was there, as promised, behind the counter.

"Good morning, sir," he said with a self-satisfied smile. "I'm happy to see you. Have you decided on the caviar for your friend?"

"Yes, in fact, I have. If you could please prepare the package to be shipped, I would like it to go out today."

"Plenty of time," Fred said, looking at his watch. "It is only ten-fifteen, and the delivery doesn't leave before eleven. I won't be a minute," he added, and disappeared through a door at the back, coming back again with a large box, filled with dry ice.

He took the caviar jar, checked its seal, and placed it in the box's center, surrounded by the dry ice. Then he took two strips of adhesive and fastened them at the box's extremities, passing over the top of the jar's lid. It was a masterly work of packaging, as far as I could judge. Still, I had to inspect it.

"Here you are, sir," said Fred, showing his work of art to me.

"May I take a closer look?" I asked.

"Certainly, please," said Fred, handing the box to me. "I'll be back in a minute," he added, and moved to inquire about another customer's needs.

He couldn't have chosen a better time to leave me alone with the box. I had planned to ask him to show me some goods I had noted on a shelf far away, to buy me time to deal with the business at hand, but now I didn't have to make an effort.

I kept one eye on him as he walked away, and with my finger, I moved aside a few pieces of the dry ice and slipped a vial into the space left. I covered it again with the ice I had moved and repeated this procedure two more times so that all the vials were now hidden within the box, under the layer of ice. I put the box on the counter and waited patiently for Fred to come back.

"Everything okay?" he asked when he returned two minutes later.

"Everything's just fine," I answered. "You have made a great package indeed, and I am confident that my friend will get the caviar in good shape. Would you mind closing the lid and finishing the packaging?"

"Not at all," he answered and firmly fixed the lid with three long strips of adhesive tape, then he packed the box into a plastic bag that he also sealed with adhesive bands. "Please write here the name and address of your friend," he said, handing me a form.

I filled in Yair's name and address, along with his phone number, and handed the form back to Fred, who inspected it and nodded with satisfaction.

"Perfect, sir. The package will go out in a few minutes. Now all that remains is the little matter of the payment. Do you have an account with us?"

"No. I'll pay now," I said, handing him my gold credit card.

I paid the mind-boggling sum that turned up on my credit card slip, which was all-inclusive of shipment and taxes, and left the shop, not without thanking Fred again.

"Miss DiNapoli?" I asked.

"Yes. Who is speaking?"

"My name is Doctor Heikki. Doctor Karl Heikki. I got your phone number from Alicia at DPV-Med."

"Oh, yes ... What can I do for you?"

"Well, it's a delicate matter in which I hoped you might help me. You do know Professor Daniel Vargo, of course."

"Of course."

"And may I assume that you, like many of us, are one of his well-wishers?"

"Well, considering that he has saved my life, you can certainly say that."

"Then I can speak openly with you. Professor Vargo has been nominated for a very prestigious prize—when we meet, I'll tell you all about it. I am here in the capacity of Chief Reviewer for the institution that is considering awarding him the prize, and I am supposed to render a report next week. In the meantime, however, someone must have heard of Professor Vargo's nomination, and we have received an anonymous letter alleging that he is pursuing improper medical practices."

"You must be kidding ..."

"Unfortunately, I am not. Much as we are disgusted by the

practice of sending anonymous allegations, we cannot afford to ignore them when a prize as prestigious as ours is involved."

"What is it, the Nobel Prize?"

"It is, miss if I am allowed an opinion, an even more important prize than that."

"Oh, okay. Of course, this is all pure nonsense. Daniel is the most wonderful doctor I ever met—and believe me, unfortunately, I know a thing or two about doctors. So what can I do for you?"

"I was hoping that you might answer a few questions that may help me in formulating a positive report that will overcome that opprobrious gossip."

"Go ahead. Ask me."

"I fear that this is not so simple. Our rules call for a face-to-face interview. You see, I must identify my interlocutor in person."

"When do you want to meet?"

"The sooner, the better. I'm in L.A. right now."

"Well, you can come now if you want. I live in San Diego; do you have the address?"

"Yes. I'll be there as quickly as possible. But I would like to impress on you that you must be discreet about the whole thing. It is one of our rules that if the fact that a review process is in progress in respect of a candidate leaks out, that candidate is immediately disqualified. Only the persons I interview are entitled to know, provided they undertake to keep the matter secret until the nomination is confirmed. Can I count on you not to tell anybody, including people in your household?"

"Oh, all right. But you do seem to have an awful lot of rules."

"I am afraid that this is the nature of our scientific institution. We go by the rules, and rigidly so. Well, see you soon," I added, and hung up.

The trip to San Diego was a pleasant one, and I got there in a good mood. At that point, I was undecided as to whether to believe Richmond's story that made Daniel an alien or to conclude that Richmond was delusional after all, and Daniel was a real genius who had found the cure for cancer. I counted on Abby DiNapoli to tip the scale and give me the confidence needed to decide which was what.

By concentrating on Daniel, I was pushing aside my fear of Paula. I hoped to find out that Daniel was genuine and knew nothing of Paula's doings. Perhaps he was dominated by her, a mere pawn in her game, whatever that game was. Maybe Paula was really an alien, and Daniel was another one of her slaves. I liked that option better because I couldn't picture him taking an active part in murder schemes. I knew that I was being incoherent, but I have always been a good judge of character, and I had liked him very much. That had to amount to something. And if he was being used by Paula against his will, perhaps I could be the one to free him and to expose her evil doings. I had to think positively, or I would never find the courage to keep going.

The DiNapoli family lived in a grand house in one of the best neighborhoods of San Diego, which is saying an awful lot. She was waiting for me in the garden by the swimming pool. She was reading a book, which she put aside and got up when her maid walked me to her. For a moment, I was blinded. I felt a strange affinity with her, a kind of attraction too intense for words. I wondered if I was becoming a philanderer as a result of my estrangement from Becky. I shook the thought away. I had to concentrate on getting the information I was after.

She was astonishingly beautiful, with a splendid smile and laughing blue eyes. I had noticed her beauty in Daniel's movie, but the amateurish video didn't do her justice. She was no more than twenty-two years old. I could have sworn that she had to be a movie star—and if she wasn't, something was terribly wrong down Hollywood way.

She must have been used to having men gaping at her because she gave me a broad smile and said:

"Are you here, Doctor Heikki?"

"Yes, I'm sorry," I said, life returning to my frozen limbs. "How do you do, Miss DiNapoli?"

"I prefer Abby. It's much easier. Please, do sit down."

I did as instructed, and we sat beside a garden table in the shade of a large umbrella. I fished out one of my fake visiting cards and handed it to her.

"If you are not in the Life Science business, you may not have heard of the Vanhanen Foundation."

"In fact, I haven't. What is it?"

"It is a scientific institute, associated with the National Academy of Sciences of Finland. The funds for it were willed by the late millionaire, Johannes Vanhanen—hence the name. Once a year, the foundation awards the most prestigious prize in Life Sciences to a scientist who has made an outstanding contribution to science. This year one of the nominees is Professor Daniel Vargo."

"Outstanding achievement ...," she mused. "That is Daniel to a measure. He is incredible. Have you seen the movie?"

"Yes, I have."

"Then you have seen the tumor I had in my brain. My parents are very well off—shamefully rich, I should say. There must be no single doctor that counts for anything in this field that hasn't seen my medical file and hasn't checked me. The verdict was unanimous: the tumor was malignant. It was located in a place where it was impossible to operate without killing me. In short, nothing could be done. Daniel checked me, told me not to worry, and that I'd be all right, gave me three shots, and sent me to get a new X-ray. In a short while, the tumor was almost invisible. Now it's gone. All the doctors who said that there was nothing to be done have been looking for it with microscopes, but zilch. Nada. Gone for good. So that's Daniel Vargo."

"And I understand that there was no question that the tumor was there when you began treatment?"

"You had to be drunk and blindfolded not to see it. And then I was fainting and having seizures every day. Even I understood all about it. I have been X-rayed so many times and in so many ways that it should have killed me."

"And while he treated you, he didn't administer any other drug? Anything that gave you side effects?"

"The only side effect it had was to keep me alive. Whoever told you all that bullshit about Daniel misconducting doesn't know what he's talking about."

"Thank you very much, Miss DiNapoli ... Abby," I said, rising unwillingly from my seat—she was delightful to talk to and to look at. "You've been very helpful to me ... I mean, to Professor Vargo. I am relieved to hear that everything in his treatment was professional and above reproach."

I started to leave, but she called my name. "Doctor Heikki," she said, gazing at me in a strange way that made me wonder if she was suspecting my story.

"Yes?"

"Have we met before?"

"Met? No, of course not, why?"

"I had a feeling like we had met before. Are you sure?"

"I'm positive. You are not someone easily forgotten. I would remember it if we had met."

She acknowledged the implied compliment with a graceful

nod, and I left. With regret, I must say.

I left Abby's house in an elated state of mind. So Daniel was real, after all. And no matter what happened next, I had had a part in it from the beginning, and nobody could take that away from me.

"Hi, Yair."

"Richard?"

"Me in person. How are you?"

"I'm okay."

"Glad to hear it. Listen, I'm calling from California right now. Do you remember that little job I asked you to do on Daniel Vargo's stuff that turned out not to be the right sample?"

"Yes ..."

"Well, you are going to receive a jar of caviar from me tomorrow ..."

"That's kind of you. I didn't do so much really, to deserve it, but I appreciate the thought."

"No, listen. You eat the caviar and enjoy it. It's good quality, believe me. But before you stupefy yourself with it, look under the ice. You will find three little vials containing samples. These are samples like the ones that I was supposed to give you then. I want you to carry out a quick analysis and to tell me what you can, by the end of the day tomorrow."

"All I can do in a few hours is to run a gel and tell you some basic information on the samples."

"That will be sufficient for starters. Then we'll see what else we want to do."

"I can do that."

"Okay. Then I'll call you tomorrow night, your time. Guard those samples with your life because there aren't any more available for the time being."

I was really curious to know whether the protein that Daniel was using was the same that I had described in the patent application. I betted it was.

CHAPTER 26

I checked the time difference with Paris. I couldn't wait to call the professor and hear what he had learned from the videotape I had sent him. It was almost seven p.m. in Paris when I reached my room, and I felt that calling his home at that time was not impolite.

I sat on the bed and dialed the professor's number.

"Mackowski" was the quick answer.

"Good evening, Professor. This is Richard Luster speaking."

"Who?"

"Richard Luster. Remember me?"

"I can't hear you. Speak up."

"***Richard Luster***," I shouted into the receiver.

"Oh, yes, of course. How are you, Mister Luster?"

"I'm fine, Professor. I'm calling you from Los Angeles."

"Are you?" Professor Mackowski sounded perplexed. "I thought you lived in Israel."

"I do. But right now, I am in Los Angeles."

"Oh, nice. So what can I do for you?"

"Have you got my DVD?"

"Yes, yes. I have received it today."

"And have you listened to it?"

"I have looked at it, and I also listened to the people speaking there. Yes. Very strange. Inexplicable."

"What?"

"I said: 'Very strange. Inexplicable.' Can't you hear me? The line is terrible."

"I understand. But what is 'very strange and inexplicable'?"

"Well, you see, the young woman is an American. No doubt about that. A born American."

"Yes, I knew that much."

"But the other woman, the one who speaks at the beginning ..."

"What about her?"

"She has the same speech characteristics as that other woman, Elise something ... Vernon, yes, Vernon it was, that you asked me to analyze before. Pretty much the same. I compared them."

"What does that mean?"

"I don't know."

A fat lot of help you are being, Herr Professor, I thought. I was running out of patience, but I needed him too much to allow myself to lose my temper. He owed me nothing, I had to remind myself. So I kept quiet and let him continue.

"You see, my young friend, what confuses me is that baseline in Elise Vernon's speech that I couldn't attribute to any known language. As you remember, I suspected it to be an artifact of the recording. But now I have heard this other woman in a much better quality recording ..."

"And ..." I prompted him.

"She has the same baseline. Exactly the same. My computer confirmed it, but my ear couldn't be mistaken either. I don't know what to make of it."

"Don't you have any idea of what that could signify?"

"None. None whatsoever. This is something that has never happened to me in my long career. I am at a loss, my friend. And you know what bothers me more than everything?"

"What?"

"The man."

"What man."

"The man in the video. He has it too. The same baseline. The very same."

The receiver slipped from my hand. Without noticing, I had started to sweat as the professor spoke. It was not so much what he had said as the tone of his voice while he said it. I lifted the receiver and brought it to my ear, but the professor was gone, and the line was dead. I hung up.

The professor's report should not have surprised me. After all, that was the answer I was expecting, but it was spooky all the same. I sat on the bed, trying to collect my thoughts. My theory that Elise Vernon and Paula Vargo were connected had been vindicated by the professor's conclusion. But then, according to Mackowski, Daniel too came from wherever Paula had, and that destroyed my hope that he might be the good guy in the story. I had the impulse of calling Erin to tell her, but I realized that it would do me no good at that point and might put her in danger. I sat there, deep in thought for a long time—probably an hour or so—before a knock on the door yanked me out of my reverie.

I don't know who I was expecting to find when I answered the door, but certainly not a stocky man in a cheap suit, waving an official-looking ID at me.

"Yes?" I said, raising an eyebrow.

"May I come in, Mr. Luster? I am Agent Frank Davies."

"What is this about?"

"It is with reference to Professor Vargo, and I'd rather we spoke in private. May I come in?" he repeated.

I stepped aside and let him in. Whatever this was about, I didn't want the whole hotel to hear it. My room had two small armchairs on two sides of a tiny, round table, and we sat in them. I looked at him inquisitively and waited for him to start talking.

"Mr. Luster," he said, speaking quietly, "I don't want to beat about the bush. We know of your visits to the offices of DPV-Med, yesterday—both the official one and the one you made at night. We want to know what this is about."

"Why are you asking, and what business of yours is it?"

"I don't want to be rude, but please understand that I am the one who asks the questions. And everything that goes on in this country is the Agency's business."

"Let me see those credentials of yours again," I said.

He handed them to me, and I inspected them. His title was unfamiliar to me, as was that of the department in which he worked. They read "Senior Assessment Agent, Investment Fraud Division." Those credentials could be as fake as my Swedish business card. He could be someone sent by Daniel to find out what I knew, but on the other hand, if a genuine law-enforcement agency was taking an interest, I might be able to pass the burden onto them. It could be my way out of this whole mess, and they would undoubtedly be able to accomplish much more than I would.

"I understand your hesitation," he said, seeing that I was taking my time inspecting his ID. "You can call the Agency's hotline and ask for me. They will put you through to my cellular phone here, and you'll know that I am who I say I am."

"Yes, let's do that," I said. Five minutes later, having verified his identity, I got us a Diet Coke each from the minibar and sat down again. "Suppose you tell me a little bit about the reasons for your inquiry, and then I'll give you the whole story, and I promise that you'll find it interesting."

"I can't tell you too much at this point. Many details of this investigation are still under wraps. Still, I can tell you that we have seen a substantial movement of cash originating from investments made in Professor Vargo's company, going places they have no business going to, which has raised a red flag. We keep surveillance on his laboratories, and this morning, when we analyzed the video taken yesterday, we saw you. With the plate number of your rented car, finding you was easy, so here I am. Now let's hear what you have to say about Professor Daniel Vargo."

"You can start by not referring to him as a 'professor.' The man is a fraud and much worse than that. I can promise you this: after hearing my whole story, you will be sure that I belong in a straitjacket. But before you discount my tale, check out the evidence that I will provide. I know this is hard to believe because it has taken me months to digest it, but if what I think is happening is true, it must be stopped immediately."

I told him the whole story from the beginning, and he listened in silence. From time to time, I paused to look at him and tried to gauge his reaction, but he was a good listener, and his face was inscrutable. When I finished my tale, he got up and paced the room, his hands in his pockets. He finally planted himself before me, his hands still in his pockets.

"Straitjacket it is. I believe that you're convinced that what you're saying is true. But if you want to convince me that a couple of aliens are loose in the States, plotting to annihilate humankind, you'll have to do much better than that. I'm not going to bring this tale to my superiors, who obviously will think I'm off my rocker for even telling it to them."

"I have given you all the facts, and you can draw your own conclusions."

"Let me put it this way—your tale is so incredible that the obvious conclusion is that you are delusional. There is indeed something off with this Vargo individual that needs looking into, but that doesn't mean that he lives on a spaceship."

"But what if you're wrong and I'm right? You are a federal agent. Can you ignore it all?"

"I investigate money laundering, not little green men. I admit that your story is intriguing, but there has to be a better explanation than yours."

By then, I was desperate and ready to beg on my knees.

"Please ... This is too big for me. I need your help. The world needs your help."

I could tell from his face that Davies was conflicted. He furrowed his brow and averted his gaze for a few moments, and then his expression became relaxed.

"I wouldn't know how to start looking at this kind of thing. I know I'm going to make an ass of myself and that I will regret it, but I have an acquaintance who works in the UFO sightings task force, who may be much easier to convince that you're telling the truth than me. He already thinks that the aliens have landed decades ago and tells everybody about it, and in spite of that, they haven't locked him up yet. He may be able to help you."

Davies' friend had a Ph.D. in physics and held the position of Senior Research Associate, which he explained with a smile, was his agency's way to put up with his crazy ideas without having to fire him. Apparently, on occasions, he was called upon to solve complex mathematical problems and was too precious to risk losing, so they put up with his theories. A quick call that Davies made to him got us an invitation to call on him immediately. Davies' credentials got us past a gate guarded by a uniformed guard with a real gun, and we parked next to a long, four-story building with darkened windows. Up on the second floor, we found ourselves in an empty corridor, which wasn't surprising since it was well past dinner time. We stopped before a door with a sign that read "Dr. Anthony Fender. Entrance restricted." Davies knocked once and pushed the door open.

Inside, a lean man of about fifty with butter-colored hair and a wrinkled business suit stood before a table, eating a sandwich.

"Hi," he said. "You got here. Have a sandwich," he added, pointing at a tray loaded with food.

It was evening already, and I hadn't eaten anything since lunch. My session with Davies had made me forget the hunger, but now I was famished. Still, one has to be civil, so first I went to shake his hand.

"I'm Richard Luster; nice to meet you, Doctor Fender," I said.

"Tony," he said.

I guess I gaped at him because he added, "That's my name. Tony."

"Oh, yes. I'm Richard," I repeated unnecessarily. "I'll take you up on your invitation. I forgot to eat today," I added apologetically.

"Go ahead. I always forget to eat. That's why they bring me sandwiches. So, Frank," he said, turning to Davies, "you said that you have something for me. Let's hear it."

We sat down at the table, and between bites, I told my story again, this time with more details than I had given Davies. Tony almost didn't interrupt me with questions until I got to the bit when I inspected the Vargos' empty home.

"Green goo, you said?"

"Greenish-blue."

"Tell me more."

"There isn't much more to tell. When I touched it, it sort of fizzled and evaporated, and that's all there is to it."

"It smelled like cheese?"

"Yes, and mint."

"Okay, go on."

I am pretty good at describing facts—that's what I make a living at—so I continued, methodically ending my story with my visit to DPV-Med's laboratories. I watched Tony's face going through different expressions as my tale proceeded, trying to figure out what he was thinking, but to no avail. In the end, he remained silent for at least two minutes, which felt like an eternity to me. He remained motionless, gazing at something far away above my shoulder. Then he stirred and looked at me.

"Your story sounds completely crazy, and nobody will believe it—"

"But—"

"Nobody will believe it," he repeated, "but me."

"So, you do believe it?"

"Let me tell you a story of my own. Five years ago, we got a call from the sheriff of a rural county. A farmer had called to say that there was a strange, cigar-shaped object hovering outside his window. He couldn't tell how far away it was and how big it was, but he took pictures, and we later used them to estimate its size, which was that of a commercial aircraft. The farm is the only inhabited place for many miles around, and the object had been there for a full day, scaring the hell out of the farmer and his wife, who hadn't dared to go out and check on it. The sheriff got there in time to see the object shoot up sky-wise at an incredible speed and disappear. By the time I got there, all that was left at the place of the sighting was bent and partly scorched vegetation and something else that I couldn't identify: a blueish-green goo that smelled like minty cheese and vanished at the touch. I tried to collect some of it, but it just vaporized."

"The same goo!"

"So it seems."

"You know that there is an important side to this story," I pointed out. "Aliens or no aliens, they have a cure for cancer. Whatever we do, we must get our hands on it for humanity."

"I don't see any objection to the principle, except that I don't see how we can do it," Tony said.

"That's why I broke into the lab. I got samples of the material they use to cure their patients, and I sent it to a first-class scientist to have it analyzed, and I expect to hear from him soon. That should be enough, but if we can get more information on it, the better."

"But what does all this mean?" Davies asked.

"I don't know," said Tony, "but one thing we can take for sure is that this goo is somehow associated with extraterrestrial activity. It is the one element that proves that Richard is not delusional. Perhaps it is also connected with the cure for cancer, who knows."

"So what do we do now?" said Davies. "I can't go to my boss with a tale about a cheesy goo heralding an extraterrestrial invasion. He'll kick me out on my ass."

"No, you can't. We need more proof. More positive proof," said Tony.

"And how are we going to get it?"

"Richard, here is going to get it for us."

I knew that this was coming, and I guess I was prepared for it. I wasn't scared anymore, now that I wasn't alone. At last, someone believed me, and it filled me with purpose and strength.

"How," I asked.

"Let's make plans," Tony said simply.

CHAPTER 27

There was nothing more to do in L.A., so I caught a flight to New York City and took up residence at the Waldorf Astoria. In the busy surroundings of the hotel, I felt assured that my anonymity could be easily maintained. Davies and Tony had preparations to make before leaving, and they would take a different flight. Davies gave me the address of the service apartment where they would be staying.

I reached the hotel in the early afternoon, checked in, and walked out immediately. By the time I reached the address of DPV-Med's headquarters, not far from Times Square, it was after five p.m., and a constant stream of people was leaving the office buildings in the area. I was lucky to find a little garden with benches almost in front of the building entrance, and I sat there with a newspaper in my hand, watching the people leaving for the day. At a quarter to six, the street was no longer busy, and I started to worry that I was becoming conspicuous. By the time I started wondering whether I should not find myself another position, the building's door opened, and Daniel Vargo walked out. He looked briefly left and right, as if to decide in which direction to go, and started walking quickly.

Daniel had long legs so that I almost had to run to keep up with him. When we reached Madison Avenue, he slowed down a little, but he still had me panting to avoid losing him. He walked purposefully, looking straight ahead until he reached Sixty-Fourth Street, where he turned right and stopped before the entrance to an elegant apartment building. He took a key from his pocket, unlocked and opened the door, and walked in.

You are doing well, Mr. Vargo, I said to myself. Apartments in this neighborhood don't come cheap. I walked along the street, passing in front of the building, but didn't see any sign confirming that it was where the Vargos lived. Still, Daniel had a key, and it was a reasonable assumption that this was his home. I walked back and stood at the corner for a minute, but then I decided that this was a futile exercise and walked back to my hotel.

I didn't have much to do for the rest of the day, and I needed to unwind, so I chose a Greek restaurant in the Village from the Zagat Survey and enjoyed a quiet dinner. I got back early enough to have a drink at the bar before turning in. I watched TV for a few minutes before turning off the lights and going to sleep.

The wake-up call shook me awake from my sleep at six a.m. The time was one p.m. in Tel Aviv and time for me to call Yair, but I needed some coffee first. I brewed a Coffee Mate cup by the minibar and then a second one, after which I felt equal to talking. I lifted the receiver and dialed Yair's number. He answered almost immediately.

"Yes?"

"Yair, it's me, Richard."

"Oh, hi, Richard. What time is it at your end?"

"It's bloody six a.m., but it doesn't matter."

"It's lunchtime here," he said reproachfully, "but I pardon you on account of the caviar. It was superb. Pity you weren't here. Quite a feast, it was. Only next time, also send some champagne."

"Okay, okay. Now, what did you find?"

"I found that you are a bit confused or something. You sent me beautiful samples of saline."

"What?"

"Saline, you know, the isotonic fluid used as a base for hypodermic injections?"

"I know what saline is." I didn't believe my ears. "Which of the samples was saline?"

"They weren't numbered, you dummy. But fortunately, they were *all* saline, so it doesn't matter."

All saline! I couldn't believe it. Still, Yair was an extremely reliable person, and if he said it was saline, that's what it was.

"Are you still there, Richard?"

"Yes, I'm here. I'm thinking. Are you positive that there is no protein in any one of them? Even in small concentrations?"

"Definitely positive. If there is any organic material whatsoever in there, it is beyond detection limits—and my detection limits are as low as they come. No, it is pure saline. Distilled water and physiological salts. Period."

"All right, Yair. Thanks."

"Anything else I can do for you?"

"No, thanks. Not now, at least. If I think of anything, I'll call you. Keep the samples, anyway."

"Okay. If you feel like sending me any more delicacies, you're welcome. Bye."

"Bye," I answered mechanically.

It didn't make any sense. The test tube was positively the one I had seen in the movie being used to treat Abby. And, unless Abby was participating in a gigantic fraud, she had been seriously ill before and had been cured. I tried to see the reasons for Abby to lie, but I could think of none. She was a rich American girl with a medical history that must have been checked thoroughly before Daniel got permission to let her participate in the experiment. Why should she take part in a scam of such enormous proportions? And besides, other documented patients had been successfully treated. And if the active material had been replaced by saline, why was it kept in the refrigerator? None of it made any sense. But then, nothing made sense.

I got back to bed, but I was too worried to be able to resume sleep. I tossed in bed for the best part of an hour, and then I got up and dressed. I called Davies' cellular to give him the news, but got no response and left a voice mail asking him to call me back.

A leisurely breakfast in the Waldorf's excellent restaurant did much to soothe me, and then I set off to find a hairdresser. I found one not too far away and walked in.

"Good morning. How are you today?" I was asked by a young man who sat by the register near the door.

"Good, good. Is there anybody free right now?"

"Of course. BARRY!" he called, and a youth of particularly repugnant looks approached us. He had a beard that failed to cover widespread acne and a recessed chin and eyes the like of which I had only seen before on a particularly stupid cow.

"Yes?" said Barry.

"This gentleman here needs you," said the young man, after which he turned around and distanced himself from the matter.

"What will it be today?"

"Well, you see, I dyed my hair last week, but I am not satisfied with the color. I'd like to dye it back to its original one. Chestnut."

"Chestnut won't suit you. It is not your color."

"That's the color I've been going around with all my life."

"Still, black would be better. Far better. Chestnut is ... how to say ..."

"Boring?"

"Yes, exactly, boring."

"Still, that's the color I want. Can you do it?"

"Yes. Fifty dollars."

"Go ahead."

With my natural color restored, I felt much better. The time was getting on for lunch, and I got a sandwich at the Trump Tower, after which I walked back to my hotel. My cell-phone rang as I walked into my room.

"Richard?" Davies' voice said.

"Yes."

"We're here. Make the call and then come to the apartment."

"See you soon," I said. I picked up the room phone and dialed the number I had memorized.

"DPV-Med. Joanne speaking," a soft voice said. "How can I direct your call?"

"I'd like to talk to Mr. Daniel Vargo."

"I'll transfer you to Professor Vargo's secretary," was the short answer.

A few clicks and a brief silence followed, then another voice.

"This is Professor Vargo's assistant. How can I help you?"

"I'd like to talk to Daniel Vargo, please."

"I'm sorry, but Professor Vargo is busy right now, and I can't disturb him. Would you like to tell me what this is about? Perhaps I can help."

"No. It's personal. I must speak to him in person."

"I'm afraid that's impossible. Can you leave a phone number and a name? Someone will call you back as soon as possible."

"You don't understand. This is not a regular call. This is a matter of life or death. Tell Daniel Vargo that Richard Luster is on the line and that he must speak with him immediately."

"That won't help, I'm afraid. Professor Vargo is tied up, and there is no way that he can spare the time now. Even if he gets the message."

"Tell him. Just tell him, and let him be the judge. Life or death, remember?"

"Yes, but ..."

"Tell him so that you won't have to regret it tomorrow."

"All right. I'll pass him a note, but I can't promise anything."

"You do that. I'll hold on."

She put me on hold with music for fully five minutes. When the music stopped, Daniel was on the line.

"Richard, is that you?"

"Yes, Daniel, it's me."

"How are you?"

"I've been better. I must see you."

"I don't think that's a good idea."

"I know everything, Daniel. I think you should see me."

"Of course you do. I knew you would get it," came the answer after what I thought was a significantly long pause.

"I need to talk to you about the saline that you've been injecting into your patients. Also about Srapatsko and a lot of other stuff. I really think that you should see me."

"As I said, I think this is a bad idea. We've been keeping you away for a good reason, for your protection. But I can feel that you are excited. You shouldn't get too excited. If you really feel that you need to meet me, I'll see you."

"When?"

"I'm tied up with meetings until pretty late today, but we can meet tomorrow. I think the last people will leave around five-thirty or a quarter to six. Say you show up here tomorrow at six?"

"I'll be there."

"You know where we are?"

"Yes. I told you that I know a lot about many things."

"Fine. See you at six, then."

I hung up and reclined back on my bed's pillows. I felt mentally and emotionally exhausted, but I still had work to do, and I couldn't afford to rest right now. I got up and dragged myself to the lobby of the hotel. In the street, I took a cab and gave the driver the address of Davies' apartment. He and Tony were waiting for me with coffee and Tony's omnipresent sandwiches. I sat down and grabbed one almost mechanically.

"All right, Richard, let's get busy," said Davies.

"Yes, let's," I said, too tired to say more.

"Here is the tape recorder that I have brought for you. I'll teach you how to use it later. The plan is simple. You go in, get them to admit as much as you can while you record them, then you come straight to the Agency's offices with it, and we'll take it from there. Tony and I will be waiting for you there and will prepare the ground for your testimony. Okay?"

"Yes, but what is plan B if I end up dead instead of bringing you the evidence?"

"There is no plan B, Richard. We have to assume that they won't dare harm you in their own offices with witnesses who know you are there. But I'll tell you frankly that I won't force you to go there if you are getting cold feet. Do you still want to do it?"

I gazed at him, weighing the question. I wasn't sure about

what I wanted any more.

"I don't want to pressure you, Richard," said Tony, "but you need to know how critical this is. You may be our only opportunity to prove that aliens walk within us. Your contribution may mean the survival of the human race."

"So much for not wanting to pressure me," I said with a weary smile. "But I want to do it. I can't go on living without knowing what is really going on."

"You are taking into account that these Vargos may turn out to be simple crooks, I hope," said Davies, speaking to Tony. "You need to be careful before you make outlandish statements at the Agency without first getting your hands on Richard's evidence. You don't want to make an ass of yourself."

"I don't expect that I will," said Tony, and picked up another sandwich.

Back at the hotel, I ordered room service and then went to sleep in front of the TV. The next morning, I got up late with butterflies in my stomach that it took me a while to calm down. I had time to kill, and I took myself to Grand Central Park. The weather was fine, and I realized that it could be my last day and my last opportunity to stroll peacefully outside. I sat for a long time on a bench, thinking of my kids and of Erin. Not of Becky. I couldn't think of her, and that bothered me for a moment.

When my feet started to ache from the walking and standing, I headed back to the hotel. I watched a sitcom for a while without actually following it. Then I decided that the time had come to get ready. I took out the small box with the recorder that Davies had given me. It was a little recorder that fit nicely into my inner pocket. It had an excellent built-in mike, but the fabric would get in the way of recording, so he had also given me an external pin microphone that plugged into the recorder at one end, to be positioned near my collar. According to Davies, that was the best place to record. I strapped the mike's cord to my skin with adhesive tape. Time to test the recording. It worked fine.

I was ready.

CHAPTER 28

The elevator stopped on the thirty-first floor, and I stepped out. A receptionist was sitting at an elegant semi-circular table, her back to a wall of beautifully polished oak with the gold letters "DPV-Med, Inc.," and the company logo, a stylized fetus, embossed on it. When I first saw it, I remember thinking that the logo was quite in bad taste, but now I paid no attention to it.

"Mr. Luster," said the receptionist with a smile, "you are expected. Please take the private elevator in front of you and press two. It'll take you to Professor Vargo's private office."

The elevator was small, and walking into it felt like stepping into a coffin, but I took a deep breath and pressed the button. I quickly turned the tape recorder on, which I had forgotten to do before entering the building. The trip was slow but couldn't have lasted for more than a few seconds. The door opened to a breathtaking view of Manhattan.

The room I entered looked more like the Vargos' living room than an office. The furniture was off-white, and there wasn't enough of it to avoid the feeling that the place was empty. I couldn't see any documents or terminals, or anything else you would have expected to find in an executive office. An open esplanade led from the elevator to a desk of a sort, near a panoramic window. Daniel was standing by the desk, looking out, and Paula was waiting for me in the middle of the esplanade.

"Richard, how nice to see you after such a long time!" she exclaimed, extending a hand, which I ignored. She managed to look genuinely happy.

"Let's cut the bullshit, Paula," I said, with a tense and hostile voice. "This is not a social visit. You know why I'm here."

"Yes, indeed, we know it, Richard. But there's no need to be sour. You are among friends here, right, Daniel?"

"Absolutely," said Daniel, turning toward me. "We owe you a lot, and we certainly are indebted to you. Please do sit down and make yourself comfortable. Can I get you a drink?"

"I won't sit down, and I don't need a drink," I said testily. Socializing was the last thing on my mind. Besides, I needed to keep my distance; letting them too close could mean that they might spot the microphone. "I am here to get answers, not to chat."

"We'll do our best to accommodate you," said Paula. "Ask your questions."

"I have done a lot of thinking lately. I have looked back at what has happened and have reached some amazing conclusions. For instance, it was you, wasn't it, who killed Tarun and framed me?"

"Tarun was struck by lightning," said Paula. "Isn't that what the autopsy said? And I didn't try to frame you. On the contrary, I made sure that you would be in a public place with a foolproof alibi while all this happened. And they couldn't do anything about it, could they?"

"But you've been walking around with my fingerprints on

your fingertips and leaving incriminating evidence everywhere. How did you do it?"

"Does it matter? It was meant to confuse the police, and that's what it did."

"But why Tarun? Why kill him?"

"Daniel," said Paula, "why don't you explain to Richard?"

"Okay. No harm in satisfying your curiosity." This was a very different Daniel from the one I knew. He no longer sounded diffident and had lost that frail look that was characteristic of his demeanor.

"You see," he continued, "Tarun started to suspect that something was wrong with my data, and he set out to prove that my work was a fake—which, of course, it was—and that was dangerous. So he had to go," he said simply.

I was starting to feel nauseous, but I had to go on. I had to keep them talking as much as possible and get everything on tape. Then it would be time to go and expose them to the world. But in the back of my mind, I doubted that they would let me go. The more they talked, the less probable it was that they would be able to allow that to happen.

"But what were your goals?" I asked. I had been sincerely puzzled by their behavior all along.

"Money, my dear, and fast," said Paula. "Lots of money for our project—not this one, this is just a way to get the money. That was the goal, and you will be happy to hear that we have achieved it in full. Our investor's money is resting in offshore bank accounts of several companies that are totally unrelated to this business. They will help us finance our project for the next ten or fifteen years. This company, unfortunately, will suffer from the disappearance of the money and of the founders, but that can't be helped, of course."

"I don't understand how you got that much money."

"It's simple, Richard," said Daniel. "Our major investor—one of the richest men in America, a billionaire—has a wife who had endometrial cancer. I cured her. It is a simple equation: wife cured equals money in the bank. Another heavy investor in our little consortium had a boy with Hodgkin's disease. I cured him too. The moment he went into remission, there was no way to keep his father from stuffing our account with millions of dollars. So we let him. The others only needed to hear from those two, and here they were, begging us to take their money. You see now?"

"So I take it that a cure for cancer doesn't exist, right?"

"Well, yes and no. Of course, the protein that I have isolated from the fetal material does absolutely nothing at all to cancer cells. It's only a blob on the gel. It's my straw drug. However, curing these people of their illnesses was simple because I know how to influence the brain's biochemical reactions to produce the signals needed to reverse uncontrolled cell proliferation. I can re-establish the needed biochemical balance in any individual person. Pretty much like I can concentrate electricity in my hand, to a lethal voltage, and channel it to wherever I want."

"You see," intervened Paula. "The only way to make the kind of money that we need, in a relatively short time, was by investments in a biotech project. And that's what we did. Even Vernon's money, which is not insignificant, was not enough for our plans."

"So you did kill Vernon!"

"Not we personally, but one of us, yes," said Daniel.

"So now you see why we had to stop Tarun?" continued Daniel. "We needed to build a credible enough story that would bring us to the investors, and that would make them try our cure without fear that they were dealing with crooks. We needed the credibility—and we haven't thanked you yet for your great help with that. Our investors' patent attorneys never stopped praising your work. But a scandal sparked by Tarun could have ruined it all."

"Yes, really, Richard," added Paula, "I've been wanting to thank you properly for all you did for us, for a very long time, and I'm glad that we have this opportunity."

She sounded perfectly charming as if she were thanking me for a successful dinner. I eyed her with hatred, remembering something else that had been bothering me.

"And all that brawl with the hospital—you created that on purpose, didn't you?

"Good catch, Richard!" said Daniel, smiling appreciatively. "We needed to create a buzz around our 'miracle drug,' and that was the best way to start it."

"So now you do realize that I know a lot about you. What do you plan to do? Am I a hazard for you, too, like Tarun was?"

"But, my dear Richard," said Daniel, sounding hurt, "don't you even think it. I don't want you to be worried for a second about your personal safety. We only agreed to meet you and talk to you because we knew that we can be candid with you now, and we can tell you all we are allowed to tell since it doesn't matter anymore. I would never put you in danger. We, Paula and I, really feel that we are your family. In fact, you could say that we truly are, and of course, we care about you."

"How can you say that you care about me when you are scheming against the human race?"

Daniel seemed taken aback and smiled an embarrassed smile like I had seen on him in the past. "So you don't know yet?" he asked.

"Don't know what?"

"But really, Richard," said Paula, looking amused, "you mean to say that you haven't already understood? We thought that ..."

"Understood what?"

Paula and Daniel gazed at one another briefly, and then Daniel turned to me, speaking softly.

"You are one of us, Richard. I thought you knew it."

"What are you saying? What is this drivel? What do you mean, 'one of you'?"

"Sit down, Richard, and let me explain." I felt weak at the knees, and this time I sat down without complaining, and Daniel continued. "When we were just starting with the project, we scoured the planet for suitable subjects—people who might become useful to us in the future and were sick without knowing it. Curing a cancer patient makes his transformation much easier than with a healthy person. However, every transformation is hard on us and takes much of our energy, so we can only do so many. Every person we cure takes a little bit of ourselves to himself and becomes one with us; that's what I meant when I said that you are family, a new member of our race, just like everybody else that we have cured."

"What are you saying? I don't understand ..."

"Do you remember that about two years ago someone made a late afternoon appointment with you to discuss an invention but never showed up? He called himself Mr. Black. Do you remember that?"

"I seem to remember. People usually keep their appointments, so that was unusual, but what does that have to do with all this?"

"I was Mister Black, and I did show up, and I cured you. Then I canceled your memory of meeting me."

"Cured me?"

"You had an undiagnosed brain tumor—a fatal one. I cured you and, in doing so, turned you into one of us. I guess that you should thank me because otherwise, you would be dead by now."

"I don't believe a word you are saying. I don't remember ever seeing you."

"Of course, you don't. I canceled your memory and made you a Dormant. You were not supposed to awaken to your true essence before Phase Two, like many others, but we thought you had awakened prematurely because of what we went through together and that this awakening was the reason for your visit today. You behaved like you had understood, and that misled us. We made a mistake. Until Phase Two begins, all Dormants must remain fully integrated and unaware of their nature. We will awaken the Dormants for Phase Two in due course, but they must lead a normal life until then. We would have awakened you only if things got complicated in the first stage and your active cooperation became needed. Luckily, that wasn't necessary. Your premature awakening was not a desirable outcome, since once awakened, your life would be much more difficult."

"You canceled my memory?"

"Just like I did to your son."

"What do you mean?"

"Do you remember that night in your house, with Elan?" said Daniel, and when I nodded, he continued. "I got so close to Elan that, somehow, he saw me for a moment for what I am. Children have that kind of intuition sometimes. So I had to cancel his memory and regret that this had, as a side effect, the fever you witnessed. There was nothing I could do to stop his fever faster, with you and Becky watching, but you may be assured that he was never in any danger. I would never have let him come to any harm."

"So you did that to me ... you say that you turned me into ... into ... and to how many others?"

"Many."

"Abby DiNapoli? Is she a Dormant too?"

"Yes. Why do you ask?"

"When I met her ... it felt strange."

"Like meeting a part of yourself, I guess. It's natural."

"So you see, Richard, we are as open as we can with you," Paula added. "Your help will be essential in Phase Two."

"I don't believe you! Why shouldn't I expose you to the world?"

"First of all, you wouldn't betray your own kind, of course. And besides, what would you say?" asked Daniel. "That a couple of alien body-snatchers have worked out a scam to steal some money from their investors? Today is our last day in New York. By the time anybody agrees to listen to you, we will no longer be among those present—nor, alas, will our investors' money. Everybody will write this off as another high-tech fraud, and the world will forget all about us in a couple of weeks. Don't worry."

Something else was on my mind, and I had to ask.

"What did you do to Becky? That evening when I found you at my house with her."

"Nothing, really. We thought it best to keep her away from you while your mind was set on investigating us, so I only manipulated her thoughts a little. There was a danger that she might believe you and get in the way of our plans, and we decided to keep you two apart."

"So, what are you going to do with all that money?"

"Many things. For one, when Phase Two begins, there will be chaos all over the planet. Some 'natural' disasters are also planned. We need to establish a base in a safe place from which we will be able to operate—we have decided on a lovely island—which will cost hundreds of millions to build to our specifications."

I had to get out. My head was throbbing. This was no longer only between them and me. I understood now that I had stumbled on—and unknowingly aided—crimes designed against humanity. I had to do something about it. I needed to warn the authorities immediately. I had to do it at once.

I started backing away toward the elevator.

"I've had enough," I said. "I'm leaving now. I don't see that there is much more to be said."

I couldn't stand their presence a second longer. I was in the elevator now, pushing the "down" button.

"You can go Dormant again, if you wish, Richard. You will feel the urge to let go and empty your mind. If you don't fight it, that will happen naturally again, and I recommend you take that route, for your sake and peace of mind," said Daniel.

"It has been a pleasure and a privilege working with you, and I look forward to seeing you in Phase Two," said Paula. "I wish you well."

The doors of the elevator were sliding now, and in a second, they would have closed. Suddenly, Paula, who had been approaching the elevator as we spoke, shoved her hand into the cabin, a few inches from my face, blocking the sliding doors.

"Oh, Richard," she said with a smirk, "one more thing. You know that little tape recorder of yours? A bad idea, but I have switched it off."

She withdrew her hand.

And the doors of the elevator closed.

EPILOGUE

"So now you have the whole picture, Tony. You know what happened. You can believe me or not. I'm past caring."

"I think that perhaps you believe what you are saying. It may all be true, or you may be an accomplice in the biggest scam of the century, and that's why you brought us nothing but fibs from your meeting."

I gazed at him through the bars that separated us. He was keeping at a safe distance as if worrying that I might somehow get at him.

"So, what happens now?" I asked.

"I don't know, Richard. Frankly, I don't know."

He shook his head sorrowfully and left.

I am losing patience. I've been cooped up in this cage for too long, and it starts to affect me. I'm having visions of strange places and partial memories that don't make sense to me. I have to get out of here.

Perhaps, next time that Tony comes, I will use my lightning.

Meet the Author:

Kfir Luzzatto is the author of eleven novels, several short stories, and seven non-fiction books. Kfir was born and raised in Italy and moved to Israel as a teenager. He acquired the love for the English language from his father, a former U.S. soldier, a voracious reader, and a prolific writer. Kfir has a Ph.D. in chemical engineering and works as a patent attorney. He lives in Omer, Israel, with his full-time partner, Esther, their four children, Michal, Lilach, Tamar, and Yonatan, and the dog Elvis.

In pursuit of his interest in the mind-body connection, Kfir was certified as a Clinical Hypnotherapist by the Anglo European College of Therapeutic Hypnosis.

Kfir has published extensively in the professional and general press over the years. For almost four years, he wrote a weekly "Patents" column in Globes (Israel's financial newspaper). His popular guide, *FUN WITH PATENTS—The Irreverent Guide for the Investor, the Entrepreneur, and the Inventor*, was published in 2016. He is an HWA (Horror Writers Association) and ITW (International Thriller Writers) member.

You can visit Kfir's website and read his blog at www.kfirluzzatto.com. Follow him on Twitter (@KfirLuzzatto) and friend him on Facebook (https://www.facebook.com/KfirLuzzattoAuthor/).